iNSiDER

AN OUTSiDER NOVEL
BOOK TWO

MiCALEA SMELTZER

Coverart design by Regina Wamba at MaeIDesign
http://www.maeidesign.com/

DEDICATION

To the dreamers everywhere

PROLOGUE.

I knew in my heart that nothing would be the same.
My scars, both physical and mental, had changed me.
I wouldn't lie down and let someone hurt me, hurt my pack.

I'm going to stand up and fight.
Starting now.

ONE.

The small black and white dog jumped into my suitcase for the third time.

"Archie," I groaned. "Please, stop it," I said picking up the little dog and looking into his sweet brown eyes. He gave me a little doggie whimper before I set him back down.

I had to finish packing. Caeden would be here any minute to pick me up.

It was the day before Spring Break officially began and we had a plane to catch to Lübeck, Germany.

The little Boston Terrier pawed my plain black suitcase and let out a cry.

"Archie," I said, "I'll be back soon. You won't even know I'm gone." I kissed the dog on top of his soft head and then scratched him behind the ear. His back right paw thumped enthusiastically. I smiled at him.

I stuffed the last of my clothes in the bag and then zipped it easily. I smiled satisfied. I'd managed to get a week's worth of clothes and essentials in one carryon bag. Success was mine.

"Sophie, Caeden's here!" called Gram from the living room.

I shrugged my shoulders at the little dog. "Sorry bud, time for me to go."

I wheeled my bag behind me and Archie nipped at my heels.

Caeden smiled when he saw me. "What, no fifty bags?" he joked.

I pretended to be offended. "Of course not. I'm a simple girl. See-- sweatshirt, sweatpants, and ponytail," I said pointing to each.

He laughed and then kissed my cheek. "I know it's part of the reason why I love you," he smiled.

"Good," I said. "Because you're not about to get me in another dress," I said referring to prom.

He chuckled. "You look good either way."

"Suck up," I said and smacked his arm.

8

Gram clucked her tongue. "If you two keep bickering like an old married couple you'll miss your flight."

"Gram's right," I said to Caeden. I pulled her into a hug and kissed her cheek. "I'll miss you Gram."

"I'll miss you too, sweetie," she said and patted my cheek. She looked between Caeden and me. She pointed to each of us and said, "You two be good. No funny business."

"Eww Gram. Please," I said shaking my head.

Caeden chuckled. "Don't worry. I don't have a death wish and I'd prefer for Sophie's dad to actually like me," said Caeden with a smile.

Gram narrowed her eyes at him but didn't say anything.

I turned to Caeden. "Alright, let's get out of here before she gives us the safe sex talk."

Both their faces blanched and I quickly scurried out the door, my laugh carrying behind me.

I turned around and Caeden came striding out the door with my bag in his hand, shaking his head at me, with Archie nipping at his heels.

"Archie!" I scolded. "You have to stay here!"

Caeden chuckled. "No, he doesn't. We're bringing the familiars. See," he said and pointed to the back of his red Jeep.

I could see a large crate in the trunk with the huge Murphy was sitting inside it looking displeased.

"I thought Murphy and leather didn't mix?" I joked.

"Hence the cage," said Caeden with a grin. "Bryce would not relinquish the use of Stella so I had to put Murphy in a cage. He's not at all happy," Caeden smiled.

He opened the trunk and put my suitcase in before petting the dog on the head.

"Sorry Murphy," he said. The dog playfully nipped at his fingers. Caeden laughed and closed the trunk.

He shook his head and then suddenly pulled me into his arms. Our bodies were so closely molded together that air couldn't pass through.

"Caeden," I said startled.

"Shh," he said and one hand caressed my cheek while the other held me firmly to him. Both my hands were flat against his hard muscular chest. His hand that had been caressing my face tangled in my hair as he pressed his lips firmly against mine. My toes literally curled. My mouth opened underneath his and he deepened the kiss with a moan before he pulled away.

"What was that for," I panted.

He tucked a piece of hair behind my ear. "With your parents around I'm probably not going to have a lot of time to do that. It's going to be a long week," he sighed.

"Very long," I added breathlessly.

He chuckled and then held my door open for me. Archie hopped in and then up on my lap. Caeden jogged around to his side and started the car.

I saw Gram peek out the front window and waved at her. I saw her narrow her eyes suspiciously but she finally waved back.

"Away we go," said Caeden with a grin as he backed out of the driveway and we began the one hour drive to the airport. He took my hand. "Are you excited to see your parents?" he asked as we got on the interstate.

"Yeah," I smiled. "Nervous though," I said with a laugh and glanced at him.

"How do you think I feel?" he joked.

"Hey, I already met your mom. Now it's your turn," I said and squeezed his hand.

"You didn't have to go to a whole other continent to meet my mom," he said, "and your dad is a Beaumont." He gulped, "This should be his pack. Not mine. What if he doesn't think I'm adequate enough for you or the pack?"

"Caeden," I said. "You're perfect. He'll love you. You're worrying over nothing. I promise you. You'll be like the son he never had."

"I hope you're right," he said taking the exit.

"I am," I said reassuringly.

10

"Welcome to Virgin Atlantic Flights," said the overly perky red head flight attendant. She was probably twenty-five or twenty-six and her eyes kept lingering on Caeden. A growl rumbled in my chest. It was the growl of a wolf. A wolf saying, back off he's my man.

Apparently she got the message because she moved away with a strained smile. Caeden squeezed my hand and emitted a low chuckle.

"Stop it," I smacked him. "What if that was some guy hitting on me? I swear you attract single females in a five mile radius like a fly to honey."

Caeden laughed outright now, throwing back his head.

"I can't help it," he said, "I'm just *so* charming and insanely good looking," he rubbed his jaw.

"Conceited much?" I joked and petted Archie who snoozed happily on my lap. Poor Murphy was too big and had to fly with the suitcases.

"Don't worry, babe," he said leaning towards me so his cerulean blue eyes dominated my vision, "I'm all yours."

I laughed and then sobered. "I love you, Caeden, with all my heart, I do."

His eyes darkened. "I love you too, Sophie. I won't let him get you," he whispered sensing my thoughts.

I sighed and leaned my head back. "I know you won't but it still scares me. He'll know I'm a shifter now."

"He hasn't shown his face in months," hissed Caeden. "Maybe we're lucky and something happened to him."

"You mean… he might be dead?" I asked.

Caeden shrugged and buckled his seatbelt. "One can always hope."

I rubbed my face. "I don't think we're that lucky," I sighed.

"I don't think so either," he said as the plane taxied.

"At least we have each other and I'm not so defenseless this time," I said flashing my wolfy teeth at him.

He grinned. "Nope, you're a natural. Travis won't

11

know what's coming for him if he tries to attack you again."

"I really hope there isn't a next time," I whispered.

"If there is we'll handle it together," he said as the plane took flight.

I clenched my teeth and tried desperately to get air to my starved brain. If this annoying red head didn't go away I was about to go all wolf up in here and it wasn't going to be pretty. My wolf was screaming at me to defend my territory. Caeden was mine and she just wouldn't get the message!

She leaned over me to hand him his soda practically shoving her ample chest in his face.

Sophie. Caeden warned in my mind. No doubt I was shimmering around the edges as my wolf form tried to take shape. My fingers dug into the leather armrests leaving claw marks.

"Can I get you anything else?" she said in a sickeningly sexy voice.

I glared at her but she ignored me, that was her new policy, ignore the angry girlfriend.

Caeden smiled politely at her and leaned over me like he wanted to have a more intimate conversation with her. She leaned down, once again giving him a great view of her, um… assets.

"I'd appreciate if you'd stop flirting with me," he smiled. "It's very rude and not at all the kind of behavior you should have on your job. I might have to file a complaint. Oh and I'm still in high school," he added and she paled.

She slowly stood and pulled her short skirt down so it was a tad bit longer. Color flooded her cheeks making her look like a tomato. She ducked her head and darted away.

"Thank you," I said and the air finally flowed freely to my lungs.

"Sorry I made you suffer this long but it was so hot watching you get all worked up," he grinned wickedly.

"I hate you," I said pouting.

He chuckled. "Oh now I know that's not true."

"You're right," I said, "but that was unusually cruel."

He grinned and gently stroked my cheek with his index finger. "You know there's only you," he said.

"I know that," I snapped. "I'm not some insecure *girl*," I hissed. "But I am a wolf. You know that. Your instincts are the same as mine if a man would come onto me. My body screams that it's wrong. You're mine, Caeden. My body doesn't like it when other women touch you," I said and found my fingers digging into the leather seats again.

"You're right," Caeden said again. "I'm sorry. I shouldn't have done that, no matter how cute you are when you're mad."

"You're killing me," I said.

He grinned wickedly. "Love you too, babe, love you too."

"Bite me," I said and playfully bit his finger instead.

* * *

As the plane landed in Germany I looked over at Caeden. He saw the fright on my face and grabbed my hand. Once we were in the air I was usually okay unless there was a lot of turbulence but take off and landings always made me sick.

"Breathe," he said.

I glanced at him and huffed, "If I breathe I'll be sick."

He chuckled and I smacked him.

Finally the plane landed on the runway and I let go of Caeden's hand. Little red half-moons dotted his hand.

"You know," I said sitting back in the seat and taking a deep breath, "when you said you'd distract me on the plane I didn't know it would entail flirting with the staff."

His laugh filled the cabin. "It worked didn't it," he grinned.

I narrowed my eyes at him. "I might have to tell my dad."

"You wouldn't," he said paling.

"Oh, I would. I don't think my dad would like to hear about my mate flirting with a flight attendant," I grinned and he relaxed.

13

He leaned over and pecked me on the lips and then cupped my cheek with his hand. "Only you," he said and then leaned close to my ear. "I might have to distract you with my lips on the way back," he whispered and I shivered.

The plane pulled up to the gate and everyone stood to gather their stuff. Caeden grabbed my bag and his so I could keep my hold on Archie. I followed him off the plane and took in the stiff posture of his shoulders.

"Still nervous?" I asked giggling.

He glanced behind him at me and gave me a small smile. "Very," he sighed.

Caeden found a trolley and loaded our bags onto it and then we went to get Murphy. The large dog barked happily when he saw us.

"Hey buddy," said Caeden bending down to pet his familiar. Murphy's large pink tongue darted out to lick Caeden's waiting fingers.

Caeden then proceeded to load the large crate on the trolley. The cotton of his shirt stretched tightly over his muscles and I gasped. He was too perfect.

He looked up at me and grinned. He glanced around quickly before pulling me in for a kiss. He kissed me long and deep before pulling away with a grin. "Last one for the week," he said.

"Oh please," I said rolling my eyes.

"Hey," he said, "I want to be on your parent's good side. That means hands off," he said and raised his hands in the air to demonstrate.

I stuck my tongue out at him and he laughed.

"Sophie!" I heard called behind me.

I turned and smiled. "Mommy!" I cried, gave Archie to Caeden, and ran into her waiting arms like I was five years old.

"Sophie," she said again crushing me to her.

"Christine, don't squish the girl," my dad said from beside her.

"Daddy!" I said and dove into his arms next.

"There's my little girl," he said and gave me his signature bear hug.

"I've missed you guys so much," I said.

"Oh, we've missed you too, Sophie," said my dad and I could swear he sounded close to tears.

I pulled way. "Mom, dad, this is Caeden," I said and motioned to the hunky piece of man meat standing awkwardly to the side with the horse sized dog and the very upset black and white dog.

"Get over here," said my dad motioning Caeden to join us. He pulled Caeden into a hug. Surprised, Caeden hugged him back. My dad pulled away and held Caeden at arm's length looking him over. "You look so much like Roger. I can't believe he's gone. He was my best friend. I loved him like a brother. He'd be very proud of you, I know that I am," said my dad.

Suddenly, tears pooled in his eyes and he hastily looked at the ground.

My dad clapped him on the back. "It's okay, boy. Good leaders know when to show emotion and when to remain stoic. Come on let's get out of here. I'm sure you two have tons of questions."

I smiled at him, "Of course we do, smart people always have questions."

My dad laughed. "I've missed you, Sophie."

My mom smiled at me. Caeden grabbed the trolley and we followed my parents out into the parking garage.

"I told you they were cool," I said.

Caeden smiled at me, "Yes, they are."

TWO.

"I'm hungry," my dad said, "What about you guys?" he glanced in the rearview mirror at Caeden and me.

Caeden grinned; it was much like the grin he wore when he was a wolf, all teeth. He patted his stomach. "I'm always hungry," he said.

My dad laughed. "It never goes away," he said. "Even when you're my age you still have an appetite equivalent to five men."

He pulled off the road and into the small parking lot of a family style restaurant. Lübeck was a port town, located right on the Baltic Sea. It was quaint but cute.

"Alright gang," my dad said. It was so typical of him. "Let's roll."

I smiled to myself. I had missed my parents so much.

Caeden and I climbed out of the back of the car. I had been amazed that he had managed to fit his long legs in the back of the tiny car.

Archie and Murphy looked at us with round, sad, eyes.

"We'll be right back, boys," I tapped the window. Archie scratched the glass and whined. I gave him a sad face but there was nothing I could do so I turned to follow my parents. Caeden kept a well-respected distance between us when all I wanted was to hold his hand. Suck up.

My dad strolled inside, said hello to someone working there, and picked a table in the corner. I was surprised when he let Caeden and me sit beside each other.

My mom and dad didn't bother picking up the menu. Obviously they had been here a lot. Neither one of my parents liked to cook so I had always been the designated kitchen person. Honestly, my mom was an excellent cook. She just didn't enjoy it.

Caeden and I perused the menu. I had lived many places growing up and spoke many languages so I wasn't as afraid of the cuisine as he was. He looked at the menu with panic on his face.

I placed my hand on his and said in his ear, "I'll order for you. Do you trust me?"

He nodded his head and said, "Thanks," with a grateful smile.

My parents ordered and then I ordered for us. I hoped he liked it. I thought by now I knew him well enough to order food. After all, he usually ate just about anything.

My dad took a sip of water and said, "Are you two ready for graduation?"

"I know I am," I said with a smile. "I may like school but it will be a relief for it to be over."

"Yeah, I guess so," said Caeden. He looked down at the table. "I know that once school is over I'll have to focus all my time on the pack."

My dad chuckled. "It's tough being the Alpha but I know you can do it."

"Thanks," said Caeden. "That means a lot coming from you."

The waitress came with our food.

"So Sophie, are you going to play soccer this year?" my dad asked.

I nearly choked and Caeden smacked my back. I took a sip of water and waited for my coughing spell to pass.

"Uh- I'm not sure," I mumbled.

"Soph," said my dad. "You have to. This might be your last chance to play."

"I don't know if I really want to," I shrugged. "There's a lot going on right now."

Dad sighed and looked between us. "This is your last chance to just be a kid, for both of you."

I looked at Caeden and voiced what we were both thinking. "Dad, I think that ship has sailed. We have to think about the pack now."

He sighed and looked at my mom. He shook his head. "Taking care of a pack is too big of a responsibility at your age. You're just kids."

Caeden's hands clenched. I knew what he was feeling

because I was feeling it too.

A challenge.

"What are you implying?" Caeden growled. "I won't let anyone mess with my pack and I certainly won't let *anyone* try and take my position." The muscles in his arms flexed. I knew he was fighting for control. I put my hand over his trying to calm him with my touch.

My dad paled. "No- I didn't mean- that's not what I meant-" he bumbled. "I just- you're both so young. I'm not asking you to give up your position. I'm so sorry, you've both misunderstood my meaning."

Caeden relaxed. "I apologize for my reaction."

My dad laughed. "It's okay. I know how it is. Being an Alpha can be... difficult."

Caeden nodded, "Yeah, it can."

"Alright," dad said, "no more wolf talk until we get back to the house. Deal?"

"Deal," Caeden and I both said, relieved.

* * *

The house my parents were living in was a quant, idyllic, little cottage. It was white with a red door and gray shutters. The roof peaked to a point above the door. Flowers overflowed around the walkway and cast a fragrant scent. Or maybe it only seemed so fragrant because of my wolfy nose.

"Get in here baby girl," called my dad from the steps.

I looked up with a shy smile. "Sorry daddy."

He smiled and came down the steps to put his arms around my shoulders. "It's nice having you home baby girl," he said and kissed the top of my head. "Your mom and I have missed you more than you can imagine. It's been far too quiet without you."

"I've missed you guys too," I wrapped my arms around him and for just a moment pretended that I was five again and my dad could scare all the monsters away. "So much has happened in the last few months."

"I know," he said and kissed the top of my head again. "You're a strong girl Sophie. I know you can handle it.

—

18

I have all the faith in the world in you."

"I'm glad one of us does," I said and let him lead me inside. He closed the door behind me. My mom and Caeden were already sitting in the living room and she had a tray on the coffee table with four glasses of water. I guess I had dawdled longer than I thought. Murphy and Archie were already snoozing on the floor.

I sat down on the couch beside Caeden and my dad took the seat across from us on the opposite couch. His standard recliner sat in the corner of the room. He put his arm around my mom and tenderly kissed her cheek. Even all these years later you could see the aura of love around them. Did Caeden and I look that gooey?

I looked over at Caeden who had taken my hand. He was staring at me with a crooked smile on his lips.

I gulped.

We looked worse than they did. It was almost comical. Almost.

"You need to shave," I said to wipe that gooey love struck look off his face. I didn't need my dad to kill him.

Caeden grinned and rubbed his stubbly chin. "But you love my scruff," he said and rubbed his jaw against my face to drive home the point.

For the moment he seemed to have forgotten my parents.

My face went red and I swallowed thickly. That plan had backfired.

I turned to find my parents watching us but instead of looking irritated they looked happy.

"So," my dad said and spread his arms wide, "questions?"

I looked at Caeden and back at my dad. "Lots."

"Fire away," he said. "I just hope we can answer them."

I tucked a piece of hair behind my ear. "Well..." I said and my mind went blank.

"Why do you think mates are coming back?" Caeden

intervened.

My dad shrugged. "No idea. My theory is that it has always been around but people just don't realize what is happening. In our case," he motioned to my mom, "we were from different packs. We met by chance and it was like... wow," he shook his head. "Had we been in the same pack, and grown up together, those feelings would've been dulled and easily mistaken for infatuation."

I looked at Caeden and wondered if he was thinking the same thing that I was. Bentley and Chris.

"That makes sense," said Caeden.

I looked down at our entwined hands. *Caeden* and *Sophie* said the elegant script.

"Do you have the tattoos?" I asked, holding up my wrist. "I don't ever remember seeing you have them."

"We have them," dad took mom's hand. "But only we can see them. Only you and Caeden can see yours."

"Really?" I asked.

"Yeah," mom began to trace lines on her wrist, what I assumed was my dad's name. "It's not meant for anybody but the two of you."

"Can you guys do the mind reading thing?" Caeden asked.

"We can," my mom answered and then took a delicate sip of water. "It's very useful," she said.

Caeden grinned and shook his head. "It's odd being able to speak in our minds when we're not in wolf form."

"What's not odd about all of this?" my dad asked rhetorically. "We turn into wolves. I think that's odder than the mind reading."

Caeden chuckled. "You've got that right."

"What about the others? The other shifters, I mean. Do they have mates?" I asked.

Dad cleared his throat. "In the legends it was all shifters but I don't know if their mates are 'reappearing' so to speak. When your mother and I left... We said goodbye to that life Sophie. It was safer for you if we cut off all ties so I know nothing about the others."

"You kept in touch with Gram," I accused.

"That's different," he said. "She didn't want to kill us."

Travis. Travis and his dad wanted Caeden and me dead. They wanted to destroy our pack and they'd destroy my parents too if they found out who my mom was. Christine Grimm. Peter Grimm's sister.

Caeden swallowed thickly. "I...we," he amended, "need your advice on how to handle the Grimm's." Unconsciously, Caeden began to trace the scar on my arm. The scar that Travis had cut into my skin to spell *Liar.*

My mom and dad exchanged a look. Dad shrugged and sighed. "I don't know what to tell you. They've always been a little strange-" my mom hit his arm. "Except for your mother of course," he amended. "She's perfectly sane."

My mom turned to me and tears filled her eyes. "I'm so sorry for what my brother did to you," she said and then the dam broke. Tears soaked her face faster than she could wipe them away. "I'm sorry," she sobbed as she stood up and left the room.

I looked at my dad and then Caeden. I patted him on the knee and said, "I should go talk to her."

He nodded. "That's okay. I'd... uh... actually like to talk to your father in private."

I narrowed my eyes. "Why?"

Caeden wouldn't meet my gaze. "Nothing important."

"Uh-huh. Sure," I said and went after my mom. I could hear her sobs coming from a bedroom upstairs. Caeden and my dad disappeared into his office. If Caeden thought I wasn't going to question him about this later then he was sadly mistaken. If he knew something about the Grimm's and was hiding it from me, he'd never hear the end of it.

"Mom," I said and softly knocked on the door before pushing it open.

Archie scampered past my legs and into the room. He hopped up onto the bed beside my mom.

She turned to me and her brown eyes were already red and puffy. "Sophie, come here," she said and patted the empty space next to her on the bed. When I sat down she pulled me into her arms and kissed the top of my head like she had so many times before when I was younger. She smelled like freesia. "I could've lost you," she whispered.

"I'm fine mom," I said. "Everything worked out."

She looked down at my arm. "I don't see how you can be fine, Sophie," she looked at my scar.

"Maybe I'm not *fine* but I'm better than I could be. I have Caeden to thank for that. Without him I know I would be the biggest mess ever."

"I'm so happy you have him," she said. "I know as your parent I shouldn't like him or want you to be so serious." She laughed. "But I remember what it was like discovering that your father was my mate. It was... magical. Just don't move too fast, take things slow, and appreciate the little moments."

"I will mom," I said and laid my head on her shoulder. "I am," I added.

"I miss you... so much," she said. "It's hard being away from my baby girl."

"I miss you too mommy," I said.

"I can't believe you're about to graduate high school. It seems like just yesterday you were a baby."

"Moooom," I whined. I hated when she became nostalgic. It usually resulted in lots of tears, a box of tissues, and her pouring over old photo albums.

"One day you'll have kids and you'll see," she said.

"Yeah, well that's a long ways down the road. Like way, way, way, down the road." I motioned with my hand just how far down the road *that* would take place.

She laughed and I laughed with her. It was great to be home with my parents again. Some might say this wasn't my *home* since I had never lived here but it's the people that make the place. My mom, dad, and Caeden were my home.

Mom patted my knee and smiled. "Want me to braid

your hair like I used to when you were little?"

A smile broke across my face. "I'd love that."

I situated myself on the bed while she went to grab a brush and ponytail holders. Sitting down behind me and spraying my hair with detangler she said, "I think we'll do something a bit more sophisticated instead of pig-tails."

"Good idea," I laughed.

She separated my hair into sections and gently brushed it. I always enjoyed getting my hair brushed. It was relaxing and always made me sleepy.

"What do you think daddy and Caeden are talking about?" I asked tentatively.

Her brush strokes stilled.

"I don't know. Alpha stuff I guess." She resumed brushing my hair. Satisfied that it was smooth she began to braid the sides. "What do you think it is?" she questioned.

"No clue but Caeden seemed nervous. Do you think something's happened and he's keeping it from me?"

"I'm sure that's not the case," she said. "Don't worry your pretty self." She fixed the braids in place and pulled the rest of my hair back into a ponytail. "Perfect," she said and patted my shoulder.

"Thank you," I said and turned to hug her. I was planning to hug both of my parents as often as possible.

She patted my cheek and said, "I know we just ate lunch but between your dad and Caeden it will take me all afternoon to make enough food for dinner. Do you want to help me?"

I smiled. "I'd love to."

I followed her into the small but clean kitchen. It hadn't been updated for a while but at least it was functional. Mom decided to make her famous chicken recipe. Okay, maybe it was only famous in my mind.

I helped her coat the chicken in mayonnaise, parmesan cheese, and bread crumbs. After the chicken went into the oven we made homemade rolls, mashed potatoes, and macaroni and cheese.

By the time we were finished nearly three hours had passed and I was covered in sweat. Caeden and my dad had long since come out of his office and were busy doing male bonding out on the back porch. It made me smile knowing that my dad approved of my mate.

"Go ahead and wash up," mom motioned her head down the hall.

In the bathroom I splashed my face with water and dabbed it dry before touching up my makeup. With my mom's amazing skills not a hair was out of place of the hairdo she had created. The woman was amazing. I washed and dried my hands before venturing back to the kitchen.

"Do you want to eat outside or in here?" she motioned to the small dining area.

"Outside!" I exclaimed. I couldn't help my excitement it had been over six months since I had seen my parents.

Mom smiled. "I thought you'd say that." She tapped the glass door and dad poked his head inside.

"Yeah?"

"Why don't you two help us set up the table?" It wasn't really a question since she shoved outdoor placemats, utensils, and plates into his unsuspecting hands.

"Uh- okay," he said and turned around. Caeden hopped up to help him.

Mom and I carried the various dishes out while the dogs circled our feet.

"Looks like a feast," dad said and rubbed his hands together. I sat down beside Caeden and we faced the back yard. I gasped at the sight. I hadn't realized the sea was just outside the door. If I had known that, there was no way I would've spent the last three hours in the kitchen. I guess mom knew that and neglected to tell me on purpose.

Caeden smiled at me and squeezed my hand before shoveling food onto his plate.

It was hysterical the amount of food my dad and Caeden had on their plates. My mom and I had more on our plates than the normal human would eat but it in no way compared to theirs.

I took a bite of chicken and sighed in pleasure. Amy and Gram were excellent cooks but when you're away from your mother's cooking suddenly nothing else compares. Especially when she rarely cooked when I was home.

I hadn't believed Caeden and the others when they said that I'd eat more once I turned but they'd been right. In record time every morsel on my plate had disappeared. I didn't even feel the need to unbutton my jeans.

"That was delicious," I said.

My mom laughed. "Thank you. Is Gram not feeding you?"

"Oh she's feeding me," I said. "I used to think Gram was the best cook ever but I'm thinking that you could give her a run for her money."

"I don't know whether to be flattered or offended," she laughed.

I smiled. "Maybe a bit of both." Caeden still had a bit of chicken on his plate. "Are you gonna finish that?" I asked.

"Huh?" he said around a mouthful of roll.

Not bothering to wait for his answer I snatched his chicken.

"Hey!" he cried with a laugh.

I shrugged. "You snooze you lose."

I quickly devoured the chicken before he could snatch it back.

Caeden shook his head and grinned. His dimple stood out and I couldn't resist kissing it. Who cared if my parents were sitting across from us?

"Mrs. Beaumont let me help you with that," Caeden said and began to clean up the table.

"Thank you Caeden," she smiled and her eyes crinkled around the edges. That was new. "And please call me Christine."

"Christine," he said and stacked the plates on top of each other.

Mom and Caeden disappeared inside with the dishes and I was alone with my dad.

He pulled a cigar from his pocket and lit it.

"What did you and Caeden talk about?" I asked, not even bothering with subtlety.

He laughed around the smoke in his lungs. "He just needed to ask me something that's all."

"Well, what was it?"

"Something he needed to talk with a father about," he said and blew out a cloud of smoke. I coughed.

I narrowed my eyes. "What is that supposed to mean?"

"Just that he needed to talk to a man."

With his vague answers I felt like I was talking to a fortuneteller. The billowy smoke from his cigar added to the mysterious aura.

"Thanks for not answering my question," I groaned and rolled my eyes.

He laughed and stretched his legs up on the table. "I have a feeling you're going to know the answer to your question soon."

"Thank you oh wise one."

"I miss your humor," he smiled.

"Garrett!" Mom yelled from inside. "Get your feet off the table."

"Busted," dad smiled and slowly lifted his feet off and planted them on the floor. "Sorry honey!" he called.

Ten minutes or so later, mom and Caeden joined us again. Caeden's hands smelled like lemon dish soap and it made me smile.

"Have you thought of any more questions?" my dad asked as he leaned forward to extinguish his stub of a cigar.

I entwined my fingers in Caeden's before saying, "Is there anything you think we should know?"

Dad cleared his throat. "Have you heard of the binding ceremony?"

"No," I said. "What is that?"

Dad chuckled. "Shifters have a traditional wedding just like humans but there's an extra element to ours and it's the binding ceremony. It's quite beautiful and still practiced today but it has a different meaning for mates. Your souls merely recognize each other right now, they've chosen the other person, but the binding ceremony binds your heart, body, and soul to the other forever; even in death."

"It sounds scary not beautiful," I snorted.

"I'm sure at your age it does sound a bit frightening but I can assure you it's anything but."

Caeden cleared his throat. "So for mates it literally binds us?"

"Yes," my dad said and looked at my mom with so much love. I would normally find it disgusting but now that I had the same with Caeden I couldn't think that anymore. "You become even more in tune to the other person thoughts, feelings, and their emotions. When you fight you're stronger, unstoppable, when you're together. The things you can do become limitless."

"Wow," Caeden breathed. "I had no clue."

"So you did the binding ceremony?" I asked my parents.

My mom shook her head no. "We did it ourselves," she squeezed dad's hand, "but in order to work properly it has to be performed by the head elder of the council. Our binding is weak."

"Oh."

She smiled at me. "Sophie, I know what you're thinking and that's not true. We could've never stayed there. It wouldn't have been allowed. A Grimm and a Beaumont..." she shook her head, "It was blasphemy. You are not the cause of this my beautiful girl."

"I'm sorry," I said and stood up, shoving the chair back in my haste. I stormed down the porch steps into the sand.

I walked as fast as my feet would carry me. When the house was no longer in my sight I fell to my knees. I didn't cry I just sat there and stared at the falling sun.

Sacrifices. So. Many. Sacrifices. And I knew that my parent's sacrifices were only the beginning.

I brought my knees up to my chest and rested my chin there. The evening air was cool and goosebumps soon appeared on my skin but I didn't move. Couldn't move.

The sky burned a brilliant orange. Tints of lavender and pink dotted the sky. It was a beautiful sunset, one you can only see from shore. With the water receding in the distance the world looked infinite. If only that was true.

Caeden sat down beside me. I knew it was him. I didn't even need to look. There was just a certain feeling of *calm* that stole over me whenever he was around.

He draped a jacket over my shoulders.

Archie and Murphy played nearby.

"I didn't ask for this life," I breathed.

"None of us did, Sophie, but it's all we've ever known."

"What if I can't do this Caeden? What if I can't be a shifter? An Alpha?"

"You can Sophie, it's in your blood."

"Everybody keeps saying that!" I snapped.

"It's the truth," he said quietly.

Tears glistened in my eyes but I dammed them back. "So many sacrifices have been made Caeden. By *everyone*. I don't know if I can do the same."

"You can, I believe in you."

"I'm glad one of us does," I laughed shakily and stretched my arms into his warm jacket. I then wrapped it around me. "Thanks for the jacket," I tried to smile.

He tentatively opened his arms. I leaned into his embrace. His woodsy smell engulfed my lungs.

"This life is a blessing, Sophie, not a curse."

"I'm sorry, I know that."

"No, you don't," he said and I could feel him shake his head. I burrowed my head against his warm neck. "Ever since you found out about this world you've only seen the bad."

"That's not true," I whispered and hated that I had caused his thoughts to wander this way.

"It is true. Between what happened to me, what Travis did to you, and hearing about Bentley's brother you must think we're all like that."

"Our pack isn't like Travis," I said and looked up into his vibrant blue eyes. Right now they were less vibrant and more stormy colored, almost gray.

He smiled, a genuine smile, "*Our* pack?"

I sighed. "It's our pack Caeden. I need to stop thinking of myself as something outside the pack and instead as an insider."

"You are an insider," he said, "to the greatest pack *ever*."

We both smiled. Our previous melancholy disappeared.

"It's beautiful here," he said. "Nothing at all like I was expecting."

He wiggled around and fixed me between his legs so I could rest back against his chest.

"Same here. I don't know what I thought it would like but it was definitely not this."

The water was gray and the town was small but its simplicity only made it more beautiful.

"I'm so happy I found you," I kissed his cheek.

He grinned. "Yeah, sorry about dropping the cupcakes on the floor."

I laughed and it felt good. "It was cute and you certainly made an impression."

He shook his shaggy head. "I was so embarrassed."

"Not as much as me when I fell off the treadmill," I added rather glumly.

Caeden hooted with laughter. "That was hilarious. Your face! Ah, that was classic. I'll be telling our grandkids about that one day."

"Grandkids?" I turned around and smiled at him.

"Well," he squirmed suddenly nervous, "I like kids and I just assumed that sometime in the future there'd be little Caeden and Sophie's running around." He shrugged and squinted into the sunset.

I settled myself against him once more. "I like kids and I want kids but it's just strange to think about it right now. Talk to me about it again in a few years." First my mom and now Caeden! Jeesh, we weren't even out of high school!

Caeden laughed. "Alright, we'll talk about it again in a few years." His chin rested on my head and he inhaled.

"Cookies?" I joked.

"Freshly baked chocolate chip cookies," he said.

We sat there until the sun went down. With the stars twinkling above us, I stood. "We better get back."

"Yeah, you're right," he said and stood as well, brushing sand off of his shorts. He pulled me to him and placed his hands on my cheeks. He slowly lowered his head until his lips touched mine. The kiss was slow and sweet. He then kissed me on my head and said, "I love you, Sophie, so much. Never forget that."

"Your love would be impossible to forget."

"That's what I like to hear," he grinned and kissed me again.

THREE.

Giggling, we opened the screened door and walked into the kitchen.

"Sophie-" mom called and I could hear her getting up from the couch.

"Sorry about running out," I said.

"Baby girl," she said and wrapped her arms around me. "You've got to stop worrying about me and your daddy. We made our decisions and there's not a single one that I regret."

"Sorry about running off," I repeated. "That isn't like me," I pulled away from her embrace.

She patted my cheek. "You've been through a lot. I think you're allowed to freak out now and then." She took a breath and pulled away. "We're going to bed. See you two in the morning. Night."

"Goodnight," Caeden said from where he was leaning against the wall.

"Nightie night mommy."

"Nightie night Sophie," she said.

When I was little she had always tucked me into my bed, read me a story, and before turning out the light she'd kiss me on my forehead and say, "Nightie night Sophie." Even when I entered my teenage years she'd stop by room and say the same words.

"I'm going to shower," Caeden said and moved away from the wall and down the hall.

"Kay," I said.

Mom had gone upstairs but dad was in the living room stretched out in his recliner watching TV. I flopped onto the couch and sighed. Down the hallway I could hear the shower come on. I yawned.

"Sleepy?" dad asked.

"It's been a long day," I replied. "I better get ready for bed but I'm just too tired to move."

Dad laughed. "I thought you might be different after being away for half a year but you're still the same," he

---

31

shook his head.

"Should I be offended?" I asked and twisted around on the couch until my head hung off and the blood went rushing to my forehead.

"No," he laughed. "You're going to give yourself a headache if you hang upside down like that."

"You suck," I said and stuck my tongue out at him before flipping backwards off the couch.

"I'm your dad, it's my job to suck the fun out of everything."

"Well, you're doing a great job," I said and saluted him. His laughter sounded behind me as I headed down the hallway. Caeden was already out of the shower. Guys were so lucky, they didn't have all this hair to wash.

I grabbed my pajamas and headed into the bathroom to take my own shower. A stinky Sophie was not a good thing.

My mom had about fifty bagillion different body washes, shampoos, and conditioners.

She was one of those people that bought it if she liked the scent, not caring that she had ten bottles at home.

I washed my hair and then scrubbed my body with a cookie scented wash. Caeden was going to love it. I should buy some when I get home. I committed the brand to my memory.

I dried my hair a bit with the towel and pulled on my PJs.

I turned the light off and slowly opened the door, creeping down the hallway to see if my dad had gone up to bed. Thankfully he was gone. Backing down the hallway I came to Caeden's room. The door was closed and I eased it open.

"Sophie?"

"Shh," I hissed.

"What are you doing?" he whispered and flicked the bedside lamp on.

I rolled my eyes. "You didn't really think I was going

to sleep across the hall by myself did you?"

"But your parents-" He protested.

"I don't care, Caeden," I pulled the sheets up and wiggled in beside him. "I've gotten so used to sleeping with you that I can't sleep without you."

He laughed and put his arm around me, holding me close. He sniffed my hair. "Is it just me or do you smell more like cookies than you usually do?"

I giggled and splayed my hand across his chest, watching it fall and rise as he breathed. "Yeah, mom had some cookie scented body wash."

He pulled the sheet up over my shoulder and snuggled closer. "Your dad is *so* going to kill me in the morning."

"He'll have to go through me first," I smiled.

"You're so hot when you're protective," he breathed against my ear, sending a shiver down my spine.

"Go to sleep Caeden," I said.

"I can't now," he said. "I just keep seeing you go all wolfy on your dad. How do you expect a guy to go to sleep with that image in his mind?"

I laughed. "Try, please? I'm tired."

"Then you shouldn't have gotten me all worked up," he said but he leaned over and turned off the light. "Night babe," he whispered but I was already asleep.

* * *

I woke up with my face pressed into Caeden's chest. He was snoring softly and the sun was beginning to shine through the blind, lighting the blue walls. I pulled myself out of his death grip and he mumbled something in his sleep. Gosh, he was so adorable when he slept, so peaceful. I tiptoed to the door, opened it, and did a quick scan before scurrying across the hall to the room I was supposed to have slept in. I pulled the covers back and quickly covered myself when I heard steps on the stairs.

The steps came down the hallway and my door opened.

I feigned waking up. Stifling a yawn I said, "Morning mom."

"Sophie Noelle Beaumont don't act like I don't know where you were sleeping last night," she said, a coffee cup in her hand.

"I don't know what you're talking about," I stretched my arms above my head.

"Oh don't you?" she quirked a brow.

I let my arms drop back down. "How do you know?"

"I came to check on you last night and found this bed empty but another one suspiciously full."

I hung my head and shoved my long hair out of my face. "I can't sleep without him anymore not since-"

"Say no more," she held up a hand. "Just don't keep things from me Sophie, kay?"

"Okay," I nodded. "Sorry mom."

"Get dressed, I'll make breakfast."

She closed the door behind her and I let out a big breath before flopping back on my bed. That went way better than I could've ever expected.

I made the bed that I hadn't even slept in, and dressed in a pair of jean shorts and a t-shirt.

I knocked on Caeden's door and he opened it, pulling on a t-shirt over his baggy basketball shorts.

"What?" he asked, rubbing sleep from his eyes, and then ruffling his wavy hair.

"My mom knows where I slept last night."

He glanced down the hallway and then back at me before whispering, "Should I expect to be hung from a tree in your backyard?"

I laughed. "No, she understands."

"Phew, that's good," he rubbed neck. "I don't think a hanging would be very pleasant."

"I don't think it's meant to be. Mom's making breakfast," I nodded my head down the hall.

He yawned. "Good, I'm starving."

"You're always starving," I said.

"Especially since you ate my dinner," he said with a grin.

I smacked his side. "It was a little piece of chicken, you baby, and that hardly constitutes dinner."

He laughed and danced down the hallway, his feet thwacking on the tile. "Just don't eat my breakfast."

I shook my head at his antics.

I took the time to stop and admire the pictures mom had hung in the hallway. The beige paint hardly peeked through, the wall was so covered. There was a picture of me on my bike without training wheels, and then one taken only a few moments after the one before it of me crying my eyes out over my skinned knee. There was one of me as a baby sleeping on my dad's chest, me with missing teeth, school pictures. The whole hallway was basically devoted to pictures of my childhood. It brought tears to my eyes.

"Sweetie?" mom said.

"Yeah?" I turned to her and wiped away a tear.

"Are you crying?" she asked and concern etched her face.

I shrugged. "Maybe."

"Why honey?" she asked and wrapped her arms around me in one of her warm hugs. Her distinct scent of freesia nearly knocked me over. Several months after my transformation most things, like my new sense of smell and sight, seemed normal but every once in a while something would threaten to overwhelm me.

"I just miss you guys," I said. "Most kids think they don't need their parents but I do. I need you mommy."

"Aww baby girl you're breaking my heart," she said and suddenly her southern accent was thick. It usually got that way when she was concerned. I hugged her for a good five minutes before I pulled away. I never wanted to let go.

"Sorry, I needed that," I said.

She smiled. "We always need our mothers pretty girl," she said and wiped my wet cheeks. "Come on," she tilted her head down the hall, "breakfast is getting cold."

I giggled. "If dad and Caeden haven't eaten it all by now."

She threw her head back and laughed. "That's very true." She patted my shoulder before leading me to the kitchen and practically shoving me into a chair.

Dad and Caeden were sitting at the table waiting patiently for breakfast. Thank the lord they hadn't started eating or it would all be gone. Mom handed us each a plate.

"Homemade chocolate chip waffles? Am I in heaven?" Caeden asked as he looked at his plate with wide blue eyes. "Sophie I don't think we're ever going home."

I laughed. "Your mom can cook."

Caeden shrugged. "Yeah, but lately she's on this health food craze. If she makes me eat one more bowl of organic spaghetti I'm gonna go all Alpha on her ass." He looked up at my parents and blushed. "Butt I meant butt."

"That's not what you said," my dad grinned and slapped Caeden on the back. He sipped his orange juice before saying, "You kids should do something fun today. Explore the town."

I shrugged. "Sounds like fun."

* * *

It was raining. No, raining was an understatement. This was a torrential downpour. I turned to Caeden. "I don't think we're going anywhere."

"Me neither," he said and took my hand. He pulled me to the couch and down beside him. "It's too bad cause I kinda wanted to check out the town." He scratched the back of his neck.

I stretched out and laid my head in his lap. "Maybe we can go out tomorrow."

He threw one of his arms across the back of the couch and then played with my hair with the other.

"If you keep doing that," I yawned, "I'm going to fall asleep."

He chuckled. "Please don't fall asleep. I'll be bored out of my mind if you do."

I sat up and rested my head on his shoulder. I nuzzled his neck and soaked in his unique smell. Pine, cinnamon, citrus, and wood. It was the best smell in the whole world.

"What should we do then?" I asked.

He shrugged. "Do you think your parents have any board games?"

"I'm sure they do," I said. "Let me ask."

I hopped up from the couch and bounced into the kitchen where mom was cleaning up from breakfast.

"Mom?"

"Oh!" she jumped and put a hand to her chest. "I thought you two had left. You startled me."

No dip. Her reaction totally hadn't clued me into the whole startled thing.

"It's raining wolves and panthers out there so we decided to put off exploring until tomorrow. Do you have any board games?"

Were board games named board games because most of the time you played them when you were bored? Hmm.

"I don't know. You know we usually don't pack that kind of stuff when we move. If there are any they'll be in the right drawer of the entertainment center."

"Thanks," I said and kissed her cheek.

She smiled and swatted my backside with a dishtowel. I danced away and into the living room.

Caeden was leaned forward resting his elbows on his knees. He brightened when he saw me.

"She said if there were any they'd be in here," I said and bent down on my knees to open the drawer. The tiles were hard against my knee. Mom had covered the white tiled floors in a fuzzy rug to add some softness. Too bad the rug didn't cover the whole room.

I yanked the drawer open and went sprawling on my backside. "Ow," I said and rubbed the spot.

Caeden cackled.

Old DVDs, magazines, and instructions to various items littered the drawer. I lifted them out and sorted them into neat little piles. At the bottom of the drawer was an ouijia board. I pulled it out and looked at Caeden. "I guess this is it. You game?"

"I'm not going to die if I mess with it right? A ghost isn't going to attack me? I don't do paranormal."

I laughed so hard that I had to wipe tears from my eyes. "You don't do paranormal? For lord's sake Caeden you turn into a wolf. If that's not paranormal then I don't know what is."

I set the ouijia board down on the floor.

"Sophie, put that thing away. I am not communicating with spirits. Nuh-uh. Not happening. *Ever*," he said and slashed his arms back in forth in a no gesture.

"Fine," I sighed and put it back in the bottom of the drawer. "No ouijia board." I packed the other various items back on top. I placed my hands on my thighs and said, "What do you propose we do then?"

"Watch a movie and snuggle?" he grinned and waggled his eyebrows.

I laughed. "For someone that was dead-set against not touching or kissing me while we're here you've really changed."

"What can I say? You're parents love me. I'm just so full of awesome sauce."

I laughed and then launched myself at him so that we ended up a tangled mess of legs and arms. He kissed my nose before untangling us. He sat me down on the couch and then crawled over to the entertainment center. He shuffled through the movies and looked at me with a quirked brow.

"Looks like it's either *Despicable Me* or *Up*? Unless you wanna watch these?" he held up a boxed set of movies on the Civil War.

"Despicable Me," I said and sat Indian style on the couch and flipped my hair over my shoulder so it would be out of my way. "I am not in the mood to watch a grumpy old man with a penchant for balloons."

Caeden laughed. "Little weird green men it is."

38

He popped the DVD in and settled beside me on the couch. He shucked his shoes before stretching out and pulling me against his warm body.

Caeden skipped the previews and pressed play. His hand gently rubbed my back in an up and down motion. His warmth felt so good and I loved the feel of my cheek against his chest. I sighed in pleasure and snuggled even closer to him.

Mom poked her head in the doorway. "Do you want some popcorn? Cookies?"

"Both please," Caeden said.

"No problem," she twirled around and entered the kitchen.

I stifled another yawn and Caeden chuckled. "You act like you didn't get any sleep last night."

"I think I'm jetlagged and you know I hate planes so that whole traumatizing experience has probably added to my exhaustion."

He laughed. "Or a flirty redhead."

I smacked his chest as hard as I could.

"Ow," he said and rubbed the spot where I had hit him.

"Do not bring up that whore-monkey again. She's lucky I didn't claw out her eyes."

"Whore-monkey?" he laughed.

"It was the first thing that came to mind," I snapped which only made him laugh harder. I was tempted to hit him again just for the fun of it.

Mom came into the living room with a big bowl of popcorn and two bottles of water. "Here you go," she handed the popcorn to Caeden. "It will be a little while on the cookies. I decided to make them homemade."

"You didn't need to do that mommy," I said.

She smiled. "I know baby girl but I wanted to. I don't have you here much longer and I just want your stay to be special."

"I'm just happy to see you guys. Homemade cookies

are just a bonus."

She started to leave but turned at the doorway. "And they're snicker doodle," she winked.

"I love you mommy! You're the best!" I called after her. I turned back to Caeden, the movie being the last thing on my mind. "I swear, when I was still living with them she hardly ever cooked. Now she cooks all the time. I think she's hoping I'll never leave."

Caeden played with my hair as a chuckle rumbled through his chest. "She misses you."

"Who wouldn't miss me?" I scoffed and feigned outrage.

Caeden wrapped his arms tightly around me and pulled me up so that I was lying on top of his chest instead of beside him. He framed my face with his hands so I had no choice but to stare into his cerulean blue orbs. "Those days-" he swallowed, "while you were gone. It was the worst kind of miss anyone can ever experience. I've never missed someone so much in my life. Now, when you're gone for a room, for not even a minute, I miss you."

Just moments ago we had been joking but now his eyes were nothing but serious.

"Caeden-" I started.

He shook his head. "Don't say anything."

And so I didn't.

FOUR.

The next morning the weather had cleared so Caeden and I went out to explore the town. We strolled hand in hand while he swung our arms back and forth like little kids tended to do.

"Caeden, you're going to rip my arm right out of the socket," I snapped.

He laughed. "Come on, let me have some fun."

"Can you have fun that doesn't include ripping my arm off?"

"Sure, sure," he said and stopped swinging our arms.

The sky was gray and so covered with clouds that it was impossible for the sun to peek through. Luckily it wasn't raining. Despite the dreary weather Lübeck was bustling. Boats zoomed around the port and people bustled in and out of the quaint little shops. All the buildings were centuries old and spires soared straight up into the sky. Several things that resembled castle turrets dotted the sky. Courtyards seemed to be on every corner their grass an insanely bright green. I would've enjoyed taking the time to explore the courtyards but everything was so wet that I didn't want to bother.

"Let's go in here," Caeden pointed to a store full of clothes.

I shrugged. "Why not."

The store was full of cozy looking sweaters that were hand-made on site. An older man sat in the back working on one. He spoke a little English and tried his best to describe the process to us. I was fascinated.

After we finished speaking to the man we walked around the store. Caeden picked up a large cable knit cream sweater. He held it up to himself.

"Do you like it?"

"It would look great on you," I fingered the soft fabric. "It'll make all the ladies go wild," I looked up and met his eye.

"All the ladies? There's only one lady that I want to make go wild," he grinned. His brown hair flopped over his forehead and he flicked it out of his eyes.

I giggled. "It would look great on you."

"I'm going to buy it then. You want anything?"

"No," I looked around. "It's kind of an engrained habit not to buy needless items. I always had to get rid of so much stuff when we moved that I just learned not to buy anything," I shrugged and stuck my hands in my pockets, following him to pay the man.

"I'm going to have to change that," he winked.

From there we ended up going in and out of the different little shops that lined the port.

As the day wore on the wind picked up and I found myself wrapping my jacket tighter around me as my teeth chattered. It wouldn't be long until my jaw fell off.

"Cold?" Caeden asked as he threw his arm over me.

"Y-ye-ah," came out of my mouth.

He smiled. "Let's get you back then. I don't want your parents to think I'm not taking care of you."

"He-av-en for-or-b-b-id," I chattered.

As we started the trek back to my parents' house it started raining. I forced the hood of my jacket over my head and Caeden did the same. He took my hand and said, "Run!"

My converse sneakers quickly became soaked as we splashed through puddles of water. I'd be lucky if I didn't end up with frostbite and an amputated toe or two. We reached the back door and plowed into the house. Caeden shook his head and raindrops went everywhere.

"Caeden," I giggled, "you look like a dog when you do that."

He gave me a crooked grin and my heart skipped a beat. "Stop looking at me and get in a warm shower."

"Okay, okay, bossy pants," I said and put my hands in the air.

I took a quick but hot shower and the cold instantly seeped out of my bones. A normal human would be sneezing their brains out by now but with my freaky wolf mojo I couldn't get sick. I pulled on plaid pajama pants, a t-shirt,

---

and a pullover sweatshirt. This was supposed to be spring break but instead I was bundling up like it was Christmas break.

By the time I came out of the guest room Caeden was in the shower. I could hear the clinking of glasses coming from the kitchen so I headed there.

With her back to me, mom said, "I thought you might enjoy some hot chocolate."

Yeah, this definitely didn't feel like spring break.

"That will be great," I sat down at the table. It was no time before she was sliding a steaming mug in front of me. Before taking a sip I studied the familiar purple mug with a Rhino on it. *Rainforest Café* was emblazoned along the side. It was cracked and chipped in places and should've probably seen the trashcan years ago but I had always loved it. "I can't believe you still have this." I took a sip.

Mom smiled and sat down beside me with her own cup. It was white with a sunflower.

"It was always your favorite and I just never had the heart to get rid of it."

"I'm glad," I stared into the pale brown depth of the hot chocolate. A mini marshmallow floated at the top. I watched it float around the top before sinking a bit below the surface.

Footsteps sounded behind us and I turned to see Caeden standing there in only a white towel wrapped around his waist. Water droplets dripped down his bronze chest and disappeared into the band of the towel. I wanted to lick all those water droplets off of his delectable chest. But then my gaze ventured up from his stomach and chest to meet his eyes.

"Caeden," I said and worry coated my words. "What's wrong?"

He held his cellphone in one hand the look on his face could only be described as something between confusion and pain. In moments like this, his dimple completely disappeared.

"Bentley and Logan just discovered Peter Grimm's body," he said.

My mom made a strangled, half-painful, sound behind me. I could hear my dad coming out of his office.

"His body? He's dead?"

"Murdered, apparently it's pretty gruesome."

Mom made a choking, gasping, sound. I could hear my dad come into the kitchen and speak to my mom in soothing tones.

"What does this mean?" I asked Caeden. I knew my eyes were wide with disbelief and my eyebrows had probably completely disappeared.

"It means that Travis is now Alpha and we can expect war."

* * *

After Caeden's loaded statement we all just sort of stared at one another for a while.

Finally I stood and said, "We need to go home."

"Yeah," Caeden rubbed his face. "We do."

"Get dressed and I'll start packing my stuff. Dad can you call the airport and try to get us a flight out? I know you have some major finagling abilities."

"Yeah, I can do that," he said.

"Mom, please don't cry. I hate to see you cry," I hugged her.

She wiped her eyes and turned to my dad. "I'm fine honey, really," she patted his hand. "Call the airport and I'll make some sandwiches for you to eat on the plane."

"Thanks mom," I said and hugged her again. I wanted to argue with her on the whole sandwich making thing but I knew she just needed the distraction.

I pulled away and headed down the hallway to the guest room across from Caeden's. Even though we had been sleeping in the same room I had left my bags in the other one. I just hadn't felt like moving them.

I closed the door and quickly changed into regular clothes. Jeans and a white t-shirt. Archie was lying on the bed and snored softly. I swear that dog slept as often as a cat.

"Come on bud we're going home," I nudged him. He instantly became alert. I stuffed the last of my items in the suitcase and zipped it closed. I trudged out into the hallway and left it by the door. Dad was on the phone arguing with the airport and mom was sliding sandwiches into Ziploc baggies. Her eyes were red and puffy and she kept rubbing incessantly at them.

Archie scampered around my feet making yipping noises.

I didn't know what to say to comfort her so I just wrapped my arms around her and rested my head on her shoulder.

Caeden came down the hallway with his bag and Murphy.

"Did your dad get the airport?" he asked.

I shrugged my shoulders and rubbed my mom's back as she sobbed. Caeden picked up his bag and went in search of my dad. Murphy followed behind him like an overgrown shadow.

"Mom," I pulled away and took in her tear stained cheeks. "I'm sorry."

She wiped her face and moaned, "I'm a horrible person. I'm not crying because my brother's dead I'm crying because I'm relieved. He can't hurt you anymore."

I stood, flabbergasted, because what did one say to a comment like that and because Travis was just as much as a threat to us as Peter had been.

Luckily, I was saved from making a comment, by my dad entering the kitchen. He leaned his hip against the counter and rubbed his face. He looked tired. "Your flight leaves in two hours. You'll have to leave now to make it in time."

"Thank you daddy. I'm sorry that our time got cut short." It suddenly hit me that I would be leaving my parents sooner than I had planned and tears misted my eyes. Three days. Only three was the time I had had with them. That just

―――

45

didn't seem fair. Who knew when I'd get to see them again? Even in death, Peter Grimm was causing me problems.

"We'll see you again soon, baby girl," he said and slung his arm over my shoulder. I wrapped my arm around his middle and leaned my head against his chest. He kissed the top of my head before ruffling my hair. "I'll miss you squirt."

"I'm going to miss you guys so much," I said. I had said goodbye to my parents in August but now I had to go through it all again and for some reason this time felt more difficult.

"I need to make some calls, so I called for a cab to take you to the airport," he said.

I took a deep breath and pulled away before hugging my mom again. She squeezed me tight. So tight, that the air rushed out of my lungs in a gush.

"You're squishing me," I choked.

"Sorry," she pulled away. She patted my cheeks and stared into my eyes. Hers were the same chocolatey brown color. "I love you Sophie. So much," she hugged me quickly before letting go.

A horn honked outside. "That's the cab," dad said a bit forlornly. He patted Caeden on the back and my mom hugged him.

"I'm so sorry ya'll have to leave so soon. It just breaks my heart," she said and my dad slung his arm around her shoulder.

"Me too," Caeden said, "but we need to get back to our pack."

"We understand," dad said.

"Love you guys," I said and blew a kiss as I walked to the door. Mom held her hand out and caught it, our ritual since I was a child. Caeden went on out with our bags and then returned for Murphy's flattened crate. By the time I made it outside he already had everything loaded in the taxi.

"Do you have everything?" he asked while his hands rested on the open trunk.

46

"Yeah," I said sadly as I looked back at the house and my parents where they stood on the front stoop.

He closed the trunk with a loud thwack.

"Come on, Sophie. It's time to go home," he took my hand and guided me into the back seat. Archie jumped into the car and onto my lap. Caeden slid in beside me and closed the door. He told the driver to take us to the airport and then took my hand in his as the car started to pull away.

I waved to my parents and they waved back. It seemed like it had only taken a matter of minutes for us to leave and I had no clue how long it would be before I saw them again. One month? Six? A year?

Caeden's thumb gently stroked my hand in circles.

"I'm sorry Sophie but we have to go home. Our pack needs us."

"I know," I turned around to watch the house and my parents disappear. "It's just hard to say goodbye. You'd think I'd be used to it. I've been doing it my whole life."

"You've been saying goodbye to friends not your parents. There's a difference."

"Goodbye is goodbye, Caeden, it doesn't matter who you're saying it to," I turned around and sat down. Archie glared at me for disturbing him and Murphy sat in between us on the seat, his head almost touching the ceiling.

I crossed my arms over my chest and soaked in my last sights of Germany. Rain splattered the windows and the wipers swung back and forth as fast as they could.

The taxi pulled up to the airport and Caeden went to fetch a cart. He set up Murphy's crate and coaxed the reluctant dog into it. I slung my suitcase on top of the cage and then Caeden's.

Archie pawed at my legs so I scooped him up into my arms and then followed Caeden to the check in and then through security. Once we were through that nightmare we collapsed outside the gate.

Caeden's knee bounced up and down with restlessness. Finally he stood and said, "I'm going to get

---

47

some coffee, you want anything?"

"No," I shook my head.

"Alright," he said and shoved his hands through his hair before stretching his back. The movement caused his shirt to lift and show off his taut stomach but I was too upset for it to get me excited. "I'll be right back."

I watched him weave through the crowd, and every woman he passed eyed him. Normally that made the wolf in me insane but I was too numb for it to matter.

Peter Grimm was dead and that meant Travis was Alpha. I knew he'd continue his father's pursuit to kill us. I was so new to this life. How would I be able to defend my pack? Caeden? Myself? I knew nothing of fighting in my wolf or human form like the others. I couldn't be a weak link for them. I was going to have to prepare myself. There was no way I was going to let Travis Grimm hurt anyone in my pack. Not Charlotte. Not Bentley. Not their parents or Gram. It was time for me to step up to the plate and take my position as Alpha by Caeden's side. He needed me. They needed me.

Caeden came back with a small coffee and sat down beside me. He was extremely jittery but I knew it wasn't a byproduct of the coffee. He was simply anxious to be back with the pack. In a time like this they needed their Alpha. Both of their Alphas, even though I'm not sure I could be included in that terminology. I knew nothing of being a leader whereas Caeden was a natural.

"Caeden?" I asked and put a hand on his bouncing knee to stop him.

"Yeah?" he said and placed his coffee cup on the empty seat beside him. A girl, probably sixteen or so, had been slowly creeping towards it. I couldn't hide my smile.

"When we get home I want you to teach me to fight. As a…" I looked around and hissed, "*wolf* and as a human."

"Sophie," he rubbed his face and then turned his blue eyes to me, "I don't know if I can do that. I don't want to hurt you."

———

48

"Then get Bryce and Bentley to teach me. Please, Caeden, I need to know how to defend not only myself but the pack as well. You know I'm right," I argued.

He groaned. "It's just that the thought of you getting hurt makes me sick, Sophie, *sick*," he repeated.

"Caeden," I said softly and looked at him beneath my lashes, "I've already been hurt. Wouldn't you rather I know how to defend myself?"

He smacked his hands against the hard plastic airport seat. It left a dent. I did a quick scan to see if anyone had noticed. Nope, old man picking his nose, two girls giggling as they pointed at Caeden and they were looking at his face so there was no way they saw the dent, and then there was a guy yelling angrily into his phone. I let out a sigh of relief.

He squished his eyes closed and then pressed his fists against them. "Fine," he said after several minutes of silence. "You're right, you need to learn. I'm sure they won't mind helping you."

I smiled. "Thank you," I threaded my fingers through his and then leaned my head on his shoulder.

"I don't like this," he said. "I don't want you to get hurt."

"A few little bruises aren't the end of the world Caeden. I've had worse," I said and thought of my scar.

"Yeah, I know," he rubbed his face. He hadn't shaved and scruff shaded his cheeks and jaw. He had been right when he said I loved him scruffy. It only served to make him more handsome.

They called our flight and we boarded the plane. Caeden took the window seat again and I settled beside him. We buckled our belts and Archie settled into my lap to sleep. Man, I wish I could fall asleep that fast. The flight attendants went over safety measures and then told us to prepare for takeoff.

My fingers dug into the leather seat as the plane taxied to the runway. Caeden took my chin in his hand and tilted my face towards his. "Remember when I said I'd have to distract you with my lips?"

I nodded.

He grinned. "Good," and then his mouth was on mine, searing into me, like he wanted to melt into me. Oh dear God he was going to make me pass out. His tongue flicked out and licked my bottom lip and I gasped in surprise. I think someone laughed behind us but I was so occupied with kissing Caeden that I didn't care to be embarrassed. My fingers tangled in his hair. He kissed me a few moments longer before pulling away. His thumb caressed my bottom lip. "Was that a sufficient distraction?"

"Oh yeah," I said breathlessly.

His husky laugh filled the cabin. "Just wait until we descent."

FIVE.

It was nighttime a day later when we arrived in Dulles. I was utterly exhausted and we still had to make the hour drive home. I yawned and leaned against Caeden's car for support. If I didn't, I was sure to fall over.

"Sorry Murphy," he said to the dog. "You've gotta stay in the crate until we get home."

The dog whimpered and I felt so bad for him being stuck in that cage. He couldn't even turn around.

Stifling yet another yawn I said to Caeden, "Does Gram know we're coming home? I don't want to scare her half to death."

"Yeah, she knows." Caeden's arms flexed as he reached up to close the trunk. It clicked shut and he poked at his face. "I'm so freakin' sleepy. You'll have to make sure I don't fall asleep behind the wheel."

"I'm not making any promises," I climbed in the car. Archie sat in my lap.

Caeden slid in and started the car. The headlights flicked on, highlighting the parking lot.

Gold eyes flashed in the darkness and I sat forward.

"Did you see that?" I asked Caeden.

"What?" he asked as he backed out.

"I thought I saw... *eyes*. But... it must just be my imagination."

Caeden's blue eyes flicked through the lot. "I don't see anything."

But I still couldn't shake the feeling that something was there.

* * *

Caeden parked on the street in front of Gram's house. With a yawn he said, "Let's just go to bed. We can unpack in the morning."

"That sounds like an excellent plan to me," I opened the door. "Go pee Archie," I coaxed as I sat the dog down in the grass.

Caeden opened the trunk and let Murphy out of his

cage. The dog stretched and rubbed affectionately at his master's legs.

I rubbed my jeans as I pulled my keys out of my pocket. I looked at the little yellow house that had become my home these past months.

"Hey Caeden," I said.

"Yeah?" he replied as he stretched his stiff back and a few joints popped.

"Since we're home early... and after we take care of pack business... maybe you could help me decorate my room? Like paint it and stuff?"

He winced. "Paint? Gosh, I don't know..." he pretended to deliberate. Finally he shrugged. "I'll do it cause I love ya," he wrapped his arms around me and kissed me with a loud smack of his lips.

"If we don't get in bed soon I'm going to fall asleep in your arms."

He laughed and nuzzled my neck. "That wouldn't be a bad thing."

I pulled away and headed to the door. After the third try it clicked and the door swung open. I let the dogs go first before I stepped inside. The dogs headed straight for my room.

"They're going to totally hog the bed," I said to Caeden as I closed and locked the door.

Grinning, he whispered, "You're right."

We tiptoed quietly down the hallway and into my room. Sure enough the two dogs were on the bed snoozing.

"Murph, Arch, off the bed," commanded Caeden.

Murphy immediately obliged but Archie opened his eyes and quirked his brow before going back to sleep. Caeden threw his arms in the air and looked at me.

"Well, I tried." He hooked his thumbs into the back of his shirt and yanked it off.

I giggled and grabbed some pajamas from my dresser before slipping into my closet to change. Caeden may have seen *everything* but that didn't mean I was comfortable giving him a strip tease every time the opportunity presented itself.

I pulled on the flannel bottoms and a pale green cami top. I bundled up my dirty clothes and exited the closet. I tossed the clothes in the hamper. "She shoots, she scores!" I staged whispered.

Caeden laughed from my bed. His jeans and shirt were on the floor so he wore nothing but his boxer briefs. Oh dear lord, was he trying to kill me? Normally he at least wore pajama bottoms. I swallowed thickly before climbing into the bed beside him. He put his arm around me and pulled me against his very warm, very naked chest. I was also very aware of the fact that there were only a few pieces of clothing separating us. My heart stuttered.

"Sleep babe," he said and kissed my forehead. His lips seemed to burn the sensitive skin. I hated to tell him but sleep was going to be nearly impossible with him practically naked in my bed.

Despite that thought sleep did eventually come and I was thankful.

* * *

My cheek burned where it was pressed against Caeden's too warm chest. Sometime in the night I had kicked the covers off of us. Sleeping next to Caeden and his too hot body temperature tended to make me do that.

Archie was pressed against the wall and Murphy slept right next to me on the floor. Based on the light coming through the window it was near noon.

"Caeden?" I sat up and pushed his shoulder. "Babe, wake up."

"Hmm," he hummed in his sleep.

"You need to wake up, honey," I coaxed.

"Kiss me," he said, with his eyes still closed. He pinched my side.

I lowered my lips to his and pressed tenderly. "Awake now Sleeping Beauty?"

"Not quite," he opened his eyes and gave me a

crooked grin. His dimple winked at me and I just couldn't resist kissing it. Despite being only eighteen Caeden looked like a man, like someone twenty-four or twenty-five, so his dimple added a bit of a childlike quality to his manly appearance.

Before I knew what was happening Caeden pulled at me and I was flat on my back. He pulled me against him.

Oh.

And then he kissed me passionately. His hand pressed into the small of my back and his warmth threatened to burn me. My hands laced around his back, holding him to me, and slowly crept up his smooth, muscled back, to tangle in his shaggy dark brown hair.

He pulled away and stroked my cheek with his thumb. His breathing was heavy, as was mine. "Now I'm awake."

"Me too," I breathed and a smile broke out across his face.

He gave me a quick peck on the lips, said, "I love you," before climbing over me and out of the bed.

"Love you too," I said and propped my head up on my arm to watch him as he stepped into his jeans. His shoulders and back were lean and muscled and his butt was amazing, even when it was hidden by boxer briefs. He had to be the most beautiful man alive and he was mine. Mine, mine, mine. I could do a happy dance over it.

He didn't bother to put his shirt on and he left his jeans unbuttoned and his belt unhooked.

He was definitely trying to kill me.

I watched as Caeden stretched and yawned. He ran his hands over his face and then through his hair. He turned back to me a smiled. Once again I couldn't help but appreciate his perfect washboard abs, that delicious v that disappeared into the waistband of his jeans, and the light dusting of hair covering his chest.

"I'll go unload the car and then we'll head to my house so I can get some clean clothes."

"You know," I said and downcast my eyes to the sheets. I began to pull at a stray thread. "You could just bring some clothes over here. I mean, you do sleep here every night."

He grinned and put his hand over his heart. "Are you offering me a drawer in your dresser?"

"Yeah, I am," I smiled.

"I think I'm gonna take you up on that offer but..."

"But?" I prompted. "There always has to be a but doesn't there?"

He grinned. "If I'm going to have a drawer in your dresser then I want you to have one in mine."

I couldn't help but smile. "Deal, I'll even take some stuff over with us today."

"I'll be right back," he said and started to leave the room.

"Wait!" I hollered.

"What?" he turned around.

I picked his shirt up off the floor and tossed it to him. "Please put your shirt on before all the neighbor ladies start drooling over you. I have enough competition as it is."

He laughed but put his shirt on anyway. "Be back in a minute," he called over his shoulder.

I hopped up from my bed and grabbed some clean clothes before shutting myself in the bathroom. I heard the TV and figured Gram was watching CNN.

I scrubbed the stale plane smell from my body and then pulled my wet hair back into a bun. I brushed my teeth before dabbing on some pale pink strawberry flavored gloss and swiping mascara on my lashes. I added a hint of shimmer body lotion, vanilla scented, to my arms and shoulders before dressing in a pair of olive green shorts and a black shirt.

I hung my towel up on the back of the bathroom door and headed into the kitchen. My stomach was rumbling something fierce.

Caeden was already there, eating a sandwich, with a dab of mayonnaise in the corner of his mouth. I leaned over

---

55

and kissed it away. It was so easy being with Caeden. I never second-guessed myself.

"I made you a sandwich," he pointed to the counter. "Barbeque loaf with mustard."

"I knew there was another reason I loved you besides your absolute adorableness."

He laughed and shook his head while I grabbed my plate and sat down beside him.

Gram ventured into the kitchen. She patted my shoulder and kissed the top of my head. "I've missed you. It's been far too quiet without you two banging around, but I am sorry that your trip got cut short."

"Me too," I said around a bite of my sandwich. I wiped my mouth with a paper napkin. "But at least I did get to see them."

"That's my girl," Gram said, "always seein' the bright side of things."

I snorted.

"I assume ya'll are heading over to Amy's?"

I looked at Caeden.

He swallowed. "Yeah, that's the plan."

Gram puttered over to the sink and began washing some plates that were sitting there. "Cate and I have the shop covered for the rest of the week since you two weren't supposed to be back yet. Take this time and do something fun."

"Like decorate my room," I said.

Gram turned away from the sink and smiled at me. "I was beginning to think you weren't ever going to do anything to that room."

I shrugged. "It didn't feel like the right time."

"Well, here. Take my debit card," she said and puttered over to her purse. She pulled out her wallet and began to dig through it.

"Gram, no," I said. "I have my dad's credit card. He won't mind if I get some stuff. Plus, I still have that gift card you got me."

"Am I not allowed to buy my granddaughter anything?" she pouted. "You never let me spoil you."

"Gram it's really not necessary," I said. "I appreciate the thought, I really do," I stood and kissed her cheek.

She slipped the card back inside. "Fine, you win."

I laughed and turned to Caeden. "You ready?"

"Yeah," he swallowed the rest of his sandwich. He dropped his plate in the sink and I did the same. "See you later Lucinda."

"Bye Gram," I hugged her.

We were almost out the door when Caeden grabbed my arm and said, "Wait."

"What?" I asked and instantly went on alert, sniffing the air.

"Aren't you going to bring some stuff to my house? You know, drawer sharing?"

"Oh," I said and put a hand to my racing heart. I was far too jumpy. "Yeah, sorry, I forgot."

"I'm offended," he joked and I playfully hit his arm.

I headed back to my room and he trailed behind me, before plopping on my bed beside the dogs, who were still snoozing peacefully.

I dug out my shiny royal blue duffel bag, which I had gotten from American Apparel on a trip to New York City, from the bottom of my closet. I grabbed some jeans, shirts, hairbands, and a bunch of other crap and dumped it into the bag. I struggled to zip it closed.

Caeden took it from me and slung it over his shoulder. "I think I'm going to get me one of these. I can rock the shiny metallic look."

I laughed as he strutted out of my room, doing duck lips, when he reached the front door he turned and struck a pose.

"Do that again and I'll take a picture and post it all over Facebook," I threatened.

"You wouldn't dare," he said.

"Oh I would," I laughed.

"You mean to tell me that you would mortify the love of your life?"

"Yes, and enjoy every minute of it," I crossed my arms over my chest and leaned against the wall. The dogs wandered out of my room and into the hall. Archie stretched and Murphy rolled around on the floor.

"You're sick," he grinned.

"What can I say?" I shrugged. "I love it when your cheeks and ears get all red with embarrassment."

Caeden shook his too long hair. "We better go."

"Come on guys," I said to the dogs. They immediately jumped up from the floor and ran to the door.

Caeden let them out and I closed the door behind us. Gram's car was gone so I figured she must have left for the cupcake shop already.

Turning around I busted out laughing when I saw Caeden struggling with Murphy. His face was quickly turning red. "You. Have. To. Get. In. The. Crate."

The large dog would not be budged.

"Come on Murphy. I don't want to hurt you," Caeden said. Murphy was half in, half out, of the crate and he wasn't budging. Caeden pushed at his backside. "Please, Murph? When we get home I'll give you a nice big juicy bone." Suddenly Murphy was in the cage and Caeden fell from the sudden movement. I was laughing so hard now that I had tears running out of my eyes. "That was not nice, Murph," Caeden chided as he slid the locks into place.

He had a cut on his cheek but it was already healing. He closed the trunk and turned to me with his hands on his hips.

"That went well."

"Definitely," I giggled.

I opened the car door and picked up Archie. As soon as I closed the door he pawed at the window. "You want it down bud? Wanna feel the wind through your pointy ears?"

He made a cute little noise as I rolled the window down. As soon as Caeden started driving he turned and gave me a cute little dog smile. All pointed teeth and rolling pink tongue.

On the ride to Caeden's house we were both quiet. I think we were both lost in our thoughts.

He came to the gate and entered his card. The doors quickly swung open and we drove through. The garage door was up and two people were in there. One with fiery red hair was pressed against a brand new green Jeep and was totally making out with the other person. There was enough passion to ignite the garage.

"Is that Charlotte?" I asked leaning forward. I knew it had to be. No one else had red hair that shade.

"Yeah, and my brother."

SIX.

Caeden parked the car and rubbed his knees. "Well, I guess I should've known this was coming."

I laughed. "Yeah, you should've. Do you think they've noticed us yet?"

Bryce and Charlotte were still going at it. Tongues, hands, it was a bit dizzying watching them.

"I don't think so," he said and tapped the horn. The noise made me jump and it did the same to the two lovers. They both looked around, with the whole deer in headlights look, before spotting us.

I gave a small wave and Caeden grinned cheekily before hopping out.

I opened the door and let Archie out. Caeden had let Murphy out and he was running around in merry circles. He saw a bird and took off after it. Didn't dogs know that they couldn't fly? If so, why did they chase birds? The bird is always going to get away.

Caeden cleared his throat and must have decided not to say anything about the intense make-out session because instead he said, "Are the... uh... others here?"

Charlotte was blushing profusely, her pale freckled skin turning crimson. She straightened her curly hair and said, "Yeah, I think they're in the kitchen."

"Did you get a new car?" Caeden asked Bryce.

Bryce's hands were shoved in his pockets and he was looking anywhere but at his brother. "Uh-hmm, Stella died. This baby is Stella Jr." He lovingly rubbed the side of the brand new Jeep.

"Okay then," Caeden said. "Well, I need to talk to everybody so you might want to head on into the kitchen."

Bryce shrugged away from the Jeep and took Charlotte's hand. "You got it commander," Bryce saluted Caeden.

Caeden shook his head and turned to me. "His sense of humor never ceases to amaze me."

I snorted. "That was pretty tame. I called your house

one time and he answered-"

"Oh lord, I don't think I want to know what he said," Caeden grinned as he followed Bryce and Charlotte to the house. I kind of wished the garage was connected to the house. I hated being out in the open like this.

Caeden took my hand as if he sensed my unease.

"Well, I'm going to tell you anyway," I smiled. "He said, 'Mel's Taxidermy. You bag em' we stuff em'.'"

"No, he didn't!" Caeden laughed. "Wow, I don't know why mom ever lets him answer the phone."

"I just wonder what strangers would think if they dialed the wrong number and he answered."

"They'd probably be thoroughly freaked out."

"Luckily I knew it was him so I just laughed. Does he answer his cellphone that way?"

"You betcha," Caeden grinned and his dimple peeked through, taunting me.

We went in the side door and straight to the kitchen. Amy was whipping up lunch. When she saw us she stopped what she was doing and smiled at her eldest son.

"Give me a hug!" she said and enveloped him in her arms. "I know you were only gone a few days but I missed you so much! What will I do when you move out?" She kissed his cheek and moved to me. "And Sophie, I missed you too. I'm so sorry you had to leave in such a hurry and under such circumstances."

"It's fine," I said and hugged her back. "We needed to be here."

"I'm making lunch," she said, as if we hadn't noticed the mess behind her. "Homemade pizza. Are you hungry?"

Even though I'd just eaten a sandwich my stomach rumbled. I blushed and looked at Caeden. "Yeah, I'm hungry."

"And I'm always hungry," Caeden rubbed his flat stomach.

"Good," she clapped her hands together. She was just a total ball of energy today. "Go sit down and when it's ready

I'll bring it."

Bryce and Charlotte were sitting side by side at the table; holding hands. Logan was sulking, at the end of the table, the front legs of his chair off the ground, and his blond hair combed back. He was scowling at no one and nothing. Dude needed a serious chill pill.

I spotted Bentley's dark head and was just beginning to scan for Chris when I saw that she was sitting in his lap. She nuzzled his neck and giggled. Bentley's smile lit his brown eyes as he whispered in her ear.

I turned to Caeden. "Holy hell, what happened while we were gone? Is it mating season for wolves?"

Caeden's blue eyes were wide. "Apparently so." He paused at the head of the table and cleared his throat. "We have some important things to discuss."

Chris slid out of Bentley's lap and straightened her honey blond hair. It had gotten longer in the past few months.

Caeden didn't sit down; instead he leaned forward, placing his hands flat on the table. He looked into each of their eyes. "With Travis as Alpha we are all in danger. He's even more unstable than his father was. Based on what... you described," Caeden winced as he looked at Bentley. "It was pretty gruesome. Travis is power hungry and I'm positive he'll come after me just like his father. We're going to have to do more scans of the woods and change up the groupings." He eyed the lovebirds. "We'll change the groupings every shift so that Travis can't predict who will be together. If you smell a hint of anything suspicious you let me know. *Anything.* We're in danger, and I can't press the importance of safety and caution enough. Don't do anything stupid, I mean it," he glared at his little brother. "First shift tonight will be Logan and Bryce. Bentley and I will take over for you. Sophie and-" He looked around with a bewildered expression.

Christian and Charlotte giggled. "I guess Sophie's all by herself," Chris said.

Bryce spoke up and said, "I'll do it."

"So, basically," Logan said as he drew random designs on the table. "We're going to be doing twenty-four hour patrols?"

"It's necessary," Caeden snapped, "for the safety of our pack."

Patrols had just been after school and the occasional one at night.

"What about once school starts back up in a few days?" Logan drawled.

"Then patrol starts right after the bell rings and through the whole night."

"Are you kidding?" Logan slammed his hand on the table. "When are we supposed to sleep?"

Caeden's teeth ground together and his nails sharpened to claws. "Are you questioning my authority?"

Logan paled. "I- I-" he was saved from saying anything more by Amy.

She brought over the five pizzas covered in toppings. They smelled heavenly.

"I'll be in my office if you need me," she patted Caeden on the shoulder and ruffled Bryce's hair.

Caeden's nails retracted and the tension slowly leaked from his body.

Caeden and I sat down and grabbed a slice of the pizza. Two whole pizzas were already gone.

I cleared my throat and poked Caeden in the side.

"What?" he said.

I gave him a significant look.

"Oh right," he swallowed. "Sophie needs more training in how to fight. I'm not sure that I'll be able to do it."

"I'll help you," Bentley said.

"I'm game," Bryce said. "Anything that allows me to knock my brother's girlfriend on her ass sounds like fun."

Caeden smacked the back of Bryce's head.

"I'll help you too," Chris said. "I may not be a wolf yet but that doesn't mean I still can't beat you."

63

Logan, of course, said nothing. I would never want to play the quiet game with him. I'd definitely lose.

Charlotte reached across the table to take my hand. "Between all of our help you'll be the biggest, baddest, wolf out there."

"So," Chris leaned forward, "when do we get to kick the crap out of Sophie's toosh?"

"Now, I guess," Caeden shrugged. Chris grinned wickedly and I knew I was in for a beating. "But don't hurt her cute tooshie too much," he pinched my hip. "I'm rather fond of it."

SEVEN.

I groaned as my body slammed forcefully down on the mat.

Was she trying to kill me?

I lay there for a moment as I tried to draw air into my lungs. I smacked the mat with my hand and stood.

Chris smirked at me. I wanted to rip every single blond hair from her head. She'd already broken my wrist and I'd had to sit for twenty minutes while it healed. Her pale green eyes shimmered. She was enjoying kicking my ass *way* too much.

"Christian," Caeden said for the one-hundredth time. "You're supposed to be teaching her, not killing her."

"Do you think Travis is going to teach her to fight before he kills her? I think *not*," she rolled her shoulders and raised her fists. "Besides I'm not hitting her *that* hard."

I could argue with that. My bruises were quickly forming bruises and I still had a round with Bentley and Bryce.

Chris lunged towards me and I ducked, swiping my leg around behind her legs to knock her down. Despite not having shifted, Chris' reflexes were much better than those of a normal human. She easily jumped over my leg. "Nice try," she laughed and dove to tackle me.

I twisted my body so that I broke the fall with my hands and not my back. As soon as my hands touched the ground I turned back around and brought my legs back so that I could kick her in the chest. She rolled off of me and then smiled. "Better."

"That's enough," Caeden said. I was about to thank God when he continued, "of that. It's time you practice in your wolf form. That's the form Travis will most likely use to attack you. Not that Chris hasn't been a most excellent teacher," he flashed her a warning smile.

"Kay, kay, I get it," she put her hands up in a surrendering gesture. I was pleased to see that she was sweating and her chest heaving. Maybe I'd given her more of a workout than I thought. "I'm going to hit the showers," she pointed with her thumb over her shoulder to the separate guy's and girls showers. We even had lockers. I swear, the basement was a better equipped gym than any around town.

"Sophie, you ready?" Caeden asked as he held out his hand.

No.

"Yes sir," I answered instead.

Caeden's lips quirked as I placed my hand in his and he hauled me up.

"Outside," he motioned to Bentley and Bryce.

Bryce hopped up like an over active puppy and squeezed my shoulder. "This is gonna be so much fun."

"Oh yeah, loads," I my words dripped with sarcasm. He grinned and ducked out the basement door and into the woods. Bentley was already ahead. "They are so going to kill me," I said to Caeden as he lifted a branch over my head.

Caeden chuckled, "Don't worry I won't let them." He led me to a thick cropping of trees and bushes. "Strip," he said.

I quirked my brow and grinned, "You want a strip tease in the woods. That's pretty kinky." I unbuttoned my shorts and began to ease them down my hips in a joking manner.

Color flooded his cheeks and he turned around with his back to me. "That was *so* not what I meant," he said.

I laughed as I removed the rest of my clothes and the laugh turned to a bark as I switched forms. It was so easy for me to become a wolf, freeing. I shook my shaggy brown coat. Sometimes, it felt like I was coming home when I entered into my wolf form.

Caeden and I switched places so that he could switch forms.

Caeden understood that I was uncomfortable changing in front of the others. I didn't grow up running around naked like they did. It took some getting used to. I didn't really mind around Caeden, since he'd been there with me the first time, but I still appreciated the gesture.

In quicker time than it took me his gray wolf was beside me. His tongue lolled out of his mouth and his eyes took on a periwinkle cast. I wondered if my eyes got lighter, took on a different tone, like his. I guess I'd have to ask him.

Can you smell them? He asked.

I lifted my muzzle in the air and sniffed. I turned my head northeast. *That way.*

Very good. He grinned but with his inch long teeth it seemed menacing. *I want you to run as fast as you can to them. Speed is your greatest weapon against an opponent. Female shifters have much more speed than males so we know to never underestimate our girls.* His human laughter filled my head. *Ready, get set, go!*

I was gone. My legs stretched faster, and farther, and I soon left Caeden behind. The speed was exhilarating. I was sure that real wolves couldn't possibly run this fast.

I jumped over a log and my claws dug in; bark chipping off. Birds, squirrels, and other woodland creatures scattered when they caught my predator scent in the air. I swung to my right and if my sense of smell was reliable I was two hundred yards from Bentley and Bryce.

I bound into the clearing and skidded to a stop.

A few seconds later, Caeden came through the brush. He shook some brambles from his fur, panting, and plopped on the ground. *Geez, I didn't know you were* that *fast.*

I came up to him and licked the side of his face. *Never under estimate me Williams.*

Wouldn't dream of it Beaumont.

Who wants to go first? I looked between Bentley's black wolf and Bryce's reddish brown one.

Me, me, me! Bryce chanted and turned in a circle.

Bentley barked a laugh. *Bryce can go first. He'll be able to demonstrate an* unskilled *attack.*

Hey! Bryce said and bit Bentley's shoulder.

Just speaking the truth pup.

Okay, okay. Caeden intervened. *Enough arguing.*

We're wasting time.

He started it. Whined Bryce.

Enough! Barked Caeden. *Get ready Sophie.* He turned to me. *Bryce over there, Sophie stay here.* He said so that we were on opposite ends.

Ready... Set...

Bryce started running towards me.

Dammit Bryce, I didn't say go! Caeden scolded but I was beyond listening.

I prepared myself for the impact but it never came. I looked to see that Caeden had Bryce pinned to the ground by the neck.

What the hell Caeden? I'm supposed to attack him, not you! I scolded my mate.

Sorry. I'm sorry. Caeden let go of his brother. *I can't do this. I can't watch it and just do* nothing*! My instincts to defend you kick in.*

I need to learn this Caeden. Maybe it would be better if you leave.

Leave! I can't leave you! What if you get hurt!

Bryce and Bentley aren't going to hurt me. I argued. *You didn't have a problem when I was fighting Chris and she broke my wrist.*

That's different.

No it's not. I said. *Besides, we heal. My wrist was better in no time at all.*

Sophie.

Caeden, I need to be able to defend myself. You're not going to be around all the time to protect me.

Caeden said nothing for a moment.

Fine. But I won't be far away and I will *be listening. If you get hurt I'll be here in no time at all.* He looked warningly at Bryce and Bentley before taking off.

Bryce looked at me and said, *Ready?* Before I could answer he attacked.

Jerkface.

He bit my shoulder and I nipped at his side. His teeth

tore into my flesh and I gritted my teeth so that no sound of pain could escape. I didn't want Caeden coming back after being gone for only three seconds.

Get angry, Sophie. Use your anger as power. Bryce coached me.

I pushed forward and pulled my skin from his mouth. Blood matted my fur and dripped from his mouth.

Speed, Caeden had said, use my speed.

Even though we were no more than a few feet apart I rushed him. He wasn't expecting that. I had him on his back and went for the sensitive skin of his belly. Distantly I could hear Bentley's cackling bark and his human laughter floating through my head.

Time! Bryce cried. *Tap out! Stop!*

I pulled away and he shakily rose to his feet. *That was... incredible. You were like a freaking avenging angel... or wolf... whatever. If I had been a true attacker you would've killed me.*

What? My voice rang through our heads as a gasp.

I definitely don't want to end up on your bad side. You're a fucking beast. Bentley cackled. *Wow.*

Travis won't know what hit him when it comes to you. Bryce shook his shaggy wolf head. *If we keep practicing with you, you'll be unstoppable. Un-freakin-stoppable.*

Let's go again then. I said.

You're on. Bryce taunted.

Wait. Bentley said calmly. *Let's try it with two attackers this time.*

I'm not sure I like those odds. My voice quaked.

I think Bryce and I need to be more worried than you. Bentley said and the two wolves began to circle me. I whined and pawed the ground. No wolf liked to be caged in.

Calm yourself, Sophie; let your instincts take over. Look for weak points.

Bryce's cockiness would definitely be a weak point for him but Bentley? The guy was built like a truck. As they circled me I watched for any muscle ticks, anything that

---

69

would give me leverage. Bentley's back legs tensed and I knew he was getting ready to spring. As soon as his back paws lifted from the ground I slid to my belly, not a wolf's first instinct, and bit into his foot. His blood rushed into my mouth, hot and fast, leaving behind the taste of rust. *Oh, yuck.*

Bentley was a seasoned fighter so a blow to his foot wasn't going to take him down completely. So I bit into his hamstring, which left him incapable of walking.

Bryce looked at me in shock.

How did you move so fast, Sophie? You were a freaking blur!

Are you going to fight me or not? I asked. I was beginning to enjoy this now that I was the one winning.

Ugh... Is that a trick question? I mean you're not going to kill me are you?

Bryce. I whined.

Alright, alright. He leaped towards me. I jumped to the side and before he could turn I had jumped on his back.

You're dead. I chimed.

Bentley lay off to the side while his leg healed. Panting he said, *You're a natural. It's the craziest thing ever, you move like a ninja. Bryce and I* know *what we're doing and you make us look like fucking amateurs. Caeden!* He called. *Get your ass back here!*

Caeden's laughter filled our heads. *Oh, she whooped you two. That was the funniest thing I've ever seen. Wow, Soph, my little she-wolf. I didn't know you had it in you.*

Hey! I exclaimed offended.

Sorry, he said, *I just expected* you *to get hurt after the way Chris tore you apart in your human form.*

I have this insane urge to bite you right now, I grinned menacingly.

He laughed. *I still think you should continue to practice in both forms. After all, practice makes perfect, right?*

At least I know now that I'm not completely

defenseless.

I'm so proud of you, he nuzzled my neck. *You amaze me more and more every day. Come on,* he said, *it's starting to get dark. Bryce you better find Logan and start your patrol.*

Oh joy, Bryce said sarcastically before taking off.

I'm sorry I hurt you, I told Bentley.

His chuckle filled my head. *How about from now on we don't take bites out of each other? Deal?*

Deal.

He struggled to his feet and started to limp away. *You were amazing, Sophie.* Bentley said as he disappeared.

Thanks. It felt amazing to be complimented on fighting skills from Bentley.

Caeden continued nuzzling me and breathing in my scent. His thoughts projected to me by accident. *Cookies, cookies cookies. Cakes, cakes, cakes. Icing, icing, icing. Hmmm.* Buttercream *icing.*

Are you done sniffing me? I chuckled.

I'll never be tired of your delicious scent. He said but pulled away. His tongue lolled out of his mouth. *Can you smell our clothes?*

I lifted my nose in the air and inhaled. The flood of scents was enough to give me a headache. As soon as I located the scent of cookies and pine in the distance I took off running. If anyone asked me my favorite thing about being a shifter I would say the speed.

I reached our clothes and shifted forms. I had worried that I'd have a difficult time changing from human to wolf and back again but it was as easy as breathing. As soon as I pictured myself in the other form, my body would vibrate, shimmer, and then I would become whatever form I wanted.

I pulled my clothes on and was just finishing buttoning my shorts when Caeden's shaggy gray wolf appeared.

"Gosh, you're so slow," I joked.

He barked a laugh before nudging my leg with his

wet nose. "Ew, Caeden! You got wolf snot all over my leg!" I left him behind the bush as I stared at the wet mess on my leg. His barking laughter quickly turned to human laughter.

"Wolf snot?" he grinned.

"Yes, and it's all over my leg. It's gross," I complained. "Just because we can change into wolves doesn't mean we need to act like them all the time."

"You're so cute when you're mad," he zipped his jeans.

"Caeden!" I stomped my foot and clenched my fists. My nails dig into the skin.

"You are," he shrugged as he pulled his shirt over his head.

"I guess we'll be old and gray and you'll still be telling me I'm *cute* when I'm mad?"

"Most definitely," he said and came out from behind the bush. He wrapped his arm around my waist. He pressed his lips to mine and I pushed at his chest. He chuckled into my mouth and only kissed me deeper. My fists soon stopped beating his chest and instead grabbed his shirt and pulled him closer. Pulling away and breathing heavy he said, "And that's how I plan to end all our spats."

"It certainly works," I breathed. "What were we arguing about again?"

He threw his head back and laughed. Taking my hand he led me through the woods. "Nothing important." We strode a few more feet before he said, "Ready to put your stuff in my room? I promise to give you a whole drawer."

His grin was contagious and I found myself smiling back. "My bag is still in your car."

"Well, let's get it," he smiled. "It would be a shame for you to cart all that home."

"Most definitely," I played along.

His Jeep was parked outside of the garage. He unlocked it and it chirped happily. I opened the door and grabbed my bag.

Caeden took my hands and pressed his face against

72

my hair. "I love you," he said, just outside the door.

I stopped and looked up into his cerulean eyes. "I love you too, more than I ever thought it was possible to love someone."

He grinned and opened the door. We were about halfway up the twisted staircase when his mom saw us.

"Is Sophie staying the night?" she asked, noticing my bag. She stood at the bottom of the stairs with some papers in her hand.

Caeden blushed and stammered. Composing himself he said, "Sophie's going to leave some of her things here and I'm going to keep some things at her house."

"Oh," Amy nodded and her eyes glittered, "I see." She smiled and presumably went back to her office.

"That was awkward," I said.

"I think it was worse for me than you," he rubbed his face.

I laughed. "I think you may be right. Your face is the reddest I've ever seen it." At my words it got even redder. I giggled.

"Stop laughing at me," he pushed open the door to his bedroom.

The warm blue gray color instantly calmed me. I sat down on his bed and placed my bag beside me. I fingered the soft quilt that was varying shades of blue and gray.

Caeden proceeded to open the various drawers of his dresser. "This one should work," he muttered to himself as he dumped the contents of the top drawer, out on the floor. Once the drawer was empty he turned to me, "All yours."

I laughed and shook my head. "Thanks but you didn't need to make such a huge mess," I nodded to the basketball shorts and socks littering the white shag carpet.

He sighed and looked at the mess on the floor with his hands on his hips. "Oh well," he said. He grabbed a few articles of clothing and started towards his bathroom. "I'm going to shower. Make yourself at home."

I nodded and proceeded to unzip my bag. A strong

scent of wood and stain wafted from his dresser and nearly overwhelmed me. Not everything was a perk of being a shifter.

Holding my breath I folded my clothes and neatly organized them in the top drawer. My stuff didn't take up much room so I picked up his socks and shorts and placed them beside my clothes. I was surprised by the amount of satisfaction I felt at seeing our stuff side by side. A smile spread across my face. I was so lucky to have Caeden. Most people never had a love like ours and here I had found it in high school. I looked towards the closed bathroom door and blushed. I could say with conviction that my future husband was behind that door.

Blushing I plopped on his bed. I hadn't even graduated high school; so I should definitely not be thinking about calling Caeden my husband or feel such pleasure from the thought.

I am so screwed, I thought, and threw my arm over my eyes.

* * *

I must have dozed off because the sound of Caeden opening the bathroom door startled me.

He wore a pair of navy gym shorts and a plain white shirt. He rubbed his shaggy hair with a towel, sending water droplets cascading through the room.

"Were you sleeping?" he asked when he noticed me rubbing my eyes.

I stifled a yawn. "I must have dozed off."

He plopped on the bed beside me. "If you want to take a nap, go ahead."

He wrapped his warm arms around me and snuggled close.

"I shouldn't," I shook my head. I eyed the guitars scattered around his room. "I really wish you'd play for me again."

He blushed. "Are you sure?"

"I love it when you play."

"I'm not that good," he said bashfully.

I poked his arm. "That mister is a big fat lie."

"What do you want me to play?" he asked as he reached over and picked up a red guitar.

"Anything you want to play." I folded my hands and tucked them under my cheek.

He grabbed up a guitar pick from his nightstand and began to strum. I quickly recognized the song as *Meet Me on the Equinox* by Death Cab for Cutie. He began to sing the lyrics softly under his breath. I soaked in the words and music, felt the vibrations under my skin, and smiled up at him. "I wish you'd sing and play for me more often. You're so talented."

"I don't know about that," he finished the song and leaned the guitar against the wall.

"Really?" I quirked a brow. "When you played at Griff's those girls were ready to throw themselves at you."

He laughed. "Okay, maybe I'm not *that* bad."

"Ya think?" I smiled.

"Take a nap," he whispered into my hair. His breath tickled my skin and I shivered. "You'll have to be up early in the morning for your duty. Get some extra sleep while you have the chance."

"Don't leave me," I gripped his shirt in my hand, wrinkling the fabric. "Stay and take a nap too."

"I'm certainly not going to deny that request," he pulled me even closer. My leg entwined with his and my head rested on his chest. My hand fingered the bumps and ridges of his exquisite body through the thin cotton of his shirt. "Sophie," he said and his voice was husky, "if you keep that up I'll never go to sleep."

I giggled and stopped tracing his chest. I took a deep breath and pine, wood, cinnamon, and citrus filled my lungs. It was such a unique scent, so purely masculine, and completely Caeden.

"Sleep, my little she-wolf," he murmured as he rubbed my neck.

—

75

"Don't call me that," I mumbled as I fell asleep in the arms of my beloved.

EIGHT

I parked my Honda Pilot in the Williams' driveway. It was still dark out, the sun not having risen, and I was scheduled for my first turn on guard duty. I was thankful that Caeden had insisted on my taking a nap yesterday. I didn't feel nearly as sleepy as I normally would. I locked my car and went in search of Bryce.

I didn't find him outside, and I couldn't smell him, so I headed for the front door.

I was just about to knock on the door when it swung open. Bryce stuck his head out and grinned. "Want some breakfast? Mom made omelets," he held up a plate.

"Don't we need to-" I pointed to the woods, "you know *go?*"

Bryce grinned. "They can wait a few more minutes. Besides, I'm not doing guard duty on an empty stomach. I'm not eating a squirrel for breakfast, blech-" he made a face as he led me to kitchen. "I did that once and I can assure you, it will never, ever, happen again."

"Ew," I crinkled my nose.

Bryce handed me a plate and I sat down beside him at the kitchen island. "Where's your mom?" I asked looking around.

"I think she went back to bed," he shrugged.

"I'll have to thank her for breakfast later then," I said.

Bryce swallowed a big bite of egg and said, "She's used to feeding all of us. This-" he motioned to our two plates, "is a piece of cake compared to what she normally has to cook up."

I shrugged. "I'd still like to thank her, this certainly wasn't necessary."

"Pish posh," Bryce faked a nasally British accent, making me giggle. "It was completely necessary. Too bad she forgot the tea and crumpets." He took a swig of his orange juice and purposefully stuck out his pinkie. I laughed a bit harder.

"I don't think British people actually sound like that,"

I mocked him around my laughter.

"Oh puh-*lease* girlfriend," he said, switching to snarky popular girl. He continued with his funny voices while we finished eating. I ended up laughing so hard that I had tears running down my face. I stood to clean the dishes when he grabbed my wrist. "Leave those for the scullery maid, dear, we can't have you pruning your sweet little fingers," he switched back to British.

"Bryce," I said, "I can't leave these for your mom."

"Oh fine," he said in his normal voice. "I'll help."

Amy walked in just as we finished cleaning the dishes. She yawned and poured her customary black coffee.

"Did you get Bryce to wash dishes?" she asked.

"Yeah," I said. "I didn't want them to be left for you."

"I don't think I can remember him ever doing dishes," she smiled at her youngest son.

"And thank you for breakfast Amy," I said.

"I didn't make breakfast," her brow furrowed.

I turned to Bryce, "But-"

He blushed and looked away sheepishly.

A smile spread across Amy's face. "Bryce Elliot did you make breakfast for yourself and Sophie?"

"Maybe," he said softly and with more volume, "You'll never get me to tell!" He edged out of the kitchen towards the front door.

"I guess that's my cue to leave," I said to Amy.

I followed Bryce into the woods before we headed separate ways to shift.

I shook my shaggy coat before stretching out my senses. I located Bryce a short way from where I was and took off in his direction.

When I found him my laughter came out in a sharp bark.

Bryce was running around chasing a yellow butterfly and trying to catch it with his teeth.

Bryce! I scolded. *Is this what you guys do when you're on duty?*

He stopped and looked at me. His blue eyes appeared almost navy. *When I'm with Logan we typically give each other manicures and pedicures.*

I should have brought my nail polish. I joked.

Actually, he said, still chasing the butterfly, *everyone's pretty boring. Logan sulks, Caeden bosses me around, and Bentley just moons over Chris. You should be fun.*

Don't you do patrols in your human form too? I asked.

Yeah, he growled at the butterfly when it landed on his nose. He shook his head and sneezed, sending the butterfly back into the air. *Caeden doesn't really like to do that but it gives Christian and Charlotte a bit of practice.*

He began to head north so I followed him.

How come Caeden never let me do that? I'm surprised he's letting me do this now.

Caeden's just overprotective. He's always been that way but he's been worse since dad died. He thinks it's his job to protect and save everybody. It's not that he thinks you're incapable; he just doesn't want to see you hurt and after what happened with Travis- He gave the equivalent of a shrug. *We better hurry. We're already late so I'm sure we'll hear hell from Caeden.*

He took off at a sprint and I ran after him. I had to hold back so that I didn't pass him. He skidded to a stop, kicking up leaves.

It's about time, snapped Caeden as he stalked towards us.

Bryce rolled his eyes. *Told ya he'd be a grumpy pants.*

I'll show you a grumpy pants, Caeden growled menacingly. His teeth flashed in the rising sun.

We're here now, Bryce said. *Go home and take a nap.*

I will, he rumbled.

Bentley's dark form joined Caeden's.

Caeden turned his attention to me and he instantly

changed. He sauntered over and began to nuzzle my neck. *I love you, be safe, and don't let Bryce do anything stupid.* From the tone of his words I knew the others couldn't hear him.

I love you too. Take a nap. You look tired.

I'll try. Bentley's dad and Charlotte's mom will relieve you. It's hard to get the older wolves to do duty. They have other responsibilities. But until Chris and Charlotte shift it's too tight for us to take turns. We'll be exhausted.

You already look exhausted.

It's necessary, he said. *Travis is unpredictable.*

I know. Go home.

His pink tongue shot out and liked the side of my face. *Later babe!* He called as he ran away.

Bentley looked between me and Bryce. *Be careful,* he said before running after Caeden.

So, Bryce said. *What did Mr. Perfect say to you?*

If I had been in my human form a blush would've stained my cheeks. I decided to give Bryce the edited version. *He said to be careful and that Jeremy and Savannah would be relieving us.* Bryce snorted. *He also said to make sure that* you *don't do anything stupid.*

Moi? Do something stupid? Never! His laughter filled my head.

Alright, Bryce how do we do this?

We walk around... And smell things.

That's it?

Pretty much. If you come across anything suspicious just call for me. If it's really *bad howl and the others will come.*

Okay, I said.

I'll head this way. He nodded to the left. *And you go that way.* He nodded to the right. *You can run if you want, just remember to smell. We'll come across each other eventually and then we'll widen the circle.*

Before I could ask anything else he was running. I shook my head and took off in the other direction.

I inhaled the scents of nature, looking for anything that screamed *wrong*. I didn't pick up anything suspicious and I quickly met up with Bryce and we stretched the circle. I easily began to notice the path they had created.

Hours went by and nothing odd came up. I was relieved by that fact but bored. Very, very, bored and my legs were getting tired.

Jeremy, Bentley's dad, and Savannah, Charlotte's mom, showed up in the afternoon. I was exhausted. Bryce and I said our hellos and our goodbyes to them before taking off.

I found my clothes and switched to my human form. My muscles were aching. I was desperate for a nap and very hot, very long, bath. I wasn't sure which I wanted first.

I pulled my clothes on and headed towards the house and to my car. Caeden was leaning against it and when he saw me emerge from the woods he enveloped me in a hug.

"Ow," I said and pulled away.

"That bad?" he asked.

"I hurt everywhere," I yawned. "I used muscles I never knew existed before. I'm going to go home and take a nap." I pointed to the car.

He kissed the top of my head, deciding it was a safe zone, and said, "Stay here. You can sleep in my bed. You have clothes here. Remember?"

"Are you sure? I don't want to invade in your personal space," I said, struggling to keep my eyes open.

"Of course I don't mind; you could never invade my personal space." A thought seemed to strike him and a worried expression clouded his face. "Do I invade your space?"

"No, no, of course not," I said. "I didn't mean it like that."

He let out a sigh of relief. "Okey dokey then, my bed it is," his mouth grazed my ear and I shivered from the contact.

He took my hand in his and led me into the house and

up to his bedroom.

"Can I have a bath first?" I asked.

"Sure," he said. He opened his bathroom door and then seemed to recall that he only had a shower. "Mom won't mind if you use her bathtub. The thing is the size of a small swimming pool."

"Let me grab something to change into," I ruffled through what was now my drawer. I grabbed a pair of cotton shorts and a tank top that would be comfortable to sleep in. "I'm ready," I said.

"Mom's room is this way," he said and led me to a side of the upstairs I'd never seen before. "Mom wanted our rooms away from hers because of my music and Bryce's games. Apparently we're too loud," he rolled his blue eyes as if them being too loud was an impossibility.

He opened a door and ushered me inside.

The walls were painted a pale but warm brown. The furniture was a rich dark wood with mostly antique pieces, only a few contemporary items. The bed covers were a golden honey color and so fluffy that it tempted me to take a dive for the bed.

Caeden opened the bathroom door and ushered me inside. Like the bedroom, the bathroom, was brown and gold.

Caeden started a tub of hot water and he hadn't been exaggerating. It was huge! There was a cluster of different bubble baths. Caeden picked one up, unscrewed the cap, and sniffed.

"Ugh! Oh! Ew!" he said and thrust the bubbles away from him. The soapy residue lingered on the edge of his nose and I giggled. He picked up another and hesitantly sniffed it. "Oh, that's better," he added a cap full of bubbles to the steaming water. The scent of vanilla permeated the air.

He ventured over to the double sink and opened the cabinets. He pulled out a downy gold towel and laid it beside the tub.

Caeden looked around and scratched the back of his head. The movement caused his shirt to ride up and flash his smooth tan muscles and light smattering of dark hair. "I'll... uh... be in my room. If you need me," he pointed his thumb over his shoulder.

I smiled. "I'll be fine."

"You're not going to pass out in the bathtub are you?" he asked. Concern flooded his eyes, turning them from their normal pool blue color, to a stormy sea gray.

"No," I laughed. "I'm tired but not *that* tired."

"Don't take too long or I'll be forced to barge in here," he said in all seriousness.

"You wouldn't dare," I stuck my hands on my hips.

"I've already seen everything anyway," he said. He tenderly caressed my face and in a soft tone said, "You don't need to hide from me, ever." His long black lashes fanned out and brushed the high planes of his cheekbones. He cupped my face in his warm, large hands. He took my breath away.

I blushed and words failed me.

He kissed my forehead, my nose, each cheek, and finally my mouth.

"Seriously," he said. "Don't take too long. I'll worry."

"Give me thirty minutes," I said.

"Twenty," he countered.

"Thirty," I said stubbornly.

He grinned. "Fine, thirty minutes and don't think I won't be counting."

"Go," I pushed him out the door. He laughed at my persistence. I finally got him all the way out the door and locked it.

I divulged myself of my dirty clothes, turned the water off, and sank greedily into its heavenly depths. An embarrassingly loud sigh of pleasure escaped my lips. I closed my eyes and leaned back; letting the hot water work its magic as it uncoiled my stiff and tired muscles. When my body began to loosen I chose one of Amy's body washes. I was happy to smell like a normal human being again and not a sweaty mess. I pulled the plug and watched the water circle down the drain. For some odd reason I'd always found the swirling motion of the water relaxing. I pulled myself out of the tub, dried, and dressed in my clean clothes. I spotted Amy's brush and ran it through my unruly locks.

Was that a stick in my hair? Ew.

I bundled up my dirty clothes to take back to Caeden's room and opened the bathroom door.

"Oh my God!" I screamed when Caeden's tall presence startled me. The clothes dropped to the floor with a plop.

"Sorry, I didn't mean to scare you," he bent down to pick up my clothes. "I was worried. You were gone for thirty-one minutes."

"Caeden," I whined. "I was fine. You worry far too much."

"That's true. But I would rather worry too much than not all."

I shook my head at him. "Nap time?" he asked.

"Now that I'm clean? You betcha."

I followed him down the hall and into his room. He closed the door and tossed my dirty clothes into his hamper. "Don't do that! I'll take them home and wash them," I tried to grab for them but Caeden grabbed my hands instead.

"It's fine," he kissed the side of my mouth while I squirmed in his grasp.

"Caeden, your mom doesn't need to clean my dirty clothes."

"It's not a problem. Besides," he said huskily in my ear, "my mom doesn't do my laundry. I do my own, just like a big boy."

I laughed.

"And you know what else?" his lips brushed my ear.

"What?"

"I even make my own bed."

He picked me up and tossed me on the bed. "Caeden!" I cried but then began to giggle.

84

He jumped onto the bed beside me, yanked the covers down and then over our bodies.

"Nappie nap time," he kissed my forehead.

I cuddled into his side and fell fast asleep.

* * *

When I woke up the bed was cold. I lifted my head from the pillow and saw that Caeden was gone. I rubbed my eyes and looked at the clock. Ah, dinnertime. That explained his absence. I swung my legs over the side of the bed and thought to myself, *if I keep this up I'll sleep my entire spring break away.*

I looked around Caeden's room for my hairbands. I knew I had stashed some somewhere. There was no way I was going downstairs with my hair looking like this. I thought I had put them on top of the dresser but none were there.

Maybe he put them in the bathroom, I mused.

I didn't see them in there either.

Caeden! I called in my mind.

Huh? Are you okay?

I'm fine. But where are my hairbands?

Your what bands?

Ponytail holders, Caeden. I left some here but I can't find them. I thought I put them on top of your dresser but they're not there.

Oh, he said, *those weird brightly colored circle things? I put them in your drawer.*

I opened the drawer and sure enough there they were.

Found them. Thanks. I said.

I smoothed my hair down with my fingers and pulled it back into a ponytail. It wasn't the best-looking ponytail ever but it was better than looking like Medusa.

I found Amy, Caeden, Bryce, and Charlotte eating dinner in the kitchen.

I went to go grab a plate when Caeden said, "I already fixed you a plate." He then patted the empty seat beside him.

I slid in and eyed Charlotte, looking between her and

Bryce. She blushed profusely and looked down at her plate.

Dinner was fairly quiet, which was a rarity in the Williams' household. Dinner was usually a raucous.

Amy had made some kind of health food dish that was barely recognizable as food. I basically pushed it around on my plate while my stomach rumbled.

Amy finished her dinner and cleaned her plate. "I'll be in the library if you need me."

When she was gone we all breathed a sigh of relief. We dumped our food in the garbage disposal and Caeden then rummaged through the fridge for something edible.

"Who wants ice cream?" he asked, now digging through the freezer.

"Me!" Bryce screamed.

"Shh," Caeden scolded. "Don't let mom hear you."

"Sorry," Bryce said. The kid seriously reminded me of an eager, over active, puppy.

"We have..." he looked through the various ice creams, "pretty much every flavor. What does everyone want?"

"Rocky Road," Charlotte and Bryce said together. They looked at one another and blushed.

"Soph?" he asked.

"Umm," I peered at the different flavors. "Banana."

"Good choice," he said and handed it to me. "I think I'll have mint chocolate chip."

Bryce and Charlotte were eating out of the carton but Caeden grabbed us bowls. He opened a drawer and pulled out a scoop. He took the ice cream carton from me and made me a bowl. Sticking a spoon it he grinned and handed it to me. "Dig in," he said.

I took a big bite. "Mmm, yummy," I said.

He laughed as he scooped his own ice cream. He put the ice cream away before it could melt and hopped up on the counter to eat.

"I have the next two days covered for duty so we can redecorate your room."

"Caeden," I said. I had completely forgotten about decorating my room. "That's not necessary. I don't want the others to have to work overtime."

He waved his hand and blushed. His feet thumped against the cabinet in a steady rhythm as he swung them back and forth. "Yeah well," he rubbed the back of his head nervously, "I realize that I overreacted. Our usual patrols are more than enough to keep check. I'm new at this whole Alpha thing and I just don't want anything to happen to the pack."

"I understand," I kissed his dimple. A smidge of ice cream was left on his cheek and I wiped it away with my thumb.

He smiled at me. "I'll get the hang of it eventually."

"We both will," I leaned my head on his shoulder.

NINE

"No, no, no. No way!" I shook my head and looked at the offending black motorcycle. "I am not getting on that *thing!*"

"Sophie, it's a motorcycle, it doesn't bite."

I turned my head to look at the beast. "Really? It looks like it could bite, to me."

"Please, Sophie," he held out a helmet.

I crossed my arms over my chest. "What if I fall off?"

"You're supposed to hang on to me, Soph. What happened to my mighty little she-wolf?"

"She packed her bags and left," I said.

"I'll go really slow," Caeden said in a coaxing voice that was meant to soothe me. It did anything but. "The hardware store is only two minutes from here. We can go there, get your paint, and come right back. I won't make you ride the bike to Target, we can take your car."

"I don't want to."

"It's safe Sophie. I wouldn't ask you to do something that isn't safe."

I bit my nail. "You'll go really slow?" I asked.

"Of course," he said, grinning. Obviously he could sense my imminent defeat.

"Give me that thing," I snatched the helmet from his hands and pulled it over my head.

Grinning like a fool Caeden climbed on the bike and started it. The loud rumbling made me jump and let out a squeal.

"No! No! I can't do it!"

Caeden began to laugh. He held his own helmet in his hands. "Just put one leg over here and hold onto me. I started towards the bike but ended up taking three steps back. I bent down at the waist.

"No! No! No! No!"

"It's fine Sophie," he said softly and held out a hand to help me.

I started once more towards the monster before

88

screaming. "I can't! I don't think I can do this!"

He grabbed my hand in his and pulled me closer to the bike. I let out a high-pitched girlish scream.

Caeden dropped my hand and covered his face in order to hide his laughter. I was too busy screaming to tell him he failed miserably.

I saw a few neighbors peek out their doors to see what the squealing was about.

"Sophie, it's fine, really," Caeden wiped away tears of laughter.

"No, no, no, no!" I squealed.

I closed my eyes. *I can do this. It's just a motorcycle. Come on, Sophie, don't be a wimp.* I told myself this with as much determination as I could muster. I swung my leg over the side of the motorcycle and wrapped my arms around Caeden; all with my eyes closed.

He revved the bike and pulled out of the driveway much too fast for my taste. I would have preferred one mile per hour. It got even worse though when he sped through the neighborhood.

"Caeden!" I screamed and my thighs dig into his sides while my fingers gripped his shirt.

When he parked in the hardware store parking lot I was still screaming and apparently paralyzed. "Sophie?" he rubbed my leg. "You okay?"

I closed my mouth in order to cut off the high-pitched keening escaping my lips. Who knew a wolf could scream like a jungle cat?

"Sophie, you need to get off now," he coaxed.

I finally found my voice a few moments later. "I can't move."

He chuckled, which shook the bike, and made me scream again.

"I'm going to help you off the bike. Okay Soph?"

He sounded like he was trying to talk a suicidal person off a ledge.

"Put your feet down on the ground," he said. I did as I

was told and a whimper escaped my lips. "Good, now let go of my shirt."

"No, no, no," I leaned my head against his back. "I can't."

"Yes, you can," he pried my fingers from his clothes. "Now swing one leg over and you're off."

I slowly swung my one leg over but held onto Caeden's shoulder for support. My heart was beating faster than it ever had before and my stomach was rolling. I was afraid I might throw up so I quickly pulled the helmet off.

Caeden climbed off the bike, locked our helmets inside the storage compartment, and then took my hand.

"You did great," he kissed my forehead.

"And you're a liar," I said. My voice sounded shaky.

He laughed as the sliding doors opened with a gush of air, ushering us inside. Caeden led me straight to the paint section.

"What do you have in mind?" he asked.

"I don't know," I picked up a few paint chips to study. "Something different."

Caeden snorted. "I kinda figured that."

There were so many colors to choose from and since I had no idea what I wanted to do with my room anything was an option.

"What do you think of this color?" I held up a peach shade to Caeden.

"Eh," he made a face. "Do you really want to sleep inside a fruit?"

"Good point," I said and put the chip back.

Caeden picked one up. "What about this one?"

"It's blue," I commented.

"Yeah, so," he glanced at it and shrugged.

"My room's already blue," I stuck my hands on my hips.

"So? That's an old, faded, ugly blue. This is a nice pretty pale blue," he said.

"No," I said and took it from him. "I don't want

---

blue."

"What about green?" he asked.

"Hmm, green? Maybe," I said, "I do like green."

I switched my focus to solely shades of green. I settled on a funky shade of green that wasn't overwhelming.

"This is it," I said.

Caeden motioned to a person working in the store. The man came over and said, "Can I help you with something?"

"Yes," Caeden took the paint chip from my hand and gave it to him. "We need a gallon of this and a gallon of white ceiling paint."

"It won't take long," the man said.

I watched as he mixed the colors and then the machine shook it. For some reason this process had always amazed me.

Caeden ventured down the aisle and returned with paint pans, rollers, and brushes. He put them down on the counter while we waited for the paint to finish mixing.

"Here you are," he handed the two jugs of paint to Caeden. "Checkout's over there," he pointed.

"Thank you," I called to the man as he left to do something else. I gathered the paint supplies in my arms and followed Caeden to the checkout.

The cashier entered the prices of the paint, scanned the other items, and I pulled out my gift card.

"Have a nice day," she said, giving me the receipt.

Outside, Caeden took the helmets out and placed the paint there instead. He tossed a helmet to me and said, "Please, no screaming this time."

"I'm making no promises Williams'."

He chuckled. "I'll probably lose all my hearing."

"What a shame," I said. "I think the punishment is just for forcing me on this… this… creature," I pointed to the bike.

He stuck the helmet on my head to shut me up.

Caeden climbed on the bike and put his helmet on. He

91

tilted his head towards me.

"Are- aren't you going to- to- start it?" I stuttered.

"I was going to wait until you got on this time," he said.

"Oh," I played with my fingers. I gulped and swung my leg over and then wrapped my arms around his muscular middle. My heart was beating so fast I was sure he could feel it through the thin cotton if his shirt.

He started the bike and it growled beneath me. I screamed and some guy turned to look at me before shaking his head and chuckling under his breath. Jerkface.

Caeden peeled out of the parking lot, going faster than he had before, and my fingernails dug into his abdomen.

I silently thanked the gods of really fast things that I didn't live very far from the hardware store.

Luckily, I did start to ease up a bit. My muscles loosened and I relaxed. Caeden pulled in the driveway and cut the engine.

"Well?"

"That was better the second time," I breathed.

He laughed as he removed his helmet. "Really? I thought you were going to forcibly remove the skin off my stomach.

"Sorry," I released him and climbed off. My legs were still shaky but not nearly as much as the first time. Caeden removed the paint and then took my helmet from my head. He locked up the helmets, grabbed the paint, and started for the door.

"Are you coming?" he called over his shoulder.

Right foot, then left foot, then right. I had to force my quaking legs to move. I'm sure I looked like a bumbling drunk.

Gram was gone; working at the store, so the house was quiet. Archie snoozed peacefully on the couch.

Caeden set the paint down in my room and turned to me. "Target first? Or paint first?"

"Let's paint first so that it can be drying while we're

gone."

"Good idea," he said.

We moved my mattress and furniture out into the hallway before draping the carpet with old sheets.

"Thank your mom again for me. She didn't need to give me that bed," I pointed to the black old-fashioned iron bed.

When Amy had heard that Caeden was helping me redecorate my room she had smiled enthusiastically and asked us to follow her. We ended up in a storage room off the basement I'd never noticed before.

"Do you like it?" she had asked motioning to bed frame.

"I love it," I said, fingering its smooth surface.

"Then it's yours."

"Oh no, I couldn't," I had said.

"Yes, you can. I want you to have it. It's just sitting down here, never being used. Take it."

"Are you sure?" I bit my lip.

"Of course," she said.

"Thank you," a huge smile had spread across my face.

"You're welcome," she hugged me and kissed my forehead.

Caeden sighed. "Sophie, you've thanked her like fifty times, now you want me to thank her?"

"I want her to know that I appreciate the gesture."

Caeden grinned and bent to open the paint before dumping it into the pans. "I think she knows," he said, and began rolling paint onto the wall.

I rolled my eyes and picked up the other roller before joining him.

The room was small and between the two of us it took no time at all to paint the walls and ceiling. Caeden and I both were covered in green and white paint flecks. Caeden pulled off the look far better than I did.

He took in our paint-splattered appearance and said,

"I think we should shower before we go."

"You're right," I touched up a spot. "You go on ahead," I nodded down the hallway towards the bathroom.

"Thanks," he picked up his duffel bag and kissed the top of my head. He hadn't bothered to unpack since we were moving my furniture around. I'd have to empty out a drawer for him later.

I touched up a few more spots before throwing the rollers and pans away and cleaning the brushes.

I had just finished putting the brushes away when Caeden came out of the bathroom. His hair was dripping and beginning to curl on the ends. He wore a pair of khaki shorts and a navy blue polo shirt. His light blue eyes sparkled at me and he tossed his duffel bag beside my bedroom door. He padded out into the living room and a second later I heard the TV click on.

I pulled some clothes out of my dresser and headed into the bathroom. The mirror was still steamed up from Caeden's shower.

It took longer than I anticipated, scrubbing the paint from my body, but eventually I succeeded. I dressed in a pair of shorts and t-shirt, my traditional hot weather garb. I pulled my hair back into a wet knot on my head and smeared some gloss across my lips.

"I'm ready," I bounced out to the living room.

Caeden sat up, dislodging Archie, and turned the TV off.

"Got everything you need?" he asked.

"Uh?" I looked around for my purse, located it, and swung it onto my arm. "Now I do," I smiled.

"Car keys?" he asked.

I grabbed them up from beside the door.

Caeden headed out and I turned to my black and white familiar. He looked at me with big sad brown eyes. "Sorry Arch, but it's too hot in the car to take you with me. Maybe Murphy will show up and you won't be so alone."

Familiars had an uncanny knack for just appearing.

Murphy and Archie were becoming nearly inseparable and since Caeden spent most of his time here Murphy did too.

I started my car and backed around the beast. I may not like the thing but that didn't mean I wanted to hurt it. Besides it would probably do more damage to my car than to it.

"So," Caeden said, as we cruised down the highway, "do you think you'll ever ride the bike again."

"Don't push your luck," I said and he chuckled. After a minute or two of silence I shrugged and said, "Maybe."

He grinned triumphantly.

"But not until I'm ready," I pointed my finger at him.

"Of course," he ran his fingers through his wavy hair. "But you will get back on it." His tone implied it wasn't a question.

"One day," I answered anyway.

I pulled into the parking lot of Target. Since it was evening time it wasn't busy.

I chuckled to myself. On that day, so many months ago, when Gram had told me I was a shifter I had gotten in my car and driven here. To escape my life, my mate, my destiny. Now here I was shopping for bedroom supplies with him. It was comical.

"What are you laughing about?" he asked as the sliding doors whooshed open and he took my hand.

"Oh nothing," I said.

"Uh-huh," he quirked a brow. When I didn't say anything further he added, "Fine, don't tell me." We strolled along slowly and Caeden groaned, "Ugh, how long is this going to take?"

"I don't know," I shrugged and turned towards the home decorating aisles.

"Please, please, please, don't be one of those girls that takes *forever* in a store."

"What would you know about girls and stores?" I teased.

He blushed and even his ears turned red. "Well Chris

95

and Charlotte-"

I smacked his side. "I'm just picking on you. I promise it won't take me long."

"Phew, that's a relief. I thought I was going to be here all night."

"We just got here," I snapped. "Five minutes in a store does not constitute all night. Why don't you go get me a shopping cart?" I prompted.

"Yeah, I can do that," he disappeared.

I shook my head. If Caeden was this bothered by shopping for bedroom items I didn't even want to think about him and furniture shopping. He'd drive me crazy.

I was looking at a comforter set that had the same green as my walls in it when Caeden returned. It was called Boho Boutique.

"Your carriage my dear," he waved at the cart.

"Thanks," I said. "What do you think of this?" I showed him the comforter.

"Um, I like it," he said and scratched the back of his head. "You should get it."

Ugh boys.

"You like it? That's all you have to say? Really?"

"It's pretty," he grinned.

"Thanks you're so helpful," I tossed it into the cart along with some throw pillows and a green blanket. I moved down the aisle to study the sheets and settled on a light brown color. I didn't even bother to ask Caeden what he thought of them before tossing them in the cart.

He pushed the cart along behind me. It made me sick that he even looked hot pushing a shopping cart. Did he ever look bad? The answer was no. Caeden always looked like he was about to pose for a magazine shoot. Even in the middle of Target or covered in sweat. Oh, definitely covered in sweat.

I shook my head to clear my thoughts before I spontaneously combusted. I turned down the lights aisle and chose one for my end table and a floor lamp. I even chose a few pictures and a mirror.

I picked up a few accessories just to add a personal touch. This made me giddy because I'd never had *accessories* before. Since we moved all the time everything had been minimalist.

"I'm done," I turned to Caeden. "That wasn't so bad was it?"

He rubbed his face. "I guess not."

"What will you do when we move in together? Hmm?" I asked as we headed for the checkout.

A grin spread across his face. "Move in together? Does that mean you want to live with me?"

I smiled shyly. "I think that's a given. We're already bonded, you're my mate, and I certainly don't plan to spend the rest of my life with someone else."

"It's so good to hear you say that," he stopped pushing the cart and pulled me to him before planting a passionate kiss on my lips. A fire burned in my cheeks and someone whistled.

He pulled away and walked all the way to the checkout with a spring in his step.

* * *

The paint was dry and Caeden and I had moved all the furniture back in the room. He'd even put the bed together his mom had given me. It was pushed against the wall, like before, because there was really no other way to fit a queen size bed in such a small room.

Caeden shoved the mattress on and I pulled the clean sheets and comforter from the dryer. They smelled strongly of lavender dryer sheets.

"I feel so domestic," I said as Caeden helped me put the sheets on the bed.

He grinned, flashing his dimple. "I could get used to this," he winked.

Oh dear God, Caeden's winks and his dimple! I was doomed.

We finished making the bed and then dressed in

97

our... Jammie Jams.

I climbed under the covers and luxuriated in the feel of new bed covers. Caeden jumped in beside me, bouncing the bed. Archie and Murphy snoozed on an extra-large dog bed we'd found at the T.J. Maxx next to Target.

"Do you like your room?" Caeden asked, putting his arms behind his head. He wore a tank top and his boxers.

"Very much. Thanks for helping," I kissed him.

"You're welcome," he said. "And one day, I'll help again, but it'll be our house and not Lucinda's.

I fell asleep as the images of Caeden's and my future home played behind my closed lids.

TEN.

Caeden and I pulled into the school parking lot. Bryce was already there, leaning against his Jeep, with Charlotte in his arms.

Students milled around the lot, moping, the back to school blues thick in the air.

I grabbed my pale orange backpack and slung it across my shoulder.

Bryce nodded his head across the parking lot. Caeden and I both turned to look.

"Holy shit," I said under my breath. It was rare for me to curse but right now someone needed to say it. From beside me Caeden dropped the F-bomb and angrily thrust his fingers through his hair.

Travis' S5 Coupe was parked in the school parking lot for the first time since I had been kidnapped. The door swung open and his tall, lean body, appeared. His blond hair glowed like a halo, giving him an angelic appearance, and we all knew he was more demon than angel.

Caeden bristled beside me, his eyes flashing from blue to gold, and growled low in his throat.

"I'm going to kill him," he hissed under his breath, "for what he did to you."

"Caeden no!" I grabbed his arm as he headed towards Travis. His arm easily slipped through my fingers. "Caeden! Come back! Bryce do something!" I snapped at Caeden's younger brother.

Bryce laughed and shook his head. "I think not. Travis deserves whatever comes to him."

"Are you crazy!?" I tapped my forehead for emphasis. "He's going to kill Travis and end up in jail for the rest of his life!"

"No he won't. Caeden has better control of himself than you think."

"He's going to go all wolf in the middle of the parking lot where everyone will see," I hissed under my breath.

Bryce still made no move to help. Jerk.

I looked around in a panic for Bentley's truck but it was absent. I did see Logan's Toyota Tundra and I sprinted towards it.

"Whoa," Logan said when I crashed into him. "Sophie? Is everything okay?" Concern flooded his pale green eyes, so much like his sisters. I was a bit surprised by his reaction. I was used to only surliness from him.

I pointed back towards the parking lot. "Caeden is going after Travis. You have to stop him. He won't listen to me."

Before I was finished speaking Logan was across the parking lot.

Caeden was on top of Travis and pummeling his face with his fist.

Lord have mercy I thought this kind of stuff only happened in movies.

Travis tried to gain the upper hand. But despite being an Alpha now, he still couldn't gain any ground with Caeden.

Caeden's fury was frightening. No one had ever seen sweet Caeden act like a... predator. He snarled in Travis' face, spittle flying, and his face turning red. Our classmates were too scared to even stay and watch. They quickly glanced at the two boys and darted off. Even the guys that were on the football team quickly left. Pretty soon it was only my pack and Travis in the parking lot. Bentley pulled in, Chris in the passenger seat, and jumped out to help Logan pull Caeden away.

"Caeden stop," Bentley coaxed, pulling on his arm.

Caeden wouldn't listen and he was too jacked up on Alpha juice for them to pull him away.

"You sick bastard!" Caeden screamed at Travis before punching and breaking his jaw with a loud pop. "You're a murderer! If you ever touch or even look at her again, hell will be a welcome sight to you compared to what I will do to you, understand Travis?"

Travis spit on Caeden's shirt leaving behind a streak

of blood. "Still keeping your little human whore around?" Travis cackled.

"You. Will. Regret. That." Caeden's hand clenched Travis' throat. Within seconds Travis began to turn purple.

"Caeden!" Bentley cried. "You're killing him! Stop! You're not like him! You're not a murderer."

I ran to Caeden's side and wrapped my arms around his shoulders before sobbing into his neck. "Please stop Caeden. This isn't you. Stop baby, stop," I coaxed him down from the ledge he was precariously perched on.

I felt him begin to loosen under my arms. "I won't be like him," Caeden said, letting go of Travis' throat. "But he will pay," he pulled back his arm and punched Travis hard enough to knock him out.

Caeden turned into my arms and began to sob. "I'm sorry, I'm so sorry, I just saw him and-"

"Shh," I cried too. "I know. I understand. I do."

"He'll be okay," Caeden said. "I didn't kill him. He's just knocked out."

"I know," I fingered the hair that grazed the back of his neck. "I know," I repeated to reassure him.

The warning bell rang.

"Caeden, we have to go inside now," I said, wiping his face and then his blood covered knuckles.

"I have some shirts in a bag in the trunk," he pointed to his Jeep.

"Okay, stay here."

The others were still standing around.

"Go on you guys," I nodded my head towards the school. "There's no reason for you to be late too."

"We're a pack," Bentley said. "We stick together."

"Thank you," I said and meant it. I opened Caeden's trunk and found a black Under Armour duffel bag. I unzipped it and found a few shorts and t-shirts. I pulled out a black shirt for him and a green one for me. Not glancing at the others I pulled off my blood stained shirt, folded it, and placed it in one of the bag's pockets. I pulled Caeden's shirt over my head and it swallowed me whole.

"Here, let me help," Charlotte said. She pulled a hairband off her arm, pulled the shirt tight to my body, and tied the excess fabric.

"Thanks," I tucked some stray hairs behind my ear.

"No problem," She smiled and took Bryce's outstretched hand.

Caeden was still kneeling beside Travis' prone form but he had removed his shirt and was using it to wipe excess blood from his hands.

"Here, you go," I handed him the clean shirt and took the soiled one from him. Thankfully there was no blood on his shorts.

Caeden pulled his shirt on and I placed his dirty shirt beside mine in his duffel bag. I closed the trunk and Caeden pulled the key from his pocket and locked it. Both our backpacks were lying on the ground he picked his up and handed me mine.

The bell rang again, signaling the start of class.

"To the office!" Bryce said and stuck his hand out in a Superman flying move.

Travis was still slumped on the ground, not moving.

We headed as a group to the attendance office. The lady working there slid the window open. "A whole group of you late? What joy," she said in a monotone voice. Someone really liked their job. Not.

Bryce opened his mouth, no doubt to make a snide remark, but Caeden sidestepped him. His frown was instantly replaced with a charming smile. He used his dimple, his charm, and those pool blue to his advantage.

"Ma'am we were out in the parking when we noticed a student passed out. He must have been drunk," Caeden's voice dripped with sticky syrup.

"Oh dear," she said and put a hand to her chest. Her anger was gone, replaced by concern. "That's terrible."

"I know ma'am."

"I'll call someone to head out there now. Just wait a

moment and I'll write your passes," she held up one finger.

"Thank you ma'am, you're so kind."

"Oh well, I try," she blushed. Apparently even fifty-year-old ladies couldn't resist the charm that is Caeden Williams.

She came back and wrote our passes. Caeden began to walk me to class when I pulled him into a quiet corner.

"Caeden, they'll know someone beat him up and what if one of the other students tells. You'll be in big trouble.

"No, I won't," he shook his head. "First off, Travis' external injuries have already healed. It'll take him longer to recover from the knock I gave to his head. So, they'll just assume that I'm right and he's passed out drunk. As to your second question the other kids are afraid of us. They can sense that we're different. Trust me, the humans won't say anything."

"They're afraid of us?" I asked.

"Yeah," he said, "they are. They can sense that we're a predator so they just… stay away."

"But we're not any different," I choked.

Caeden put one hand beside either side of my body against the wall. "Yes, we are Sophie." A dangerous look glinted in those cerulean blue eyes. "We're faster, stronger, and-" his voice turned deliciously husky. "Sexier."

His lips brushed against mine in a tantalizing gesture. "*You're* definitely sexier," I breathed.

Caeden was so close to me that my hands were flat against the wall and his chest pressed right up against me. My breath stuttered.

"I'm going to kiss you now," he said.

"Do it already," I whispered, my voice held a begging quality to it.

His lips quirked, "So demanding."

"You ain't seen nothing yet," I said and mauled him in the middle of a school alcove. My lips, my body, couldn't get enough of him. He grabbed my thighs and wrapped my legs around his waist. My arms wound around his neck and my fingers dug into his hair. The worry about getting caught making out in the school hallway was the last thing on my mind.

I extracted my mouth from his and pressed kisses down his neck. Caeden's very presence seemed to make me do the craziest things. I knew I needed to stop but I just... couldn't.

Apparently Caeden had more willpower than me, "Stop Soph. Sophie, we have to stop," he said.

I unlocked my limbs and reluctantly dropped to the ground.

My lips felt tingly and I hesitantly brought my fingers to them. Caeden gripped my waist and put his forehead against mine. "It's getting harder," his breath caressed my cheek.

"What is?" I asked.

"To resist you," his fingers flexed against me.

"Oh," was all I could say.

"As much as I want to stand here all day we better get to class," he smiled.

"You're right," I said, reluctantly.

He laughed softly. "What happened to your 'studying' and 'I have to make straight A's' attitude?" he punctuated with air quotes.

"We have some quarterly assessments coming up," I said, "you'll see my studying powers at their best then."

He laughed. "Maybe you'll show me a thing or two," he suggested.

"You bet," I smiled and glumly extracted my hand from his.

* * *

I stared disgustedly at the pile of homework before me and the school day was only halfway through. I mean, come on, it's only the first day back from spring break. Can't they give us a break? An essay in Spanish, a power point for History, and a science project! I wanted to hit my head against the desk. Just because I like school doesn't mean I want a crap load of homework the first day back.

I pulled out my notebook and began writing a rough draft for my Spanish essay. The sooner all of this was done, the better.

Caeden sat beside me in the study hall classroom trying to balance a pencil on top of his lip. I rolled my eyes.

The power point that contained school announcements droned on in the background.

I read over the directions for the Spanish essay once more.

Write a three page paper, in Spanish, on your overall high school experience. "Sophie?" said Caeden. I studiously ignored him. *Talk about classes you enjoyed/didn't enjoy, teachers, friends, extra-curricular activities, and anything else school related.* "Soph?" poke. *Also talk about your plans after high school. Work? College? Dreams? Goals? Ambitions?* "Sophie," he said again and pushed me hard enough to knock me out of my seat and onto the floor. Dang shifter reflexes. Weren't they supposed to keep this kind of thing from happening?

"Caeden!" I hissed under my breath.

"Oopsy daisy," he blushed.

I picked myself up and brushed dust off of Caeden's shirt and my shorts. Ugh, gross. That dust had probably been on the floor for twenty years.

Straightening my disheveled appearance I said to Caeden, "What was so flippin' important that you had to *push* me out of my chair? I was trying to work on an essay."

"Flippin'?" he quirked a brow.

"Yes, flippin'," I said and slid back into my seat. "Now what was it?" I asked, picking up my pencil. I tapped the eraser against the desk.

He pointed to the power point and I rolled my gaze towards to it. "Chess club? Why should I be concerned about chess club?"

Caeden shook his head and chuckled under his breath. "No, it was before that. Soccer tryouts are next week."

"And?"

"I think you should do it," he rubbed his scruffy chin.

"Wouldn't that... I don't know... be *unfair*? I mean, how come you and the others don't play sports?"

"Sophie," he tipped his chair back on two legs. "I think it would be good for you."

"To play soccer?" I organized my papers.

"Yeah," he said, rocking back and forth in the chair.

"Mr. Williams! Put your chair down on all four legs!" the study hall teacher huffed.

"Yes sir," Caeden saluted him and the chair smacked back down on the concrete floor.

"Caeden, I have more important things to worry about. I just don't have the time. Besides, with the whole Travis thing-" I looked around. "Speaking of, where *is* Travis?"

Caeden's grin lit the whole room. "He was escorted out of the school parking lot by the police."

"You're serious?" I asked, doodling on my piece of paper. I could never get any work done with Caeden around.

"As a heart attack."

"I'll think about it," I conceded. I really would like to play again. I had always found soccer to be therapeutic.

Caeden grinned. "Excellent. I can't wait to see you running around in those tight little shorts."

I quirked my eyebrow at him. "Have you ever watched women's soccer before?"

"Er... no," he said.

"That's what I thought. We don't wear 'tight little shorts'. We wear baggy shorts that we can move around in."

"Oh," he blushed. "That sucks; I was really looking forward to that."

I couldn't help laughing. "I'm sure you were Caeden."

* * *

Caeden dropped me off at Gram's cupcake shop and then went to do a scan of the area with Bentley. I had a feeling he may be gone for a while. They'd probably be much more thorough since Travis was apparently back.

In the back of the shop I pulled off Caeden's shirt and grabbed up my black *Lucinda's* shirt. I slipped it on and pulled my hair back into a ponytail.

Gram strode through the swinging door, "Oh good you're here." She noticed the too large shirt tossed over my arm and quirked a brow. "Do I want to know?"

"Probably not," I said.

She shook her head and straightened her cap. "I've got some cupcakes coming out of the oven and I'd really appreciate it if you would ice them while I man the front."

"No problem," I smiled and headed over to the sink to wash my hands.

"Thanks," Gram flashed me a relieved smile. The bell over the door chimed several times. "After school crowd," she headed to the front to tend to the register.

I checked the ovens and refilled the icing bags so they'd be good to go. When that was done I tried to get a head start on cleaning the dirty pans in the sink. The timer went off and I scurried around trying to find an oven mitt. I finally found it and slid out the various cupcake trays. I then slid those into the fridge to start cooling. I found myself constantly glancing at the clock and calculating the length of time that Caeden had been gone. I was close to wearing a hole in the floor. I breathed a sigh of relief when the cupcakes were cool enough to icing. At least I now had something to do to occupy my mind.

I pulled out the blueberry cupcakes first and grabbed the blueberry icing. I loved the way the blueberries were swirled throughout the cream cheese frosting. It always looked pretty. I quickly finished icing that dozen and moved onto the next one, pink lemonade with pale pink icing. Gram always tried to have different flavored cupcakes for the different seasons. There were some cupcakes that she kept year round but most were different.

After icing several dozen cupcakes Caeden still

hadn't shown. I began to bite my bottom lip with worry. What was taking so long?

Sighing, I picked up the trays and carried them to the front and loaded them into the display. Gram was tending to a row of customers and waved her hand in thank you.

I smiled and hurried to the back so that the kids from school wouldn't see me covered in icing. I knew I had a big streak of lavender honey icing on my cheek. I headed straight for the sink and scrubbed the icing from my face and under my nail and was that-? Ew, there was icing in my *hair*! Gross! I tried to get as much icing out of my hair as possible but my actions proved futile.

Since no more cupcakes would be made for today, I proceeded to clean up the kitchen, and look out the window for Caeden. With each passing second my worry escalated to epic proportions.

Some time later Gram came into the kitchen and found me pacing the floor.

"I just closed the shop up," she said.

Her words went in one ear and out the other as I tugged on my lip and searched for a red Jeep.

"Sophie?"

"What if something bad happened to him Gram?" I asked her, not turning away from my search.

"You'd know," she said.

I shook my head back and forth. "I'm not so sure about that."

Gram wrapped her arms around me. "Let's go home Sophie. You can worry there just as easily as you can worry here."

"But-" I started to protest.

"No buts," she said, leading me to the back door and turning the lights off. "You need to go home and have a hot bath and just... relax your mind."

"Thank you sensei," I crossed my arms over my chest as she locked up the door.

Gram chuckled and said, "Oh Sophie, your sarcasm

never ceases to amaze me."

She started towards her Nissan Altima and I scanned the area as I walked for any sign of Caeden. A lump had formed in my stomach and I knew it wouldn't go away until I knew he was safe. And once I was assured of his safety I'd be sure to beat the crap out of him... and then make him sleep on the floor. Yeah, that would teach him not to worry me.

"Sophie?" Gram asked and I jolted back into motion. I slipped into her car. "I'm tired and I don't really feel like cooking. Why don't we go to Roma's? Hmmm? Does that sound good?"

"Uh-hmm," I said.

Gram's hand wrapped around. "Dear child, you're going to worry yourself sick."

"I do feel like I'm going to throw up," I confessed.

"If something were truly wrong, we would've heard something from one of the others, okay? Caeden would have called the pack and you would've heard it. You're worrying for nothing, Sophie. Trust me. I'm sure Caeden and Bentley are just being very thorough, maybe they even found something, and they're taking their time. Being cautious."

Her words made sense but the ill feeling inside me just wouldn't go away. Caeden was my mate and the thought of him in danger was just too much for me to handle.

Gram parked in front of the restaurant and turned to me. "Come on, Soph. Eat something, be merry. I'm not worrying and neither should you."

I swallowed and nodded my head. "Okay."

"That's my girl," Gram patted my knee and hopped from the car with much more agility than most people her age. I followed along behind her at a sluggish pace. Inside, she spoke with the hostess and we were led to our seats. I moved in a robotic motion. Or maybe it was more zombie like?

I slid into the booth and the girl handed me a menu. "Thanks." Just because I felt like I was getting an ulcer didn't

---

mean I couldn't be polite.

She smiled and disappeared.

I opened the menu and picked a random item so that I'd have something to tell the waiter or waitress.

Right on cue the waiter turned up with a steaming basket of freshly backed rolls and a notepad in hand.

"Hi ya'll I'm Harley, do ya know what ya want to drink?"

"I'll have water with lemon," Gram said and then rose her eyebrows at me.

"Uh… I'll have diet coke," I said.

He scribbled in his note pad. "If ya'll know what you want to eat I can go ahead and get that in for ya."

Gram ordered a pasta dish and then Harley turned to me. "And what will little Miss Pouty Pants have?"

Gram snickered and I shot her a scathing look.

"I'll have a cheese pizza."

"Small?"

"No, large," I smiled and shoved the menu into his outstretched hand.

He laughed and disappeared around the corner into the kitchen. I think Harley need a good kick to his knee.

Gram continued to chuckle under her breath. If she didn't watch *she* was going to get the kick to the knee and not Harley.

To resist the urge to kick my grandma I grabbed a roll, ripped it in half, and proceeded to slather it with butter. I took a bite and was surprised by how good it was and the fact that I could actually eat something.

Gram finally managed to gain control and fixed herself a roll.

The restaurant was surprisingly nice with granite tables, yellow stucco walls, and accents of royal blue. I also appreciated the use of hand painted art.

"So, how was your first day back to school?" Gram asked.

I raised an eyebrow just as *Harley* returned with our

drinks. "Horrible. Caeden and Travis got into a fight."

"Oh," said Gram and her voice rose two octaves higher. "What was the cause?"

"You seriously don't know?"

"Oh," she said again. "Caeden was defending you."

"Yeah," I tucked a piece of hair behind my ear. "And Bryce wouldn't do anything to stop him. Logan and Bentley could barely get him off of Travis. It was pretty messy. He hurt Travis pretty badly. I'm worried that maybe Travis has gotten ahold of Caeden and done something."

"Bentley wouldn't let that happen," Gram said. "Besides, the Grimm pack is weaker. Not just number wise but in general."

"That doesn't mean they can't do some serious damage Gram. Travis *did* murder his father. It takes a sick person to kill their parent no matter how evil said parent may be."

Gram's smile was wide. "Spoken like a true Alpha."

* * *

I paced in my bedroom, biting my nails, getting absolutely no homework done. Caeden was definitely going to get a kick to the shin for this as soon as I was sure he was whole and unscathed.

"Sophie!" Gram called from her bedroom. "Go to bed! I can't sleep with you pacing!"

"I can't sleep!" I called back.

I heard Gram's dramatic sigh and then the shuffling of her shoving the bed covers off. "I declare Sophie Noelle, you will be the end of me."

She shuffled into the kitchen and I left pacing my room to see what she was up to.

Gram puttered around the kitchen; opening and closing cabinet doors.

"What are you doing?" I asked.

"Making you a tea that will *hopefully* make you sleep," she sighed dramatically. "You're driving me bananas."

She pulled out a teakettle and a mug. She set to making the tea and I sat at the table watching her. "I really don't think tea is going to help me sleep," I said and propped my head up on my hand.

"Well, it can't hurt," she huffed and put her hand on her hip. Her gray hair was sticking up wildly around her head. I glanced at the clock, which I had been trying to avoid, and saw that it was after midnight. "And don't think," she said, "for one minute that if you stay up all night you're going to get out of going to school tomorrow."

"School is the least of my problems," I mumbled.

The teakettle went off and Gram dutifully poured it into a mug. "Please try to drink it," she said as she handed it to me. Its warmth was a welcoming comfort. I blew into its amber depths and watched the steam coil above it in ever evolving shapes.

Gram patted my cheek. "Go to bed, Sophie."

"How come you're so calm about this?" I asked.

She slowed her footsteps and finally stopped. With her back to me she said, "I was married to an Alpha for a very long time. I got used to having him leave me behind while he went out. Sometimes he'd be gone for days but he'd always come back to me." She turned towards me and tears glimmered in her eyes. "Caeden will always come back to you, Sophie, always."

"But I don't want to be left behind," I whispered, wrapping my hands tighter around the cup of tea.

"Well, you better get used to it Sophie. You're going to be left behind a lot. It's an Alpha's nature to protect his mate and that usually means you get left behind and lied to." Sighing, she said, "Go back to bed, Soph, you need your sleep and so do I."

She looked so forlorn that I couldn't possibly argue with her.

"Thanks for the tea, Gram," I said and stood up to kiss her cheek.

"You're welcome," she patted my hand and

disappeared into her bedroom.

I picked up my tea and headed to my own bedroom, admiring Caeden's and my handiwork. I perched on the end of the bed and sipped my tea while willing sleep to overcome me. Archie jumped up on the bed beside me, and Murphy looked up at me from the floor with a sad, helpless, look. I reached my hand out and scratched his head.

"I'm worried too bud," I said and he looked into my eyes with far too much intelligence.

I finished my tea and set the empty cup on my nightstand. I pulled the covers back and crawled under, turning my light out in the process. I patted the large empty space beside me where Caeden usually slept.

"Murphy, get up here boy," I coaxed the large dog onto the bed beside Archie. He jumped agilely over me and plopped down beside me. Archie turned in three circles and then lay down on the pillow. I scooted over and cuddled both of the dogs. I rhythmically stroked their fur and counted backwards from one hundred. Then I counted sheep. Eventually, sleep mercifully took me.

* * *

I awoke to a loud banging noise and sat straight up. I reached for the light, not to turn it on, but for a weapon. All I could think was that Travis had killed Caeden, and now he'd come for me. My heart thudded in my throat.

"Hey, hey, it's just me," sounded a voice I'd know anywhere.

"Caeden!" I cried and threw myself in his arms.

"Whoa," he said, as he rocked back from the force of my impact.

He flicked on the overhead light and I did a quick survey to make sure he was okay. Once the elation of his safety had passed I beat his chest and tears flooded my eyes and coursed down my cheeks.

"Soph?" he said.

"Don't you ever, ever, *ever*, do that again, Caeden. I've been worried *sick*. I thought something really bad

---

113

happened to you. I thought you were dead somewhere and I'd never know what happened to you. Please don't go off like that anymore without letting me know that you're safe."

"I didn't know," he said softly. "I'm really sorry. You're completely right. I should've let you know something. Nothing bad happened so I just didn't think about the time."

"How would you feel," I threw my arms out, "if I went off to do a scan and was gone for hours and hours when I was supposed to come right back?"

He swallowed. "I'd tear the ends of the earth apart looking for you."

The fight went out of my body and I buried my face in his chest. I wrapped my arms tightly around him and inhaled his scent. I instantly felt comforted by pine, citrus, cinnamon, and wood.

He picked me up, motioned the dogs out of the bed and climbed inside. The sheets were still warm from my body heat and the dogs. He slipped his jeans off and tossed them across the room before pulling me against his body, spooning me.

"I'm really, truly, and completely sorry for worrying you," his lips brushed my ear as he tenderly played with my hair. "We caught a strange scent and ran with it and we ended up in Maryland."

"Did you figure out what it was?" I asked.

"No," he said and the pillow and sheets ruffled as he shook his head. "I'm sure it has something to do with Travis though."

"Could it be another shifter? A different type?"

"No," he said again. "I'd know that. All shifters can distinguish the scent of other shifters. This was... it smelled like death."

"Death?"

"Murder," he said. "It was awful," he buried his face in my hair.

"How do you know it was murder? Did you find a

114

body?" I asked.

"No," he said and his heart thudded against my back, "we didn't find any bodies. But the smell..." he trailed off. "There was just this feeling of emptiness, of sadness, I just can't explain. It's like I felt these lost souls floating around."

"What makes you think it has something to do with Travis?"

"Intuition," he answered immediately. "It's just this gut feeling I have and I can't shake it."

I rolled over to face him and tucked my hands under my head. He reached out and gently traced my forehead, my nose, and my mouth, before brushing my hair from my face. His hand was warm and instantly soothed me. My eyes fluttered closed and he laughed. I blinked them open and found him smiling at me.

"What?" I asked.

"Sometimes I feel like this is all a dream and one day I'm going to wake up and you'll be gone."

"This isn't a dream Caeden. I'm real and I'm not going anywhere. Ever."

He smiled but it quickly faded. "I *have* to figure out what Travis is up to. It's not good, whatever it is."

I took his hand and held it to my heart. "But this time we do it together."

He kissed me and said, "Always."

ELEVEN

Travis' car was already in the parking lot but fortunately he was nowhere to be seen. Caeden relaxed beside me and his grip loosened on my hand. The crescent shaped marks his nails had left on my skin quickly healed and returned to its normal color.

"Please don't get in a fight with him today if you see him, please," I begged.

"I won't," he sighed. "I promise to be on my best behavior," he said in a brighter tone and playfully nipped my chin.

We headed into the school and found an empty cafeteria table. I looked around for any sign of Travis or his pack in case I was going to have to tackle Caeden. I didn't quite trust him *not* to hurt Travis. Bryce sauntered into the school and found us easily. Charlotte's hand was held snugly in his.

Bryce plopped dramatically into the seat across from me, his backpack bouncing. "Ready for Harding?" he asked.

I groaned and buried my face in my hands. "Don't remind me." Mrs. Harding was bound to give us a ton of homework and I still had all of my homework from yesterday to do.

Bryce flashed a lopsided grin. "It's going to be epic. Mrs. Harding is always a bitch after spring break."

"Isn't she always?" I retorted.

"That's true," Bryce shrugged. "Maybe bitchier is a better term," he quirked a brow for my approval. He suddenly hopped up and said, "I'm going to go get some breakfast."

"Didn't mom feed you?" Caeden asked.

Bryce's mouth turned down in a frown, which was rare for him. "She made me eat a spinach omelet. Spinach!"

Caeden laughed. "I'm so glad I didn't have to eat that."

I shook my head. "When will you boys learn that

green food is good for you. If I recall correctly you did enjoy your salad that one evening," I remembered back to the early stages of our relationship. We hadn't even been together a year yet and I was already thinking about the *early stages.*

"Yes, but you also made steak so that made it okay to have a little bit of salad."

"You're logic is whack," I said with a laugh.

"No, it's a proven fact. If a man has to eat something green then he needs some meat," he paused and grinned, "and of course something pretty to look at."

"Of course," I rolled my eyes.

Bryce returned with a tray of various items. "This is ridiculous," he said as he pointed to his tray. "I'm going to starve to death. I mean, do they really think this cardboard is healthy," he picked up a granola bar. He bit into it and said. "Ew, it has nuts in it! I'm not a horse so why are they feeding me this stuff." Bryce then picked up an apple. "Ugh, sour," he said and made a face. "This was a big waste of money," he said and got up, stalking towards the trashcans.

Charlotte giggled and looked at me before shrugging. "What am I going to do with him?" she said.

"I wish you luck," Caeden said and slung his arm across my shoulders.

"Hey guys," Chris said brightly. Bentley was right beside her with her hand in his. Those two were permanently glued to each other's hips. I'd think it was disgusting if Caeden and I didn't act the same way.

Logan sulked behind them and came around the table and sat beside me. He pulled a book out of his backpack and began to read.

Chris and Bentley sat down and Chris leaned across the table towards her older brother. "Logan, seriously?"

"What?" he asked in his deep monotone voice.

"You're reading?"

"Uh, yeah. I think that's pretty obvious," he pointed to the book with a thin hand.

"You're such a recluse. You need to hang out and talk

with us more often," she said.

"And you need to stop being such an annoying pest," he snapped and closed the book with a bang. He stuffed it into his bag and walked off.

"I swear he's moodier than a girl," Chris said. "Men have no room to talk about girls and their mood swings. I mean, really?"

"It's because he's gay," Bryce said as he sat back down.

"What?" we all said.

"Oh come on," Bryce said in that drawled out, dramatic way of his. He looked at all of our stunned faces and said, "Seriously? None of your gaydars go off when he's around?"

"No," we said.

"Geez," Bryce said and his eyebrows went up his forehead in surprise. "That's why he's so grumpy all the time."

"Why would being gay make him grumpy?" I asked.

Bryce sighed dramatically. "He's not grumpy because he's gay, he thinks he has to hide it from us."

"But none of us would judge him for being gay. There's nothing wrong with that," I said.

"But the council of elders would," Caeden said softly. "He would be executed."

I gasped. "Executed? For being gay?"

"Yes," Caeden said sadly, "it would be seen as impure and a disgrace to our heritage and if they didn't execute him he would be cast out of the pack. And a castaway never survives."

"That's... that's sickening," I said. "No wonder Logan acts the way he does all the time."

Chris frowned. "How could I not know this? I'm his sister. Are you sure?" she turned to Bryce.

"Positive," he said.

Her shoulders slumped sadly. "I wish he would've trusted me enough to confide in me."

"Babe," Bentley, rubbed her shoulder.

She shrugged off his touch and said, "I have to go find him." She melted into the crowd of students just as the bell rang.

Bryce turned to me and waggled his eyebrows, "Show time."

* * *

Bryce was right, Mrs. Harding was even more of a nightmare than usual and I had the added luxury of having Travis sit behind me. This was just *fabulous*. At least he didn't play with my hair this time or try to touch me. He was probably afraid his hand would be torn off and even though shifters can heal fast that doesn't mean we can regrow limbs. The idea of a handless Travis brought a smile to my lips.

"Ms. Beaumont what are you smiling about?" Mrs. Harding snapped, spittle flying.

Quick, think Sophie, think. "Um... math makes me happy."

Travis snickered behind me which made me want to turn around and stab him in the eye with a pencil.

"Math makes you happy?" she asked.

"Yes," I said and nodded.

"You're in trouble now," Bryce whispered under his breath.

"Well," Mrs. Harding smiled, showcasing crooked yellow teeth, "if math makes you so *happy* then you can stay after school with me and we'll see just how happy you are."

"Uh, I can't do that. I work after school."

Mrs. Harding smiled even broader and I swear she looked like a toad. "Tomorrow morning then. I expect you in this classroom at seven-thirty and you will not be permitted to leave until the morning bell rings."

"I'll look forward to it," I said around the lump in my throat.

She smiled through the rest of the class.

* * *

Mr. Collins, the woodshop teacher, was eager to start

a new project today.

Pushing his black-framed glasses up his nose, he said, "Today, we're going to start building cabinets. I've run out of storage areas and I thought this would be a good learning experience for you. You should see a sheet in front of you that shows that dimensions that I need. You can either make a plain cabinet or you can add detailing for extra credit. And Sophie?" He looked at me.

"Yes?" I asked.

"Please, I'm begging you, stay away from the power tools."

"Will do," I said.

"Thank you," he breathed a sigh of relief. "Caeden can build the cabinet and you can stain and I'll grade you on that. Get to work."

Caeden was already reading over the directions. Since I didn't want to interrupt him I cleaned out my backpack.

He got up and began to gather wood and tools. I dumped the items I had cleaned out of my backpack into the trashcan and headed over to our workstation. I pulled my hair back into a ponytail. Even though I wasn't the one using the tools that didn't mean my hair couldn't still be caught in one of the various devices.

I watched Caeden work, his muscles flexing, and sweat dotting his forehead. This had to be the best class ever. I mean, I got to watch Caeden for a whole hour and thirty minutes, and not do anything. Plus, I was getting an A. Why had I ever been worried about this class?

Caeden flicked a piece of hair out of his eye and smiled up at me. "What are you watching?"

"You," I said.

"Me?"

"Who else would I be watching?"

"I don't know," he shrugged and began aligning pieces. He picked up the nail gun and quickly assembled the cabinet. The rest of the class was still cutting pieces.

"Looks like I've found myself a handy man," I

smiled.

"Oh yeah," he grinned, "I'm as handy as they come."

"I can see it now," I fantasized, "leaky faucets, fixing lights, painting walls."

Caeden's laugh filled the woodshop classroom. "And let me guess, you're not going to help me, you'll just watch."

"It's what I do best," I laughed.

Caeden stood the cabinet upright and grabbed some trim pieces for detailing. "That's okay, at least I'll have something pretty to look at," he winked.

"And I'll always be there to hand you tools," I said.

"Just not the power ones," he grinned crookedly.

Caeden finished building the cabinet and I started staining. We only had thirty minutes of class left and everyone else was still trying to figure out how to piece together the pieces of wood.

"Williams!" A guy named Sid, called, "Come help us out."

"You okay?" Caeden asked me.

"I can handle this," I said, "all you have to do is follow the grain. It's not rocket science."

"Alright, I'm gonna go help them out," he pointed over his shoulder. He looked around and quickly, before I could react, pressed a kiss to my lips.

My cheeks flamed as the roomful of boys stared at us. "I hate you," I whispered.

"No you don't," he grinned. "I'm to cute to ever be hated on," he put a hand to his chest.

In the time that was left in class Caeden managed to help almost all of the groups and I finished staining the cabinet.

Mr. Collins came over to check out our cabinet. "Good job you two," he said and clapped us both on the shoulder. "I don't have anything else for you to start on so next class will be a free period for you."

The bell rang and we gathered up our stuff. Like always, Caeden was nearly impossible to keep up with.

"Ugh, forget this," I said under my breath and vaulted

myself at his back.

"What?!" Caeden explained from my sudden onslaught.

"Just go," I said, clinging to him monkey style.

He laughed. "You got it," he held onto my thighs. I wrapped my arms around his neck but held them loosely so I didn't choke him.

He wove through the hallways just as quickly as he usually did despite my added weight.

"'Scuse me," he said while I giggled. "Otta my way."

He carried me around the bus loop and all the way to his Jeep. He let go of my legs and I dropped down from his back. "Hurry," he ushered me into the car and tapped the side of it for emphasis. The way everyone hurried to leave, the parking lot became a major danger zone.

"Oh, by the way," I said.

"Oh dear God, no conversation ever ends well when you start it with, 'by the way,'" Caeden said and stopped at the stoplight coming out of the school.

"I have to come into school early tomorrow morning to do math with Mrs. Harding."

"Like I said, never ends well. What did you do?"

"I smiled," I crossed my arms over my chest.

Caeden snorted. "You smiled, so you got morning detention? That woman is twisted."

"At least you don't have her as a teacher," I grumbled. "I swear her whole goal in life must be to make me miserable."

"I think her goal is to make *everyone* miserable," he said as he drove to the cupcake shop. "Maybe you and Bryce more than others."

Caeden parked the Jeep and hopped out. I climbed out after him and asked, "You're coming? You're not going with Bentley?"

"Well," he said with a smirk, "if I remember last night correctly, after my girlfriend was sure I was safe she attacked me with her fists." He put his hands on both sides of my face, cocooning me, and said, "I hate it when you're upset. Especially when I know it's my fault."

"And that's what makes you the perfect boyfriend," I said.

"I don't know about perfect," he said. "I can never-"

"Remember to put the toilet seat down, I know, I know," I said.

He laughed. "We better get in there before Lucinda comes out here to kick our tooshies."

"You're right," I said and started to pull away but he pulled me back to him.

"One quick kiss won't hurt a thing," he said and pressed his lips to mine. This kiss was anything but quick and I began to worry that someone would see us. But quickly that thought, and all others, disappeared from my mind. Caeden always seemed to be able to do that to me.

Licking my bottom lip, he pulled away. With a smile he headed to the door and opened it. "You coming?"

"Uh- yeah," I forced my feet to move.

He laughed at my dazed expression.

Caeden and I tossed on our Lucinda's hats and shirts. Gram came from the front and said, "Thank goodness you're here. I've got to go, I'm already five minutes late," she looked at her watch and blew her gray hair from her face. She untied an apron from around her waist and tossed it over her arm. "Bye Soph," she kissed my cheek. "Caeden," she waved and he tilted his hat down.

"She was in a hurry," I said to Caeden as the door closed behind her.

He chuckled and flipped his baseball cap backwards. "A council meeting was called."

"Aren't you supposed to go to those," I said.

"Yeah," he shrugged. "But I never do, so why start now? I think you should work the front today," he tilted his head to study my reaction.

My limbs locked and the color drained from my face. "Um-"

"Soph," he said, "it's okay. I'm not going to let anything happen to you. You can't let Travis keep you from living your life and doing your job."

I wiped my sweaty palms on my jeans. "Fine," I snapped. "I'll do it. But for the record," I pointed a finger menacingly at him, "I hate you."

He laughed and his blue eyes sparkled. I turned on my heel and strode through the swinging door. "No, you don't!" he called.

A mom with her rambunctious toddler was sitting at one of the tables. The kid had blue icing and chocolate cake all over his face. Why were little kids always so dirty? Did they just enjoy being covered in goo?

"Timothy," the mom scolded when the toddler stood on the seat and wiped his dirty hand on the wall. She sent me a sympathetic glance and grabbed a handful of napkins to try and clean it off. Sighing, I grabbed a wet cloth from the kitchen.

"Here, I'll get it," I told the woman.

"Oh, thank you," she breathed and sat back down. This close up I could see just how exhausted she was and I instantly felt sorry for her. I wiped the wall clean and then turned to the dirty kid.

"Hey bud, is that cupcake good?"

He nodded his head.

"Do you mind if I clean your hands for you? It can't be fun trying to eat a cupcake with all that goo on your hands."

He looked at his mom for approval. When she gave it he shoved his chubby little fingers in my face. I proceeded to clean his fingers off and then I even wiped his rosy pink cheeks.

"Thank you," the woman said and patted my hand. "I'm so sorry for the mess he made."

"It's not a problem," I said.

The door opened and several school kids came in as well as a man dressed in a suit with his cellphone glued to his ear who I assumed worked at the bank across the road.

I opened the door to the kitchen and tossed the cloth in. It hit's target, the back of Caeden's head, and he yelled, "Hey!" before I closed the door. I turned to the waiting customers, a giggle escaping my lips.

Fixing my hat, I said, "May I help you?"

TWELVE.

I was getting stronger. I was amazed by the amount of strength I possessed. I had never imagined that I could have this kind of power. I struck out with my fist and caught Bryce square in the jaw with enough force to bring him down to the mat. He spat blood on the blue mat before jumping up and coming at me again. I ducked down and grabbed the back of his knees. He twisted to the side and came down with a thud on his hip.

Caeden laughed from the corner, clapping, and I could hear him say, "That's my she-wolf."

Bryce's stunned blue eyes met mine for a second before he jumped at me. I pushed him off and using my body weight slammed him down on the ground, holding him there. It seemed that I wasn't completely useless in my human form.

"I'm done," Bryce said, blood dribbling out of the corner of his mouth. "My bruises have bruises and those are quickly forming more bruises."

I released him and he began to rub his arm. I felt a rush of power knowing that I had taken down someone Bryce's size.

"Who's next?" I looked around, pushing sweaty hair off my brow. "Caeden?"

He paled.

"Come on," I coaxed. "I promise I won't hurt you."

Bentley slapped him on the shoulder. "Go on, Caeden, show your girl who's boss."

I narrowed my eyes, daring him to turn me down.

Sighing, he uncrossed his arms, and said, "I'll make you regret this."

"Prove it," I challenged.

Caeden stepped onto the mat and said, "Whenever you're ready."

Within a second we began our dance. I knew to the others we appeared beautiful but deadly. Two Alphas squaring off. We circled, we feinted, every move was so perfectly matched by the other that I quickly forgot who made the first move. We were both hesitant to hurt one another. I heard the guys yell, "Caeden take her down!" and the girls screamed, "You can beat him, Sophie!"

We continued our dance undeterred by their cheers. Caeden threw a punch and caught me in the shoulder. It hurt but not as bad as it could have. He was holding back and that made me mad. I put more force behind my kicks and caught him in the side. His breath whooshed out like a deflated balloon. While he was bent over I shoved him with my body weight and he fell to the mat with me on top of him. His blue eyes met mine and I gasped. That look... Wow, it did strange things to a girl.

"Got you," I rasped.

He flipped over so that I was on the floor and he was hovering over me. He grabbed my hands and held them above my head. "Now I've got you," he lowered his lips to mine and slowly pried them open. A girly breath escaped my throat.

"Ew! Are you guys going to have sex? At least let us leave first!" Bryce groaned.

Caeden chuckled and pulled away. Still holding me down he met my eyes and said, "For the record, that's how I plan to end *all* our fights."

"I think you might've mentioned that," I breathed.

Oh dear God I was doomed.

Caeden pushed himself up and held out a hand for me. Instead of letting me go he pulled me against his chest.

"Thanks for ruining the moment Bryce," Caeden grinned.

"Ugh," Bryce held his hand out. "I just don't want to be witness to any *moments* between you two. Excuse me while I throw up a bit in my mouth."

Caeden smacked his younger brother on the back of the head.

"That hurt," Bryce rubbed his head.

"Good," Caeden said.

"Oh it's on," Bryce said and attacked his brother. Caeden pushed me out of the way but Bryce's fist still caught me. Caeden growled and tackled his brother to the ground. I rolled out of the way and joined the others a safe distance away.

Chris turned to me, her pale green eyes silently laughing, and said, "Want to get a lemonade? They'll be at it for a while."

"Sure," I said. I no longer worried about Caeden getting hurt during a practice spar. With Travis? Now that was a different story.

I followed Chris up the basement steps. Her honey blond hair hung in a long ponytail. She had that thin hair that always looked perfect while mine was a thick mess. Chris opened the refrigerator and pulled out a glass pitcher of fresh lemonade. Amy had even cut up a lemon and the slices floated around. Having basically grown up in the Williams house Chris went right to the cabinet of glasses and grabbed two. I filled them with ice and she poured the pale yellow lemonade into them.

With a glint in her eye she said, "Wait," and dug through a drawer. "Aha!" she said and pulled out little drink umbrellas. She put a blue one in hers and an orange one in mine. "Now they're pretty," she smiled.

She sat on the counter and I pulled out a stool. The lemonade was tangy on my tongue but refreshing.

Chris tucked a piece of blond hair behind her ear and wiped lemonade from her lip. Blushing she said, "I don't know why but I have a feeling that I have you to thank for Bentley's sudden change of heart."

I nearly spit out a mouthful of lemonade her comment was so surprising.

"What?" I gasped, trying not to choke.

"Bentley always… avoided me. No, not avoided, more… I don't know," she rambled. "He just always fought the attraction between us."

"I-uh-I did talk to him one day," I stammered.

"I don't know what you said but thank you Sophie. I love that boy more than I ever thought it was possible to love someone. He's my everything."

"He's your mate," I said.

"Yeah," she swirled a finger around the rim of her cup, "he is and it's…"

"Magical?" I supplied.

"That's the perfect word for it. Magical," she tested the word on her tongue. "What… what did you say to him? I mean- you don't have to tell me if you don't want to," she added.

"I told him that he deserves to love and be loved despite what he thinks," I shrugged. "I honestly didn't say that much."

"I didn't know he felt that way," she said.

We finished our lemonade in companionable silence, both lost in our thoughts.

"I guess we better go back down there," Chris said with a small smile. "I just hope they haven't killed each other."

"Caeden can control himself," I winked, "and I don't think Bryce can take him."

Chris' booming laugh filled the kitchen. She placed our glasses in the sink and threw her arm over my shoulder. "Oh, Sophie, I don't know what we did before you came along."

"I'm sure it was very exiting," I said.

"Yeah, it was, but it always felt like something was missing. You're that missing piece."

The guys hadn't killed each other. Caeden and Bryce were now sitting on the floor sipping from water bottles and wiping sweat from their brows. Caeden jokingly pushed his brothers shoulder and Bryce toppled over. With a laugh, Bryce pushed back but Caeden didn't budge.

"Come on," Chris motioned her head towards the mats. "I want to see if I can still take you now that you're super wolf."

"I don't know," I bit my lip. "I don't want to hurt you."

"Puh-lease," Chris rolled her eyes. "It'll take a lot more than little ole you to hurt me," she flexed her impressive arm muscles. "I'm not as pathetic as that weenie," she giggled and pointed at Bryce.

"Hey!" he quipped and threw a water bottle at her head. The bottle shot forward like a missile and Chris caught it despite still having human reflexes.

"Nice try," she smirked.

Bryce stuck his tongue out. "Guess I'll just have to take your boy toy on and see if you still like his pretty face when he's covered in bruises."

Bentley cracked his knuckles. "And we'll see if Charlotte still likes you when you can't walk and have to eat through a feeding tube."

The boys went at it and the room filled with the sounds of punches, grunts, and kicks.

"Let's do this," Chris said, straightening her tank top strap.

"Better call 911," I said, "because when I'm done with you, you'll definitely need an ambulance."

"Hardy-har-har-har," she rolled her eyes. "All talk and no action."

Lightning fast I struck out and she fell down to her back and the air whooshed out of her lungs. "Freakin' ninja," she muttered under her breath as she slowly began to stand. She rubbed her backside. I smiled in satisfaction.

With my new and improved shifter abilities I was able to slow down every movement she went to make. She'd draw her arm back in a punch and I would see it in slow motion so I could either duck or grab her arm. "Incredible," I murmured under my breath. I had never wanted this kind of strength, power, I had been fine being perfectly normal, but there was a sense of satisfaction in my abilities. I knew that if

I went up against a seasoned shifter I'd probably fail but someone like Travis? Yeah, I was pretty sure I could do some serious damage to his pretty face.

After hitting the floor for the fiftieth time Chris held a hand out and said, "Done, I'm done." She was breathing heavily, her chest rising and falling rapidly, and I wasn't even winded. "You're a natural Sophie. I don't know what's happened to you. That one day you fought like a human and now you fight like a super wolf."

"My she-wolf," Caeden came up to me and kissed my cheek.

"Didn't I tell you never to call me that?" I smiled.

"I seem to remember that conversation but I chose not to listen to you."

"Ah, of course," I laughed. "Is this what I have to look forward to for the rest of my life? You not listening to me?"

"Yeah, pretty much," Caeden nodded. "I'm going to shower," he kissed me.

I looked down at Chris and held out a hand to help her up. She took it and I easily hauled her up. "Need some ice?"

"Yes, please," she limped over to the couch.

I went to the kitchen and brought a couple of ice packs down for Chris. She gladly took them and sighed in relief when it hit her skin. I sat down beside her and saw Bentley and Bryce in the corner. Bryce held a towel to his bloody nose and Bentley was snapping a bone in his arm into place so it would heal correctly. The sound was sickening and I made a face of disgust.

"I didn't mean to hurt you," I said to Chris, wiping my hands on my purple workout pants just to have something to do.

She waved her hand. "It's okay. I know you didn't do it on purpose and I didn't tell you to stop."

After a few moments I asked her, "Where's Logan?"

Her eyes filled with tears. "I don't know. He

disappeared from school yesterday after I talked to him and he didn't come home last night. I'm really worried about him."

My heart filled with leaden dread. What if Travis had gotten him? Instead of voicing my concerns to Chris I patted her hand and said, "I'm sure he's fine. So he knows that we know?" I asked.

"Yeah," she leaned her head back. "I hoped he'd deny it but he didn't." Turning her head towards me she whispered, "I don't want to lose my brother."

I swallowed. "Caeden and I won't let anything happen to him. This is the twenty-first century, I think it's time for some new rules."

She smiled. "That makes me feel better."

"I mean it," I said fiercely. "I won't let anyone hurt him."

"Thank you," she wiped away a tear.

"Christian?" Bentley said from across the room, sensing her upset. "What's wrong?"

"Nothing," she said. "Everything's alright."

His dark brows knitted together and his golden brown eyes seemed unconvinced. "You sure?"

"Yep," she smiled for good measure.

Bentley went back to tending his arm.

"Do you want us to go out and look for him?" I asked.

"Not yet," she said. "I think he just needs time to… process."

"Just let me know," I said, "I'll be the first one out there."

"You're so nice, Sophie," she said. "There aren't many people willing to help at their own expense."

"You guys are my friends, my pack, I'd do anything for you and I'm not saying that as your Alpha."

She smiled. "I know."

* * *

Caeden and I decided to spend the night at his house.

I tied my wet hair into a knot on my head and padded into his bedroom. Archie and Murphy, who had shown up all on their own, were plopped on an oversized doggie cushion. Archie all but disappeared into the massiveness that was Murphy.

I hopped onto the bed, bouncing it, and Caeden wrapped me into his arms. He pulled the blankets over us even though his body heat was more than enough to keep us warm.

He was so quiet and his breath so even that I was sure he must have gone to sleep but then he spoke. "You amaze me more and more everyday. Sometimes I don't think I deserve someone like you."

I laughed. "Are you kidding me? I don't deserve you. You're perfect. You're kind, smart, funny- should I go on?" I turned my head and smiled at him.

Even in the darkness his blue eyes were bright. With his index finger he began to trace my features. "I think we were chosen for a reason Sophie. We compliment each other in every way."

"Isn't that the point of mates?" I asked. "To compliment each other?"

"Yeah," he breathed. "But I think maybe we're meant to do something important. Something big."

"Like what?" I laughed.

"I don't know," he shrugged and got quiet once more. Thinking I had fallen asleep, he said, "Soph?"

"I'm awake," I scooted closer to his body, resting my head in the crook of his arm.

"Do you..." He paused. "Do you ever think about what may have happened if we'd never met each other?"

"No," I said, "you do?"

"Yeah, and it scares the crap out of me to think of a life without you. You're my light. You brought me out of the darkness."

"What do you mean?" I asked and pressed a kiss to his naked chest.

"After my dad died I wasn't myself. I didn't really

———
133

live. I was a sucky Alpha, a sucky son, and a sucky brother. I knew I was hurting my mom but I just couldn't seem to snap out of it until you. You walked into the shop and suddenly I just knew that everything was going to be okay. You're my shooting star."

"Wow, I- I didn't know," I breathed, my breath tickling his light dusting of chest hair.

"Now you do," he said.

I fell asleep to thoughts of wolves, mates, and light. A very bright light.

* * *

"Wake up, Sophie," Caeden said against my ear.

"Go away," I mumbled.

"Rise and shine," he said and shook me slightly.

"I'm going to stab you in the eye," I mumbled into the pillow.

"Ah, you wouldn't do that, you like my pretty blue eyes too much."

Sitting up I snapped, "What is so important that you have to wake me up at-" I glanced at the clock, "-seven o' clock on a Sunday?"

"Soccer," he grinned and tossed a ball at my face. I deftly caught it.

"Soccer? Caeden, I told you I don't want to try out for the team."

"You don't have to try out for the team. I just want to see you play. Think you can beat me?"

"I know I can," I tossed the ball at his chest as hard as I could.

He grunted form the force but didn't drop it. Still, I smiled in satisfaction. Caeden tossed the ball from one hand to the other. "I'm not leaving until you get out of this bed," he grinned.

"Fine," I threw the covers off. "Now, shoo," I motioned him out the door. "I have to get dressed."

"Score one for Caeden," he grinned. I shook my head and closed the door behind him.

———

I dug through my designated drawer and found a loose pair of shorts and a tank top. I changed clothes quickly, tossing my Jammie Jams into the hamper, and scurrying into Caeden's bathroom. I could hear Bryce's snore through the wall. At least someone was getting to sleep in. I brushed my teeth and hair before pulling it back into a high ponytail.

I found Caeden downstairs in the kitchen. "Here," he tossed me a breakfast bar. "Eat this now and I thought later we could have a picnic." He pointed to an actual picnic basket. I thought those things only existed in movies.

"Wow," I said, "you might just win boyfriend of the year award." He grinned but I held up a finger. "Unless you wake me up at the crack of dawn again."

"You're cranky," he grinned.

"You bet I am," I smiled, rubbing sleep from my eyes. "But it's impossible to stay cranky for long when you're around a bright ray of sunshine like you."

"Aww," he put a hand to his heart, "I'm touched."

"Are you done?" I motioned to the basket as I unwrapped my breakfast bar. It was drizzled in caramel and actually didn't taste that bad. All the other ones I'd eaten had always tasted like cardboard.

"Yep," he said and closed the top. "We are good to go."

I picked up the soccer ball and held it in the crook of my arm. "I hope you're ready to get owned by a girl," I said to his back.

"Baby, you can own me anytime."

I blushed at his words and decided to keep my mouth shut. He loaded the picnic basket in the trunk of his Jeep and Murphy was already in his cage. I looked around and said, "Where's Archie?"

About that time my cute little black and white dog came scurrying into the garage. I picked him up in my arms and showered him with kisses. "You're so cute," I cooed. "The cutest dog in the world."

"Sophie, we've got to go," Caeden said.

135

"Oh, right," I opened the car door. I put the window down and let Archie stick his head out. Murphy whined from the back, wishing for freedom.

The early morning air was cool so I had to eventually tug Archie back inside and put the window up. He looked up at me with round, sad, brown eyes. "Sorry bud," I said, "mommy's cold."

Caeden snorted.

"What?" I asked.

"Did you just call yourself 'mommy' to the dog?"

"Yes, doesn't everyone do that?"

"I don't call myself daddy to Murphy," he grinned.

"Well I don't care, if I want to call myself mommy to my dog I will," I petted Archie's soft fur.

Caeden just chuckled.

I didn't know where we were going so I closed my eyes and leaned my seat back to take a nap. In no time Caeden was telling me to open my eyes and that we were here.

Here, turned out to be the park connected to the school. The sun had fully risen and some cars were already in the parking lot. Probably people out for a morning jog on the trails.

Caeden popped the trunk and let Murphy out. The horse of a dog stretched his long legs. Caeden pulled out a tennis ball and tossed it. Murphy took out after it while Archie yipped.

Murphy came skidding back with the ball in his mouth. The ball looked so small in the large dog's mouth that I was surprised he didn't swallow it. He lay down on the ground with the ball and began to chew it.

"We'll come back and get the basket when we're ready for lunch," Caeden said, closing the trunk and locking the car.

Archie walked beside me and I held the soccer ball. "Look Archie," I said and the little dog looked up at me, "you look like a little animated soccer ball." The dog snorted and trotted ahead as if I had offended him.

Caeden looked behind us for Murphy. He was still on the ground, chewing his ball. Caeden whistled. "Here, boy, bring the ball to daddy," he turned to me a winked. I blushed. You'd think after all this time Caeden wouldn't be able to make me blush but he still could. Murphy held the ball in his mouth and ran towards us. He stopped in front of us and spit out his ball for Caeden to toss. He did and Murphy took off after it. Archie stuck his nose prissily in the air. "Soccer field's this way," Caeden guided me to the front right of the park. "Murphy!" he called and the dog came jogging back. Caeden didn't take the ball this time and Murphy stayed beside us.

We stopped in the middle of the field and I dropped the soccer ball down on the ground. Murphy and Archie sat by the bleachers.

"This is going to be kinda weird, playing against just one person," I said and tapped the ball with my foot. It moved a few inches.

Caeden laughed. "Stop trying to get out of it, Sophie, we're playing."

"Alright," I said. "I'm ready whenever you are. In fact, I'll let you have the ball first."

"Aren't you sweet," he said, and kicked the ball before jogging after it.

"Only because you won't have it for long," I laughed, jogging after him.

He went to kick it in the goal but I intercepted. I sprinted towards the other goal.

"Hey!" Caeden called behind me. "That wasn't fair!"

"That's how you play," I called back to him, taking aim, I kicked the ball and it soared into the top right corner.

"So not fair," Caeden said, wrapping his arms around my middle and swinging me around, before dropping me on the ground and going after the ball.

"And that's cheating mister," I yelled, already standing up and running after him. I stole the ball from

137

Caeden again and he cursed behind me. My laugh filled the air. I hadn't been this carefree and just... *happy* in a long time. The stress of the move, of finding my mate, becoming a shifter, *Travis*, it just all melted away. For a minute, I could just pretend to be normal. I was just a girl, playing soccer, with her amazingly wonderful boyfriend. I liked that picture. I shot the ball into the net once again. I cheered for myself and said to Caeden, "You're already losing and we've been playing for two minutes."

"Well, we're not done yet," he winked, flashing his dimple.

* * *

By lunchtime we had amassed quite a crowd. Actually, *I* was the one that the crowd was gathered for.

Six or seven guys sat on the bleachers hooting and hollering. I had gotten used to girls jaws dropping around Caeden but it weird to have the attention turned to me. Weird and a bit unnerving.

"I am going to give each and every one of those guys a piece of my mind," Caeden huffed under his breath.

"Jealous?" I asked, before flitting away with the ball. We'd been playing for hours and I still wasn't tired and Caeden still hadn't scored a single point.

After I scored yet another point I grabbed up the ball and said to Caeden, "How about lunch?"

"Thank you! I'm starving!"

"Sorry, I forgot you have to eat every five minutes," I joked.

"I'll be right back," he said, loud enough for the other guys to hear the warning tone to his voice.

"Hurry," I said and pecked him on the lips. A little bit of the tension leaked out of his body.

Once Caeden had disappeared the seven guys hopped down from the bleachers, clapping.

"That was fucking incredible," the guy in the middle said. He had floppy red hair and pale blue eyes.

"I've never seen anything like that before," another

guy said, running his hands through spiky blond hair.

"I'm Evan," said the red head.

"Oh right, we should probably introduce ourselves," another guy said. He was the tallest of all the guys with sandy hair almost to his shoulders. "The name's Riley," he produced his fist and I bumped it with mine.

"This is Tyler," he pointed to the blond guy and he waved.

"Cam," a brown hair guy said.

"Brody," the guy on the end smiled. He had wavy black hair and olive colored skin.

"I'm Kyle," a shorter guy with white-blond hair said, sticking out his hand to shake.

"And I'm Shane," the most muscular of the guys said. His brown hair skimmed his jaw.

"You whooped that guy's ass," Riley said.

"He's my boyfriend," I looked over my shoulder for Caeden. "So, he probably just let me win."

"I don't think so," the guy with the light blond hair said. Was his name Shane? No, that was the muscular guy. Kyle, his name was Kyle.

"Are you thinking of trying out?" Evan asked.

"I don't think so," I shook my head.

All seven of the guys' jaws dropped. "Are you fucking crazy?" Riley asked. "You have to try out."

"Yeah, definitely," Shane nodded. "I think coach would let you on the boys team."

I laughed. "The boys team?"

"Well, the way you took on your boyfriend you'd eat the other girl teams alive."

"But you think the boys' teams can handle me?" I quirked a brow.

"Oh yeah," Cam said and flexed his arm muscles. "We can definitely handle you."

Brody snorted. "Maybe if you're on the team we'll actually win a game."

One of the guys pushed Brody.

"Come on," said Kyle, "at tryout."

"Maybe I will," I rolled the ball back and forth. "But do you really think your coach would let a girl on the team?"

Riley snorted and crossed his arms over his chest. "He'd be a fucking idiot *not* to."

"When are tryouts?" I asked.

"This coming Friday," Cam said.

I turned around once more and this time saw Caeden. I breathed out a sigh of relief. I had started to worry that something had happened to him.

"Please, please, please, tryout," Evan begged.

"Sure, why not?" I shrugged and bounced the ball on the end of my foot before catapulting it into the air and catching it.

"What happened to, 'Caeden, I don't want to play soccer anymore,'" Caeden mimicked from behind me.

I laughed and turned around, meeting his gaze. "I guess you showed me how much I missed it."

"And do I get a thank you?" he grinned.

"Thank you," I said and went to kiss his chin but he turned his head at the last second so I caught his lips instead.

"Why are the hot ones always taken," one of the guys muttered.

"Uh- because they're hot," another piped in.

I laughed and turned to them. "So I guess I'll see you guys at tryouts on Friday?"

"You bet," Riley said.

I watched them head over to the adjoining soccer field. They pushed and mocked one another. They reminded me of our pack with their easy banter.

Caeden spread a checked blanket out on the field and sat down.

"This is just like a movie," I whispered under my breath as I sat down beside him.

Caeden pulled some sandwiches out of the basket and held them up. "Except in a movie the guy usually makes some extravagant meal. I brought peanut butter and jelly sandwiches."

I laughed. "PB and J is good with me," I took one from him.

"Phew," he wiped his brow. "I was worried for nothing."

I giggled again and bumped his shoulder. I took a bite of the sandwich. "Best PB and J I've ever had," I assured him.

"Good," he said and bit into his own sandwich.

Archie sat in front of me, licking his lips, and looking at my sandwich like he was two seconds away from snatching it from my hands.

"Here buddy," I said and picked off a piece of bread with just peanut butter. He took it greedily.

"Hold up," Caeden said and began to dig through the basket. He unwrapped a half a sandwich and a quarter of one. He tossed the half to Murphy and the quarter to Archie. Both dogs were obviously in doggy heaven.

"Thanks for today," I said and wiped a dot of jelly off of Caeden's arm. "It meant a lot to me."

"Even though I drug you out of bed early on a Sunday morning?"

"Yep," I said.

I finished my sandwich and tossed the trash in the basket. I wiggled around, trying to get comfortable, before lying on my back and watching the clouds. I instantly felt my heart rate drop. Something about watching clouds calmed me down. Caeden did the same, lacing his hand in mine.

"Do you think Logan's okay?" I finally asked after staring at the sky for a good five minutes.

I heard Caeden's sigh. "I don't know."

"Are you worried?" I asked.

He said nothing for quite a while so I figured he either chose not to answer or fell asleep. But finally he said, "Yes."

My heart stopped for a second and my hand clenched his. "I don't want anything to happen to him."

141

"I can't hear him," Caeden whispered.

"What do you mean?" I rolled over.

"In my wolf form. I can't hear him. It's just... silence. Wherever he is, he's in his human form or..."

"Or?" I prompted.

Caeden's swallow was audible. "Or dead."

I gasped and sat up. "Caeden! Why are we sitting here? We should be looking for him!"

"I did... all night."

I began to study Caeden and realized I'd missed how tired he was. Gray circles framed his eyes and his movements had been sluggish.

"Caeden-"

"I think he's dead," Caeden said.

"No," I shook my head.

Caeden continued like I hadn't said anything. "And when I get my hands on Travis I'm going to make him suffer through every unimaginable thing before I kill him. And when I kill him I'm going to make sure he begs for mercy. He hurt you and if he's hurt or killed another member of my pack, none of you will be able to stop me."

"Caeden," I said, tears in my eyes. I placed my hands on his cheeks, the stubble scratching my palms. "This isn't you."

He sat up. "Sophie, you don't understand. If he's not killed he'll just keep killing. He has to be stopped and I'm the only one that can do it. I'm the Alpha," he sighed and buried his head in his hands. He gripped the dark brown strands so tightly I was afraid he'd pull them out. "This is my responsibility."

"It's mine too," I said, trying to calm him. "We're a team Caeden! No, we're a pack! Why do you act like you have to do everything by yourself?"

"Because," he said, "I don't want anything to happen to any of you."

"And what about you? Is your life unimportant? Do you know what would happen to me if you got hurt or killed?

I don't want to even think about it," the tears finally broke from my eyes and flowed down my face.

"Soph," Caeden said, snapping back to reality. He wrapped his arms around me and held me to his chest. "Please don't cry. I hate being the cause of your tears," he wiped them with his thumb. "Sophie, please, you're far to beautiful to cry."

"I just hate it when you say things like that," I sniffled. "You act as if your life means nothing when it means everything to me," I gripped his shirt so tightly that my knuckles turned white.

"Babe," Caeden rubbed my cheeks. "I'm sorry, I shouldn't have said that."

"But you mean it," I breathed. "And I know you'll do it if you have the chance. I can't-" I swallowed and tried to calm myself down, "I can't see you hurt again." I shook my head and my hair rubbed against his shirt. "That night, when you came to Gram's and Peter had hurt you, changed things for me Caeden." I purposefully lifted his shirt up and over his head. "Look at this Caeden," I rubbed the scars on this side. Caeden's perfect tanned skin was marred by five pale white scars; all several inches long.

"But what about you?" he grabbed my arm and held it out so the light hit it. *LIAR*. "They hurt you too, don't you want to do something?"

I clenched my teeth and then spat, "Of course I want to do something! But I don't want to do something that's just plain out suicidal!"

"I'm not being suicidal," Caeden pulled away from me and brought his legs up to his chest where he then rested his arms. His muscles were tense and his jaw ticked.

I pulled at the emerald color grass. Before I shifted for the first time grass had always seemed bland. Now it shown with a kaleidoscope of colors.

Finally Caeden collapsed on his back and laughed. His laughter was contagious and I quickly joined him even though I had no idea what he was laughing at.

143

"What is it?" I finally asked.

"I've really ruined today. I wanted to take you to the park and have a date," he laced his fingers through mine, and the sun made his blue eyes glow. "We never get to have dates anymore."

"No, I guess we don't," I shrugged.

"And of course, I had to mess this one up. I hope you can forgive me?"

"Only if you promise not to go on a suicide mission of revenge. We're a pack Caeden."

"I promise," he said.

"Good," I said and wrapped my arms around his neck before kissing him senseless.

THIRTEEN.

After we left the park Caeden called the pack and told them to meet us at his house. We were going to find Logan.

I really hoped that Logan had simply left, needing time to think, and that Travis didn't have a part in this. I wasn't sure if I was ready to fight against another pack and I didn't want to be a weak link. I want to be strong. I don't want Caeden to worry about me. I want to be able to stand on my own.

Caeden reached over the middle console and laced his fingers with mine as if he sensed my inner turmoil.

We didn't talk on the drive back to the house. Caeden occasionally received a call from one of the pack. "Bring Lucy," he said into the phone.

When he hung up I asked, "Who's Lucy?"

"Logan's familiar," he said.

"Oh right, I forgot." Swallowing I said, "I don't know if I can kill someone. I'm not as confident about that as you are."

Caeden gently squeezed my hand and turned into his driveway. "I wouldn't say I'm *confident* that I can kill someone but if he's hurt another member of *my* pack," he growled, "he's not going to live to see the next day."

Caeden parked the Jeep and we went over to greet Bentley and Bryce who were both sitting on the hood of Bentley's black GMC truck.

Lucy, Logan's chocolate lab familiar, paced nearby.

Caeden nodded towards the woods, "Let's go find Logan."

* * *

Power surged in my muscles as I ran. Nothing could touch me. Caeden's silver form flickered in front of me. Bryce and Bentley flanked me. My wolf instincts could since a fight coming. Blood was in the air. Caeden stopped and through his head back, howling. His howl promised death.

145

He took off again and I stretched my legs farther to better keep up with him.

Lucy barked somewhere up ahead. I knew we were deep in the woods, deeper than I had ever gone, and maybe even states away. Adrenaline spurned me forward. Bentley and Bryce struggled to keep up. My eyes narrowed in determination and I stuck my nose to the ground, smelling everything.

I really hope my little bit of training pays off. I said to no one in particular.

Don't worry my she-wolf, Caeden said.

If I had been in my human form I would have smiled.

Suddenly, Caeden skidded to a stop, and dirt went flying. Lucy pawed at the earth and Caeden helped her.

With a shimmer he shifted to his human form. I couldn't help my reaction to turn my head. The rest may be okay with nudity but I hadn't grown up that way. Cautiously, I turned my head back. Caeden was covering his bottom half with a bloodied shirt. I sniffed. The scent of grass, water, and air hit my lungs. Mixed together it was a scent that was uniquely Logan's.

The shirt dropped from Caeden's hand as he shimmered once more and became a wolf.

He's close, was all Caeden said.

The guys and I followed Caeden and Lucy.

Lucy came to a stop in front of what could only be described as a cave. But instead of being made of rock it was formed from dirt.

The five of us crept forward.

The smell of stale earth and blood assaulted my lungs and I gagged. As a wolf it sounded like I was trying to cough up a hairball.

I focused on picking out distinct scents to identify any shifters that may have been here.

Malice floated through the air, bearing the spicy sent that was Travis.

Flowers. Carnations to be exact belonged to Hannah.

I couldn't pick up a scent belonging to Robert, but I hadn't been around him enough to connect one with him, so I had to assume that three wolves were waiting for us.

The cave, if it could even be called that, widen out.

Logan! Caeden cried. He ran forward.

I stopped in my tracks at what I saw. If I had been a human I would have clapped a hand over my open mouth.

Logan was tied to the wall with metal chains that dug into his wrists and ankles. His shirt, obviously, was gone. His naked chest was crisscrossed with claws marks. In those marks something glittered and with renewed horror I realized what it was. Silver.

"Silver is deadly... to werewolves too, more so, than it is to us... For shifters it gives us an injury... that doesn't heal fast... which can lead to death..." Caeden's voice echoed through my head from that long ago day when he was bleeding on my couch.

With the injuries Logan had sustained and the amount of silver... I'd say he didn't have much time left.

Caeden and Bentley shifted to their human forms and began to untie Logan.

Bryce suddenly whimpered and I turned my head towards him.

"Well, well, well, what do we have here?" Travis clapped his hands as he entered the widened out portion of the cave. He was shirtless and his jeans hung low on his hips. His black eyes were void of any compassion. They were the eyes of a killer. A murderer. Robert and Hannah hovered behind him. "Come to rescue an impure? Tsk, tsk, Caeden. Don't you know they're not allowed to live?"

Caeden growled, despite being in his human form.

"You are the impure," Caeden spat. They finished untying Logan and the blond boy slumped forward, passed out; completely unaware that rescue had come.

Bentley and Caeden gently helped Logan to the floor, careful not to hurt him, even though he was completely

147

oblivious to the world.

"Travis," Caeden's teeth groaned together. "If you know what's good for you, you'll run."

"Oh, are we playing cat and mouse?" Travis grinned, showing elongated teeth. Hair began to sprout and he started to shimmer. "I love games. I choose cat," his words were muffled around his teeth. He dropped to his paws and a blondish-white wolf stood before us with black eyes. Robert and Hannah shifted too. Robert's color was ashy where Hannah's was almost a peach color. Travis barked in warning. Run.

Caeden and Bentley shifted.

Sophie, stay here, Caeden instructed.

What? No! I protested.

Please, I need you to stay with Logan in case they come back for him. Please. He said all this with his eyes zeroed in on Travis.

Okay. I said.

Let's go boys, Caeden said and the three large wolves rushed the smaller ones.

Travis and his pack took off like bullets out of the cave, after all there was no where else for them to go.

I padded over to Logan. His chest rose and fell painfully. His breaths gurgled and I worried he may have a punctured lung. Strips of skin hung off of him like a torn shirt. How did anyone do this to another human being?

Logan hadn't always been nice, most of the time he was downright rude, but no one deserved this.

I switched to human form to inspect his wounds better. When I found that there was nothing I could do I switched back so I would be better prepared to defend if need be.

I heard a howl outside and my hackles rose. I knew Caeden was right, that I needed to stay with Logan, but I couldn't help feeling like I needed to be out there. Four against three was better than three against three. I began to pace the perimeter of the cave for something to do. Logan obviously wouldn't be waking up anytime soon.

Another howl sounded close to the entrance. It was a howl of pain. Of distress and I knew it belonged to one of my own. Bryce.

With a quick look at Logan I sprinted from the cave and towards the howl. I saw Bentley straight ahead fighting Hannah. To my left, Caeden and Travis disappeared behind some trees; they were making the most noise. But immediately to my right Robert had Bryce down on the ground, his teeth seconds away from biting into Bryce's neck and killing him. Bryce whimpered and that noise alone spurned me into action once more.

A power like none I'd ever felt coursed through my veins and I hit Robert in the side. I heard several ribs crack and break.

Kill him. Kill him. I will KILL HIM.

In that moment all my humanity disappeared. I was nothing but a wolf. A wolf intent on protecting its pack mate. A wolf intent on the kill.

Fear flooded Robert's eyes.

I struck down and slashed his neck open with my teeth, cutting through his pelt and skin. His blood rushed into my mouth, hot and rusty. The light went out of his eyes and with death he reverted back to his human form. His coppery blood coated my mouth and soaked the earth.

I had killed a man, a boy really, in a matter of seconds and hadn't felt a thing.

I padded cautiously towards Bryce, who wasn't making a noise.

His eyes were closed but his chest rose and fell. He must have passed out because he was now in his human form. When we're wolves we only change back to our human form if we want to, we're killed, or we pass out.

His throat had a pretty big cut but it was healing. It would heal faster if he was in his wolf form but I didn't want to attempt to wake him up. It would be better if he could heal without feeling the pain.

Bentley limped over. Hannah had bit his leg and blood oozed out, dripping with little, plop, plop, plop, sounds to the ground.

She's dead. Bentley said.

Robert's dead too. I said.

Remind me, I never want to be on the receiving end of your anger. His tongue lolled to the side in a wolfish grin. His gold eyes seemed so bright against his black fur.

A bark and howl sounded a few miles away.

Caeden and Travis.

Worry coated my tongue with an acidic taste. I tried to spit it out but instead only succeeded in looking demented.

Bentley and I looked at each other as we listened to the sounds of the war raging nearby. We were both breathing heavy and the same fear that resided in my soul was reflected in his eyes. I could hear the blood rushing through my body.

The sounds from Caeden and Travis increased in pitch. Someone howled in pain. If I had been in my human form I would have covered my ears with my hands. As it was, I pawed the earth and whimpered.

Growls and the snapping of jaws filled the air.

There were many times in the past months when I'd thought I'd been truly fearful.

When I found out I was a shifter.

Caeden being my mate.

Caeden showing up to my door, bleeding, and dying.

Being kidnapped.

Being tortured.

But it all paled in comparison to now, to this moment.

This was true fear.

The sun began to set, igniting the sky into a fireball of reds, oranges, and pinks. My eyes began to adjust to the different light. My ears prickled at every little sound and then… all sound seemed to disappear.

It was as if the forest was holding its breath. No animals moved, the trees did not stir, everything was on pause.

And then there was a cry.

The cry of a wolf.

Dying.

I held my breath and watched the trees where Caeden and Travis had disappeared.

Please let him be okay, I pleaded with God, with Bentley, with whoever cared to listen.

And then a wolf emerged between the trees. It stood mightily, it's fur stirred by the wind, and then I was running.

Running as fast as my paws would carry me.

Running and then crashing into the wolf.

FOURTEEN.

We both shifted to our human forms at the same time. I wrapped my arms around his neck and pressed kisses there, to his cheeks, his chest, and finally his mouth. I didn't even care that we were completely naked and Bentley was bound to be watching. Nothing else mattered except that Caeden was alive.

"Caeden, Caeden, Caeden," I said, over and over again. "Caeden, Caeden, Caeden," I could never tire of saying his name. That was something people took for granted. A name. I couldn't imagine never being able to say his name again so I just said it over and over. "Caeden, Caeden, Caeden," in between kisses.

"I'm okay, it's okay," he said, his hands rubbing soothing circles on my back. His hands moved slowly up my back, over my shoulders, and to my cheeks. Holding me away from him he said, "Sophie, I'm okay." He wiped my tears away.

Tears? I was crying? When did that happen?

"I'm okay, really, it's over. It's over," he said.

"It's over?"

"It's really over," he said.

"Are you hurt?" I asked, looking him over.

"No," he said. "I'm fine."

"But there's blood on you," I accused.

"His, not mine," he said.

We were resting on our knees, twigs pressing against my skin, but I didn't care.

"Oh Caeden," I sobbed and tightened my arms around his neck. "I love you so much."

He buried his face in my hair. "I love you too, my light, my she-wolf, my mate." Seeming to finally realize that I wasn't supposed to be out here, I was supposed to be with Logan, he said, "Why are you here? I told you to stay put!"

"I heard Bryce get hurt. I couldn't just do nothing!" I began to cry harder. "I killed Robert. Oh my God, Caeden! I killed someone! I killed him!"

"Shh, shh," Caeden tried to calm my hysterics.

"I just couldn't let him hurt Bryce!"

"Sophie, calm down, it's okay. You did good."

"I killed him, Caeden, like it was... *nothing*. I didn't even hesitate. It was so quick. So quick."

He rubbed my arms up and down. "Sophie-"

I shook my head. "We need to get Bryce and Logan. We need to *go*," my voice cracked.

I pulled away from him and shifted back into my wolf form. It was easier to deal with what I had done in this form. For a wolf, death and murder was normal, not so much for my human brain.

I heard a rustle behind me and knew that Caeden had shifted.

I got Logan. Bentley said as Caeden and I approached. I turned my head and saw Logan slumped against the ground. Lucy was curled up next to him. *He still won't wake up.*

How's Bryce? I asked.

Still passed out, he pointed with his muzzle.

I examined Bentley's wounds and found that he was close to being healed.

How are we going to get them back? I asked.

We'll have to wake them up, Caeden said. *We'll wait a little while though.*

Is it really over? I asked no one in particular.

It's over, Caeden affirmed.

It seems too easy. I said.

I'd say it was far from easy. Bentley said. *We can't all be super wolf like you Sophie*, he joked.

Super wolf, I snorted.

I saw you attack Robert. It was amazing! You were like a ninja!

I don't know why you guys want to call me a ninja. I am not *a ninja.* I huffed.

Bentley chuckled. *We'll stop calling you a ninja when you stop acting like one.*

153

I growled. *Do you* want *me to bite you?* I let a little bit of laughter trickle into my voice so he would know I was joking.

I'm going to check the perimeter. Caeden said. *Make sure the rest of Travis' pack isn't coming.*

Before I could ask to go with him he was gone.

I turned my gaze to Bentley and asked, *Does it bother you?*

What?

Killing? Murdering?

It's not like I wanted to, Bentley said. *But I had to protect the pack. Protect myself. It was my life or Hannah's.* We were both quiet for quite a while but eventually Bentley added, *All I could think about was Christian and that I couldn't die because I belong to her. I knew no matter what I* had *to make it out alive, for Chris. But it wasn't easy ending someone's life.* He hung his head. *But it had to be done. We have to keep the pack safe and they were a threat.*

So you think it's normal that I'm... remorseful?

I'd think you were psychotic killer if you weren't *upset. Death should have an affect on us, even when we're killing crazies like these, it reminds us that we do have a heart. That even though we turn into a wolf, at the end of the day we're still human. Remember that Sophie, you're only human.*

I soaked in Bentley's words and I instantly felt better.

Thank you. I said.

No problem, he said. *After all, someone has to be the voice of reason.*

* * *

Caeden returned and we managed to wake up Bryce and Logan. Bryce wasn't a happy camper.

"What the fuck?" Bryce looked around. "Oh fuck, I feel like a truck ran over me."

Logan seemed startled and then afraid. He tried to scramble away but once he realized it was just us he collapsed on the ground, letting out a sigh of relief. When he looked back up, tears coursed down his face. I had never seen someone as stoic as Logan break down like this.

Caeden switched to his human form. "Language Bryce," he scolded before going to Logan. "You're okay. You're safe. We aren't going to hurt you."

I wondered why Caeden felt the need to assure Logan we weren't going to hurt him when it clicked in my head. Logan would think we were going to kill him.

"You are a part of my pack," Caeden continued, "and I will protect you."

Logan sobbed. "Thank you, thank you, thank you."

"Can you shift?" Caeden asked, his voice soft, not demanding.

"I think so," Logan said.

"Bryce?"

"Oh? Now you worry about me?" Bryce snapped.

Caeden glared at his younger brother. His blue eyes seemed to burn like fire. "I always worry about *you*. Can you shift?"

Bryce rolled his blue eyes; just a few shades darker than Caeden's. "Of course I can shift, dumb shit, I'm awake aren't I?"

"Lang-" Before Caeden could finish, Bryce had already shifted. Caeden shook his head. "Let's go home."

He shifted and a mighty gray wolf stood before us. A moment later Logan shifted. His jeans exploded into the air before falling to the ground like flakes of snow. He shook his blond pelt and his green eyes were vibrant.

He pawed the ground before his voice filled out heads. *You're really not going to kill me?*

We could never hurt you, Logan. Bentley said.

You have nothing to worry about. I added.

Just try to keep this hushed around the elders. Most of them aren't as cool as Lucinda and might see fit to... eliminate the problem. But we will protect you. Logan, you're safe with us. Caeden said.

Are you losers coming or not? Bryce asked,

appearing on the hill above us. *Or are we going to stay here and have share and care time?*

We're coming, Caeden snapped. *Maybe Sophie should have let Robert take a chunk out of you.*

Hey! Bryce said. *You know you'd be beside yourself if something happened to me. I am irreplaceable.*

You're one of a kind that's for sure. Caeden muttered.

Bryce flashed a lopsided wolfy grin before sprinting off into the woods

Ready? Caeden asked.

We didn't bother answering, we just ran.

* * *

To say Amy was pissed was an understatement. She was so red in the face I was surprised she didn't explode.

"Caeden Henry Williams!" she spat. "How could you be so careless going off after Travis like that? Why didn't you tell me? I would've gone with you! So would have all the parents! You were stupid and reckless and anything but an Alpha!" she growled. Fur started to sprout on her arms and she took a moment to calm herself. As she calmed the fur receded. "And why didn't you two stop him!?" she pointed an accusing finger at me and Bentley. "You could've all been killed!"

"But we weren't," Bryce said from the corner, where he leaned against the family room wall. He held a book in his hands and flipped through the pages, obviously unaffected by Amy's anger.

Amy marched up to him, snatched the book from his hands, and unleashed her full fury on her youngest son. "Bryce, I am so sick and tired of you acting like an immature pup! Grow up! Be a man, dammit!"

Bryce straightened.

Amy shoved the book forcefully onto the shelf. "I've already lost my husband. I *can't* lose my children too," her voice cracked. She turned her wrath back to Caeden. "Think things through, Caeden! Think! You could've led your friends to their deaths! Your own mate!"

———

156

"I had to save Logan."

"Yes, I understand, and I commend you for that. But you should've informed us. I could've helped you. So could Jeremy and don't you think Logan's parent's would have liked to have helped?"

Caeden didn't say anything.

"You're all so young," Amy whispered. "Far too young to have to go through this."

I could see her anger was disappearing and soon the tears would commence.

"Mom-" Bryce said.

Amy turned so quickly she nearly blurred. Oh dear, I think there might be some anger left after all.

"So, help me God, Bryce, if you try and crack a joke I just might lose it."

Bryce's eyes widened and he ducked his head down. Shuffling his feet back and forth. "I wasn't going to make a joke. I just think you're overreacting."

"Overreacting!?" she shrieked at such a high decibel I wanted to cover my ears.

"Just shut the hell up, Bryce," Caeden said and buried his face in his hands.

Amy turned to all of us. Logan, Bentley, Caeden, and I were lined up on the large leather couch. "You are all very lucky to be alive right now, I hope you know that. Logan, I'm glad you're safe."

With a breath she turned out of the room and we could hear her marching towards the front door.

"I'm so angry I could *spit*." She said spit, like speet.

The door opened and slammed closed behind her.

For a moment we all just sat there, not saying a word.

"Oh shit," Caeden finally said.

"Language," Bryce smirked.

* * *

It was past midnight and Amy still had not returned after she stormed out of the house.

"Are we in trouble?" I asked Caeden as I played with

the neckline of his blue shirt.

"No," there was a strained quality to his voice. "She'll cool off eventually."

"Babe, you seem stressed about something."

"I'm fine," he pulled away from my arms, rolling onto his back. Caeden *never* pulled away from me.

I rubbed his back. "Caeden?"

"I'm really tired, Sophie, please go to sleep."

Whaaaaaaat?

"Okay," I said and rolled onto my side, away from him.

I waited and waited and then waited some more for sleep. But I was wide-awake. I made sure Caeden was asleep, or pretending to be asleep, before I pushed the covers off and climbed from the bed.

I slowly cracked the door open and eased into the hallway, closing the door softly behind me.

I crept down the steps and into the family room. I turned the TV on and was dismayed to find only infomercials on. I stopped on one featuring a fancy vacuum that could apparently do *everything!* I heard a noise behind and jumped.

"Sorry," Bryce said and collapsed beside me. "I didn't mean to scare you." He had a bag of BBQ chips in his hand and offered me some. Bryce was shirtless, gray sweatpants hanging off if his hips, he winced when his bare skin encountered the cold leather. "Geez," he wrapped a blanket around his upper body. "That was cold." He crunched on a chip and covered the couch in crumbs. Boys. "What are you watching?"

"Infomercials," I said.

Bryce laughed and wiped his hands on his pajama pants before grabbing the house phone off the side table. "These are the best. I love calling and asking them questions."

"Like what?"

"You'll see," he grinned mischievously, waggling his eyebrows, and punched in the number.

Someone answered and Bryce said, "Yes, I'm calling about this magical vacuum that claims to do everything."

The person said something and Bryce came back with, "If it does everything, does that mean it mows the lawn? Ah, I see, so it doesn't do everything. That sir, is false advertising!" he hung up the phone and we both dissolved into fits of giggles.

"Mow the lawn?"

"It claims to do everything," he retorted. "Let's try another one."

Bryce and I took turns calling for a good hour before I said to him, "Does Caeden seem okay to you?"

"Yeah," Bryce said. "You don't think so?"

I shook my head. "He's being weird."

"Caeden's always weird," Bryce snorted.

"No he's not," I said. "He's never like this."

"He did kill someone today."

"So did I," I whispered and picked at the frayed ends of my pajama shorts. I leaned my head back and looked at the dark wood beams crisscrossing the ceiling. "And besides, he doesn't act regretful, he seems stressed."

"Regretful? Why would he be regretful about killing Travis? Are you regretful about killing Robert?"

"Not regretful per say... just... I don't know... I know I had to save you, I don't take that back, but I killed someone. I killed him," I said again. I pinched the bridge of my nose. "It's just a lot to deal with. Killing someone. Deserved or not."

"I don't know what to tell you, Sophie. Caeden seems fine to me."

"I guess I'm just being paranoid."

"We should go to be," Bryce looked at the clock. "It's two in the morning." He stood and stretched, heading out of the room.

"I guess I better try and get some sleep," I said but made no move to leave.

"You coming?"

"Nah, I think I'll sleep here," I said and grabbed the blanket Bryce had been wrapped in. It still held the warmth of his body heat.

Bryce quirked a brow. "Trouble in paradise?"

"No."

"Huh," Bryce walked away.

I cupped my hands under my head as a pillow and fell asleep.

* * *

"Sophie! Sophie!" a panicked voice cried.

I sat up and rubbed my eyes. The gray blanket fell from my lap to the rug of the family room.

"Sophie! Where are you? Soph! Oh God, oh God, oh God!" Feet pounded down the steps. "What have I done? Oh no, oh no, oh no!"

"Caeden?" I sat up and pushed my dark locks from my face.

I heard more muttering and some thumps.

I pushed my tired body up from the couch and out into the entryway. "Caeden?" I said into the hallway.

"Sophie?" Caeden stuck his head out from the mudroom. "Oh thank God! You're safe!" He wrapped his arms around me, his breath stirring the hair at my neck. "I thought-"

"What did you think?" I pushed at him and he reluctantly pulled away.

"I thought..." he rubbed his face, I could hear his hands rasp against his scruff. "Nothing," he finally muttered.

"Really? Because you seemed really freaked out." I crossed my arms over my chest.

He ran his fingers through his hair making it stick up wildly around his head. His blue eyes were darker than normal. "Nothing, it was nothing," he started up the steps.

The front door opened then, startling me, and Caeden whipped back around and down the steps. He stood protectively in front of me but it was only Amy.

"Geez mom," Caeden said.

"What?" Amy said.

"You scared me," he said. "I thought someone was breaking in."

"Since when do burglars carry keys to the house they're breaking into?"

"Um, never."

"Exactly," she closed and locked the door. "I am going to take a long hot bath and sleep until noon. Do not disturb me," she went upstairs.

"This house is full of nuts," Caeden muttered. He turned and when he saw I wasn't following he said, "Coming?"

I looked at the couch and my neck and back screamed in protest.

"Yeah."

FIFTEEN.

"You want to tryout for the *boy's* team?" the coach asked with a look of stunned disbelief.

"Coach!" Evan cried. "You didn't see her play! She's amazing!"

The coach looked me up and down. "I don't know."

I sighed. "Just let me try out. If I suck I don't make the team. Easy as that," I leaned against the bleachers.

Coach Johnston narrowed his eyes and gave me a look. "Fine, you can tryout," a challenging quality to his voice.

Challenge accepted, bud.

Evan noticed my smirk and winked.

Evan, Cam, Riley, Tyler, Kyle, Shane, and Brody welcomed me with open arms but the other guys were pissed.

"Coach, you can't let a girl tryout for the boy's team! That's what the girl's team is for!"

"Shut it Jake," the coach snapped. "There's no rule that says girls can't tryout or be on the boy's team. Besides, she'll probably suck," he muttered under his breath. Without my shifter hearing I would've never heard him.

"Don't worry about coach," Brody said, shaking his dark hair from his eyes. "He'll come around when he sees how amazing you are."

"I don't know," I shrugged, getting into pushup position, "he seems a little old school."

Cam snorted. "Coach is a bit stuck in the past."

We all looked over at Coach's short shorts. "Ew," I said. "Get me some bleach to clean out my eyes."

The boys laughed. "I swear, if Coach Johnston doesn't let you on the team I'm quitting," Tyler said.

"How many pushups do we have to do?" Shane asked, pulling his chin length hair back.

"One-hundred!" Coach called, overhearing our conversation.

Shane grumbled before dropping down on the ground and starting his pushups.

I finished and sat back on my heels.

"You're done?" Evan asked in disbelief.

"Yeah," I said, tightening my ponytail.

"But you're not even sweating!" Kyle said.

"Or out of breath," Brody added.

I shrugged.

"This girl is bad ass," Shane said as he pushed off the ground.

"Beaumont!" Coach yelled. "Why aren't you doing your pushups?"

"I'm done... sir," I added.

"Huh," he pondered for a moment. "One-hundred sit-ups and I'm going to count."

"No problem," I said.

Coach held the end of my feet and started counting. When the guys finished their pushups they formed a circle around me, counting along with the coach.

"Ninety-eight! Ninety-nine! One-hundred!"

Coach stood up wordlessly. He marched off before returning and said, "Let's see if you can play some soccer."

I smiled.

Coach divided us up, tossing a group of us red jerseys to wear.

Evan clapped me on the back. "Let's do this Beaumont."

* * *

Coach paced back and forth, muttering under his breath. I sat on the bleachers with the seven boys that were quickly becoming my second pack.

Coach Johnston picked up his clipboard; ticking over various points, and muttered some more.

"Is he –uh- *okay*?" I tapped my skull.

Cam shoved sweat-dampened hair away from his eyes. "He's a bit cracked but he's the best soccer coach I've ever had."

"I'll second that," Shane said. "Even if we've never won."

Finally the coach tossed his clipboard down. It smacked against the bleachers with a clang.

"I'll post the names of those who made the team on the bulletin board outside my office on Monday."

Coach started to leave but one of the other boys- Carter I think his name was- called out to him. "But Coach- what about the person with the highest score? The automatic spot on the team."

Evan leaned towards me and whispered in my ear, "Coach always scores us on everything we do at tryouts. The person with the highest score automatically makes the team."

Coach put his hands on his hips. His belly extended from the waistband of his way too short, shorts.

"Sophie."

"Excuse me?" The guy assumed was Carter asked.

"Sophie has the highest score. She makes the team. And close your mouth before you catch flies with that thing. I'll see ya'll on Monday," he stalked off towards the parking lot.

Cam, Tyler, Shane, Brody, Evan, Kyle, and Riley took turns giving me fist bumps.

We gathered up our gym bags and made our way to the parking lot.

"Sophie needs a nickname," Kyle said.

"Super Sophie," Evan grinned.

"Sassy Sophie," Riley suggested.

"I am not sassy," I laughed.

"True," Riley shrugged.

They bounced more nicknames around as we walked. When we reached our cars a voice called out, "What about she-wolf?"

I turned to find Caeden leaning against his motorcycle, arms crossed over his chest. His hair was still damp from a shower, little droplets of water dripping onto his shirt.

"She-wolf? I like it," Brody said and then howled into

the night sky. The other guys joined in.

"See ya later Sophie!" They called.

"Bye guys," I waved over my shoulder. I couldn't help letting out a little laugh.

"Since it's a short ride I didn't think you'd mind taking the bike," he handed me a helmet.

I worried my lip with my teeth.

He smiled; it was a little smile, not his typical megawatt one. "Don't worry, I can see perfectly in the dark."

Just then car lights swung by us, and Caeden's eyes glowed an eerie green color, just like that of an animal's.

I stuck the helmet on my head and he did the same. He swung his leg over the bike and turned the key. The engine thrummed.

Sophie, don't be a wimp. I thought to myself.

I climbed onto the bike and gripped Caeden's shirt before I could talk myself out of it.

Remember, we're two minutes from your house. Caeden projected his thoughts to me.

Two minutes too long.

He laughed, but like with his smile, it was half-hearted.

Knowing that I was terrified of the beast Caeden drove as slow as was safe and it ended up taking us five minutes to get to Gram's.

I was handing Caeden the helmet when he thought to ask if I made the team.

"I did," I tried to flatten my helmet hair. "Apparently I had the highest points so I got the only automatic position on the team."

Caeden raised an eyebrow.

I shrugged. "What can I say? I rock."

He laughed and this time it was closer to his normal chuckle. Relief flooded my veins.

My stomach rumbled.

"I think Lucinda made spaghetti," he started towards the house. "When I left it looked like enough to feed a small

---

165

army."

"Or a very hungry wolf," I followed behind him.

The door was unlocked so Caeden just walked right in.

"Gram!" I called. "I hear you made your famous spaghetti!"

Gram came around the corner from the kitchen and kissed me on the forehead. She had to stand on her tiptoes to reach. "I heard you were trying out for the soccer team so I figured we had cause to celebrate. You did make the team, right?" She raised a gray eyebrow.

"I made the only automatic position on the boys team," I said.

Gram hooted and hollered, bent over with laughter. "That's my Sophie girl! Making the boy's team! I bet you made them all look like idiotic five year olds stumbling over their feet!" She led me to the kitchen and handed me a plate of steaming noodles before she spooned her homemade sauce on top. Yum.

"I do feel a bit bad though. I mean, my shifter abilities make me a lot stronger."

Gram shook her head. "Sophie, you were an amazing soccer player before you shifted. You're just a little extra amazing now."

"How would you even know? You never saw me play."

"Your dad used to brag about it, he sent me a few home videos. They're still around here somewhere," she puttered away, probably in search of old VHS tapes.

I grabbed a spoon and fork from the drawer and sat down at the table. Using my spoon I made a perfect swirl of spaghetti.

"Where'd you learn to do that?" Caeden asked, shoveling the noodles into his mouth. Red sauce sat adorably in the corner of his mouth.

"A Barbie movie."

Caeden snorted. "A Barbie movie?"

166

I pointed my fork at him. "Listen here bud, Barbie can be far more educational than stuff boys watch."

"Did you also learn how to hold a tea cup?"

I threw my fork at him but he caught it midair. Stupid shifter reflexes.

"Are you going to throw it at me again?" he held my fork hostage.

"No," I held my hand out.

He handed it back to me and I swirled some more spaghetti.

"And don't diss boys shows, I learned a lot from them."

"Like how to survive in a sewer?" I quirked a brow.

Caeden laughed. "You never know when that might prove useful."

"Hopefully never."

* * *

Caeden and I finished eating and cleaned up the kitchen. I finished wiping the table clean and tossed the cloth in the sink.

"Wanna watch some TV?" he asked.

"Sure," I said, "let me grab my homework."

I grabbed my backpack from my room and sat down on the floor. I pulled my books out and piled them on the coffee table. Caeden settled the TV on some wrestling channel.

I pulled out my math worksheets and finished the few problems I had left before tackling my English essay.

"Do you ever do homework?" I asked Caeden.

He grinned, dimple flashing into view. "Of course I do, I don't want to fail."

"I never see you do any," I tapped my pencil against the wood table.

"I'm just that awesome," he said.

"Seriously, when do you get it done?"

"Usually after you go to sleep. I like to watch you-"

"And that's not creepy at all," I rolled my eyes.

"What? You're cute when you sleep. You wrinkle your nose and say my name."

"I say your name?"

He leaned forward. "Apparently I star in all your dreams."

I blushed, but before I could retort, loud cursing filled the house.

"Gram?" I asked. "You okay?"

"Damn men," she said. "I fell in the toilet."

I busted out laughing. Tears of laughter coursed down my face. "Oh God," I said, still laughing.

Caeden was blushing. Even his ears were red. "I did tell you I can never remember to put the toilet seat down."

SIXTEEN.

I managed to finish my English essay, my Spanish essay, and start on my history powerpoint. Caeden called me an overachiever.

It was lunch, on Monday, and I kept getting angry stares from several of the guys who had been at the soccer tryouts. Since I knew I made the team I hadn't bothered looking at the list but I knew there were going to be a good many that didn't make the team.

"I feel like I'm going to be shanked after school," I muttered under my breath to Caeden.

He looked up and his gaze met that of one of the guys who'd been giving me the stink eye.

"Don't worry about it, babe," he squeezed my leg. "They're just pissed they got beat by a girl."

Bentley snorted. "I'd be pissed too."

Bryce balanced a fry on his upper lip. "I just can't wait to go to a game and watch Sophie beat a bunch of guys asses. It's going to epic. I can see the looks on their faces now." Charlotte swiped the fry from Bryce's lip and ate it. "Hey!" Bryce pouted at her.

She smiled. "And that's what they're faces will look like," she pointed to Bryce and giggled.

Chris sat beside Logan and was not her bubbly self. I think knowing how close she'd come to losing her brother scared her. I was glad that Logan was okay. I didn't want anything to happen to any of my pack but I also had to live with the fact that I'd killed someone.

"Sophie," Caeden said, sensing my thoughts.

I looked up at him.

"You did what you had to do. Don't beat yourself up about it."

I tore a fry in half and watched its potato guts spew out onto the green tray. "It just seems wrong that we're sitting here, laughing, talking, having fun, when they're dead. When we killed them."

"Sophie-"

169

"I know they were bad, evil, whatever. But they were still *people* just like us."

"They're nothing like us," Caeden spat. "You did what you had to do, to save my brother. We did what *we had to do*," he lowered his voice and whispered in my ear. His lips tingled the sensitive skin.

"I know," I said. "But that doesn't make it any easier to deal with."

I pushed my tray away and let my pack have their pickings. I wasn't hungry, not at all.

"I feel like I'm losing my soul," I said to Caeden. "Like I have no control over anything anymore."

"Sophie, that isn't true."

"But it is," I said. "From the moment I got here I've had no control over my future, over my destiny."

Hurt flooded his blue eyes.

"I didn't mean it like that," I grabbed his arm. He pulled away.

"I think you did," his voice was soft, full of hurt.

"No, Caeden," I put my hands on his cheeks and forced him to meet my gaze. "I didn't mean *you*. I love you. You are *my* choice. Always." I pressed my forehead to his and said again, "Always."

Caeden let out a breath. "Good... and I do sort of understand what you're saying. And about the whole Grimm thing."

"Doesn't it bother you?" I played with his ears. "Killing?"

He turned his head and looked out the back window of the cafeteria. "I don't know," he said.

"You don't know? That seems like something you would know."

He stood and picked up his backpack. I looked around and realized that the cafeteria was completely empty. He grabbed my tray and said, "We better get to study hall."

I tucked my hair behind my ear and grabbed my backpack off the ground.

170

Caeden and I walked to study hall, not holding hands, not even talking. I felt like there was an invisible wall between us. I wanted to reach out and bang my fists against it in the hope that it would fall. Crumble. Shatter.

For the first time in a long time I didn't do any homework in study hall. I was too absorbed in my thoughts. Robert. Hannah. Travis. A distant Caeden. It was all just too much.

* * *

"Welcome to the first day of practice," Coach said. "I expect the most from my players," he looked at me, "and I want to *win* this year!"

Evan snickered and leaned towards me. "Johnston may be the best coach we've ever had but we've yet to win a game."

"A single one?" I asked, astonished.

Evan shook his head.

Coach dumped out a bag of soccer balls. "I want you to do two laps around the field dribbling. Get to it!"

As we dribbled around the field I said to the seven guys, "I'm glad to see you all made the team."

Tyler grinned. "Of course we made the team."

"We couldn't let these fuckers terrorize our girl," Brody dribbled past me.

"Should I be worried that they'll do something?"

"Nah," Cam shook his head.

"And if they try something," Shane winked, "we'll be sure to stop it."

"Yeah," Kyle said, "we can't have our best player taken out. We need you."

"You're our secret weapon," Riley said.

Evan chimed in with, "The other teams are going to see you and think, 'She's hot, what can she do?' and then you'll just get out there and show them how soccer's really played."

I laughed. "It helps to have an awesome team backing you."

"Awesome?" Riley said. "We are dynamite! Dynamite! Dy-na-*mite!*" The other guys joined in, even the ones that hated my guts, and I couldn't help laughing. It felt good to laugh after the day, no not just the day but the week, I had had.

But once I thought of lunch today I couldn't get the image of killing Robert out of my mind. I understood that he was evil and that he was going to kill Bryce, but that didn't make it any easier for me to deal with. A life was life.

* * *

Caeden wasn't waiting for me in the parking lot but he had dropped of my Pilot. The key was in the ignition. I tossed my bag onto the passenger seat and then leaned back, closing my eyes. I sighed and pinched the bridge of my nose.

I thought that the Grimm Pack being gone would solve our problems but obviously they were just beginning.

Opening my eyes I started the car and drove home.

Caeden wasn't home but Gram was. She'd made grilled chicken for dinner.

"How did practice go?"

"It went," I muttered, going into the bathroom. I took a long shower and when I got out I even took the time to blow dry my hair. I clipped a portion back so that it wouldn't be hanging in my face.

When I joined Gram at the kitchen table Caeden still hadn't come home.

"Gram," I said, pushing a piece of chicken around my plate. "Does Caeden seem a bit strange to you?"

She wiped her mouth on a napkin. "He seems a bit distracted. Distant," she resumed eating.

I felt better knowing that I wasn't the only one picking up on Caeden's odd behavior.

"But," Gram shrugged, "going through something like you all did changes a person. Wouldn't you say that you're changed?"

I swallowed. "Of course."

She smiled reassuringly and patted my hand. "I'm

sure Caeden's struggling just like you are. He's a man so he's not going to be as open about his feelings. Give him time."

Give him time. "I can do that."

She sat back and pointed at my plate. "Now stop worrying and eat your dinner."

* * *

Caeden slipped into my bed around midnight. I folded my hands under my head and rolled over to face him. "Where were you?" I asked. I tried to keep any tone of accusing out of my voice. I honestly didn't even know what I could be accusing him of.

"I went for a walk. I needed to clear my head."

"You went on a walk for nine hours?"

"I was looking for something."

"Did you find it?"

"No," he sighed. "I didn't."

"What you're looking for... is it important?"

"Very."

"I could've helped you," I said.

Even in the dark I could see his brow furrow. "No, this is something I have to do on my own."

"Are you mad at me?" I asked after several tense moments of silence.

"I can never be mad at you," he rolled over to face me. He smiled. "Besides, as far as I know you haven't done something I should be mad about. Have you?"

"No," I said. "I just feel like there's a wall between us," I pointed at him and then me.

Caeden let out a breath and wrapped his arms around me. "I'm sorry I'm being such a crappy boyfriend," he kissed the top of my head. "I just have a lot on my mind. From this moment on I'll just be Normal Caeden not Grumpy Caeden."

"That sounds good," I said as his hand smoothed down my back causing me to shiver. I was sure we'd be ninety and Caeden's touch would still affect me the same way.

SEVENTEEN.

I knocked on the door and Evan opened it, grinning. "Our girl is here!" he called into the locker room. "Don't worry, we're all dressed."

I blushed, that had been what I was worrying about, was it written so plainly on my face? "Coach told me to come for the pre-game speech."

"You should've run the other way," Brody said as he made room for me to sit down.

"Are they that bad?" I asked.

"Yeah," all the boys chorused.

Well then.

"Is princess here?" Coach called from his office.

"The she-wolf has arrived!" Evan yelled back.

Coach emerged from his office and stood in front of us.

Oh God, he had the short shorts on again.

"I think I just threw up a bit in my mouth," I said to no one in particular.

"Me too," Cam said.

Coach smacked his hands together, completely unaware of his nausea inducing shorts.

"I want ya'll to go out there and show that team what we're made of! Show them that we're not a bunch of pansies! We are Warriors!"

"Warriors!" The guys' fist bumped the air and I joined in with much less enthusiasm.

"And this year we have a secret weapon! The she-wolf!" he pointed to me.

"Oh God, kill me now," I whispered under my breath.

The boys began to howl.

The other guys had reluctantly accepted me as part of the team. They no longer gave me dirty looks but there was a particular iciness radiating from them. That was fine with me.

"We're gonna win this year," Coach rubbed his hands together, "I can feel it." There was a bit of a manic gleam to

---

174

his eye. "Win! Win! Win!" He fist bumped the air. "I want to *win*," he said.

My eyes widened and I looked at Evan. He shrugged. "Normally it's worse."

"Now let's get out there and show those pussies what real men are made of!" Coach pointed to his shirt.

"Red and black! Red and black! Red and black!" We all chanted.

The boys filed out of the locker room but Coach held me back, grabbing me by my jersey top. I eyed his hand and he let go. I smoothed out the red and black mesh material.

"Ready princess?" he asked.

"I've been ready."

"Good," he put his hands on his hips.

"Can I… uh… go now?" I pointed to the door.

"Yeah, course princess." I was pushing the door open when he said, "I'm really sorry about the way I acted at tryouts. You deserve to be on this team."

"Thanks Coach," I said.

* * *

I was nervous. So nervous, and I didn't even know why. I was wiping my sweaty palms on mesh shorts when Shane walked up to me.

"Don't be nervous she-wolf," he clapped me on the back. "You're going to rock this."

As if to back up his words a chorus of, "She will, she will, rock you!" I turned to see my pack, Gram, and Amy in the stands. Bryce had obviously been the culprit to start the chant. His face was painted with our team colors, red and black.

"Do I look that nervous?" I asked him.

"You look like you're going to throw up."

"*Great*."

He chuckled and sat down on the bleachers. There was a sizable enough crowd but nothing compared to football nights. This town made a big deal out of football games.

Before I knew what was happening the game was

starting. A guy from the other team looked me over. "But you're a girl," he yelled and looked over at his coach. "She's a girl!"

Bryce stood up in the stands. "No dip dumb shit! Of course she's a girl! She has boobies and a-" Caeden tackled Bryce before anything else could slip out of his mouth.

"Just play the game!" the other team's coach yelled back.

The boy in front of me looked me up and down. "I can't believe they let you on the boy's team. Do you even know what a soccer ball looks like?"

"Apparently you don't," I said as the soccer ball flew in his direction from one of his teammates.

"Huh?" he said but it was too late, I had control of the ball.

I ran down the field, I could hear howls and chants of 'she-wolf', but it didn't faze me, not when I was in the zone.

The goalie seemed confused to see me so I used that advantage and sent the ball soaring straight into the net.

"Goal!"

My team ran to me. "Guys it's just one point," I said.

Evan stopped in front of me. "Who cares? That was fucking awesome! Did you see that dude's face?"

I ignored them and stole the ball from one of the other team's players, who was almost to our goal.

"I don't think so bud," I said as I swiped it out from under him.

"She-wolf! She-wolf! She-wolf!" the people in the bleachers chanted.

"Goal!" someone called.

Before I knew it, the game was over. I didn't need to look at the scoreboard. I was well aware of the outcome.

"We won!" Coach screamed, throwing his arms out. "We won! Oh my God we won!" He took his baseball cap off and threw it on the ground before jumping up and down like an ecstatic five year old girl. "Yes! We won! In your face Franklin! In. Your. Face." He pointed at the other team's coach.

Evan bumped me with his shoulder. "You were incredible, she-wolf. We couldn't have done it without you."

I smiled. "That was so much fun!"

Evan laughed. "Most fun we've had on the field in a long time."

"I'm glad I could be a part of it."

Brody jogged over. "Hey Sophie, are you going to come get pizza with us?"

"Pizza?"

"Yeah," he said, "the team always goes out for pizza after a game. Did no one invite you?"

"I was getting to it," Evan bit out.

I laughed. "I'd love to come. Is it okay if my friends come too?" I pointed to the stands.

"Of course," Kyle came up to us, rubbing a towel over his sweat-drenched face. "Friends, family, the more the merrier," he grinned.

"Great," I smiled, "Let me go tell them."

I ran up to the bleachers and into Caeden's waiting arms.

"Babe, you were great," he said and kissed me. "Absolutely fantastic."

"And covered in sweat," Bryce said, giving me an icky face.

I turned towards Caeden's younger brother, "That's what the showers in the locker room are for. Water comes out and then you're clean."

"I always wondered what those nozzle things were for," Bryce grinned. "Showering? Who would've ever guessed?"

"I'll meet you in the parking lot?" I asked Caeden.

"I'll be in the Jeep."

I waved over my shoulder to the others before running back onto the field.

Riley caught me in his arms when I reached the field and threw me over his shoulders.

"Put me down," I giggled, beating his back.

"No can do, she-wolf," he said.

"Help me!" I implored Brody and Evan.

They just laughed.

Riley carried me into the school and didn't let me go until we reached the girls locker room. "I hate you," I stuck my tongue out him.

He laughed. "No you don't, she-wolf."

He sauntered off towards the boy's locker rooms. Shaking my head I pushed the door open.

The girl's locker room was nothing special. Gray floor tiles and cement walls. At least it didn't smell too bad.

I showered and piled my wet hair on top of my head, securing it with a ponytail holder and a couple of bobby pins. I had brought a pair of shorts and plain t-shirt to change into. Nothing fancy since I thought I'd be going home right after the game. I dropped my dirty jersey and shorts into my duffel bag and then tossed it over my shoulder.

I jumped back three steps when I opened the door.

"Caeden!" I put my hand to my heart. "You scared the crap out of me. I thought you were waiting in the parking lot."

"Sorry," he pulled away from the wall, where he was leaning, "I didn't mean to scare you."

"It's fine," I said as my heart began to slow to its normal pace.

He took my hand and we headed out the side entrance.

"Why aren't you waiting in the car?" I asked, a bit confused.

Caeden scratched the back of his head and I knew he was purposefully stalling for time. "No particular reason." He pushed the door open and we greeted by the cool night air. He scanned the parking lot before leading me to his Jeep. "That game was epic by the way," he grinned. "You were incredible."

"Thanks," I said. "I had so much fun out there. I felt-"

"Normal?" he smiled again and I knew he was trying to sidetrack me from my previous questioning. I'd just let him think he succeeded and then I'd hit him with it again later. He was just being far to weird.

"Yeah," I shrugged. "It's nice to pretend to be normal. Even if it is only for a little bit."

* * *

Ledo's pizza was crowded between my teammates and my pack.

It was a cozy place with golden walls and brown leather booths.

Caeden and slid into two empty seat between Bryce and Evan. Evan clapped me on the back and said, "Boys! Our she-wolf is here!" And then they all howled in the middle of the restaurant making strangers look at me funny. I bowed my head and blushed, praying for them to stop. Why, oh why, did Caeden have to suggest that nickname? I think I'd prefer Sassy Sophie.

"We already ordered the pizzas," Bryce said.

"Did you get enough?" Caeden grinned, leaning back in his chair with his hands behind his head. His shirt road up a bit, showing off smooth, tan, stomach.

Bryce grinned. "We can always order more."

"More?" Cam leaned towards Bryce. "We ordered like twenty pizzas."

I laughed. "You haven't seen this gang eat yet."

Caeden leaned towards me, "I'll go get our drinks."

"Thanks," I said.

"So," Evan started, "you and Caeden."

"Me and Caeden."

"How long have you been dating?"

"Since October."

Evan's eyebrows shot up.

"What?" I asked.

"I just figured you guys had been together longer than that. You seem like an old married couple."

I laughed. "Are we that boring?"

179

"Pretty much," Riley chimed in, chewing on a breadstick.

Ooh, breadsticks! I grabbed one and nibbled on the end. Caeden returned with our drinks and took my hand when he sat down. I was comforted by his soothing warmth.

"They said the pizzas should be ready in the next ten minutes."

"Good, I'm starving," Bryce patted his flat stomach.

"You've already eaten a whole basket of bread sticks!" The guy named Carter said. "How can you possibly still be hungry?"

Bryce looked at the empty basket. "I have a fast metabolism," his lips quirked.

Carter grumbled some sort of non-sense.

I leaned my head on Caeden's shoulder. "What are you so worried about," I whispered under my breath, low enough that the humans wouldn't even know I was speaking.

Caeden swallowed. "It's nothing," he said. "Really," he smiled.

I narrowed my eyes, sick of this song and dance, but I knew that Caeden was stubborn and wouldn't tell me whatever was on his mind until he was ready. Men could be so darn frustrating.

My teammates continued to praise my soccer skills to which I blushed and ducked my head a lot.

They brought our pizzas out and Bryce grabbed a large one. Rubbing his hands together, he said, "Pizza time." The red and black face paint was starting to fade from his face a bit.

Caeden grabbed a box for himself and opened the lid on another before handing it to me. "Don't worry," he leaned towards me, "I made sure Bryce ordered you a pepperoni."

"How'd you-"

He winked,

Oh, right.

Our special mate powers gave us the ability to pick up on the other person's favorite things, even their fears.

180

I lifted the lid and my stomach rumbled. I dug into the cheesy, gooey, goodness.

So, good.

By the time the pack and I finished eating the soccer players were looking at us, mystified.

"Do you *all* have high metabolisms?" Shane asked.

"Something like that," Caeden shrugged with a grin.

Evan looked at my empty pizza box and then held up three fingers, "You're hot, you play soccer, and you have a very healthy appetite. Please marry me?"

I laughed and leaned into Caeden who then put his arm around me. "Sorry, you know I'm taken."

"Darn," Evan smiled. "Have any sisters?"

"Only child."

"So not fair," he said. Evan looked over at Caeden. "You better put a ring on that before someone tries to sweep her out from under you."

Caeden grinned and kissed my cheek. "I'm not worried," he winked at me.

EIGHTEEN

"Watcha doin'?" Caeden flopped down on the couch beside me.

"Homework, you should really try it sometime."

He snorted. "You don't even know what grades I make."

"I'm sure they suck."

He grinned and his blue eyes sparkled. His dimple flashed and he licked his lips. Oh sweet baby Jesus, those lips! They were so perfectly sculpted, just enough of a curve to be seductive.

Sophie! Snap out of it and stop looking at Caeden's lips! You need to do your homework. Don't be one of those girls!

Caeden started laughing. The kind of laughter that had you clutching your stomach and making everyone around you laugh too.

I started to giggle when I realized why he was laughing.

I had broadcast my internal rant loud enough that he had heard it. Great, just great.

I hit his leg with my fist. "Stop laughing at me!"

He only laughed harder. I tried not to get too mad. After all, it was a relief to hear his carefree laughter again. It had been missing for so many weeks.

Caeden finally managed to gain control of himself and then began to play with my hair.

Curse him! He was making this very difficult for me. If he didn't watch himself I might just maw him with my lips.

Finally I tossed my pencil on the coffee table and scooted back against the couch. I traced one of its flowers with my finger and noticed a small blood stain. No doubt from the night Caeden showed up as a wolf, bleeding on my doorstep.

I drew my knees up and turned to look at him. "I can't get any homework done with you around. What do you need?"

He grinned. "Apple Blossom is coming up."

"What is that?"

"Just a festival we celebrate here. There are two parades and a carnival. The circus comes too," he twisted a strand of my hair around his finger before bringing it to his nose and sniffing. "Cookies," he grinned.

"What are you getting at?"

He leaned his back against the couch and then rolled to face me. His eyes were glowing as he grinned. "I'm saying I want to go. I need to do something fun. We both do," he entwined our fingers together.

"That sounds fun. I've never been to a carnival."

"Never?" his jaw dropped.

"Never ever," I shook my head. "Remember, we moved a lot."

"I can't believe you've never been to a carnival. That's insane."

"When is it?" I asked.

"The carnival starts tomorrow and the parade is next Saturday."

"Caeden Henry, are you asking me on a date?" I grinned, drawing my legs up.

He pretended to think, rubbing his jaw. "Maybe."

I smacked his shoulder.

He smiled, his dimple winking at me just as seductively as he winked his eye. "I am definitely asking you on a date."

I leaned over and kissed his scruffy cheek. Caeden was right; I loved his scruff. It managed to make him even more ruggedly handsome.

Caeden picked up the remote and began to scroll through the channels so I picked up my notebook and went back to finishing my science homework. With the last quarter of our senior year winding down it was crunch time. Teachers were already assigning our finals, knowing that in the next few weeks seniors would be unlikely to show up.

Me? I'd be there till the end. Once it's over, it's over and I know that the only thing that I will have to consume my time will be shifter related.

Bentley, Caeden, Logan, and I, still planned to enroll at the local community college but anymore I wondered what the point was. For Caeden and I the pack, being Alphas, would always come first. The others did have choices. Like to go to college and get a job. Gram hadn't started her cupcake shop until after Caeden's dad had become Alpha. Amy had yet to get a regular job. I didn't see how she'd have the time. She was always doing something for the pack.

I felt bad that I wanted a life outside of the pack, after all, they had become my extended family but... But I wanted to pave my own way.

I sighed and pulled my hair off my neck before letting it drop. I shook my head and forced myself to focus on my homework.

* * *

"Bryce and Charlotte are picking us up," Caeden leaned against the doorway. He was dressed casually in khaki shorts, a red shirt, black Nikes, and a baseball cap turned backwards. I had to say, it was my favorite look on him.

"Are you sure that's a good idea?" I asked, finishing my hair in a fishtail braid. I tied the end in a pink and green ribbon.

"Why?" Caeden raised a dark brow.

"Because, I might explode from all the gushiness that comes out of their mouths. 'Oh Bryce you're *so* funny.' Or, 'Charlotte, your red hair is like a flame and I'm a moth. I'm zapped by you.'"

Caeden threw his head back and laughed. "They do talk like that don't they?"

"It's gross," I said, dabbing some glittery lotion onto my arms. Cookie scented, of course.

Caeden pinched my side. "I bet you wouldn't think it was gross if I said it."

I smiled. "Probably not." I dabbed on some peach

gloss and said, "I'm ready."

"Perfect timing," Caeden pointed towards the living room where the bay window looked out onto the street, "Bryce and Charlotte are here."

Gram was sitting in the living room watching TV. She was staying home more and more. It was beginning to make me worry.

"Bye Gram," I bent down and kissed her cheek.

She smiled. "Bye Sophie, I love you." She turned her wise brown eyes on Caeden, "And you tell that idiotic brother of yours to drive safely. There's gonna be a lotta drunks out there."

Caeden laughed and stuck his hands in his pockets. "Don't worry, I'll make sure he drives carefully."

"You do that," Gram said and picked up a drink off the side table. The ice clinked together.

As soon as Caeden opened the front door Bryce started honking his horn.

Oh dear lord.

"Bryce! Knock it off!" Caeden hollered.

"Get your butt in this car and I'll stop!"

Caeden and I both jogged to the Jeep as soon as we were seated Bryce took his hand off the horn.

Bryce had removed the roof and sides of his Jeep for the summer; which meant that the braid I had worked so hard on would be ruined by the time we made it to the carnival. Darn it!

Bryce tore off down the street and without the seatbelt I would have fallen out. I grabbed Caeden's arm to steady me, and my nails dug into his skin. I think I preferred the beast over Stella Jr. and that was saying something.

Bryce drove into town; all the while I tried not to throw up on anyone, and parked in a field. Once the car stopped relief flooded my system.

Oh thank God.

Caeden chuckled.

"Did I say that out loud?" I blushed.

"Yeah, you did, not that I can blame you. He does drive like a maniac. Although, I think my arm could have done without the squeezing you gave it."

I glanced down at his tanned arm and saw little rivulets of blood slinking down his arm. The cuts inflicted by my fingernails quickly closed up.

"Sorry," I bit my lip.

Caeden opened his mouth to say something when Bryce called from a few yards away, "Losers! Hurry up! Are you going to sit in the car all night?"

Caeden grabbed my hand and grinned like a little boy in a candy shop. "Carnival time!" He drug me from the car and then behind him as he headed to a ring toss game. "I think I need to win my girl a prize," he said.

I laughed.

"What?" he shrugged. "It's like a rite of passage. Every boyfriend has to win his girlfriend a prize," he winked, turning my stomach to jelly.

He paid the guy and grabbed up the rings. With a flick of his wrist all the rings landed easily around the bottles. A couple of people stopped to stare. The guy working the booth was stunned.

"Which one do ya want?" Caeden pointed to the various prizes.

"Um… that one," I pointed to a stuffed panda bear. It was either that or a bee.

"We'll take that one," Caeden told the guy.

"Uh, yeah, sure," he unclipped the stuffed panda and handed it over to Caeden.

Caeden went to hand it to me and I said, "Nuh-uh mister. You're the boyfriend, *you* carry it."

Grinning lopsidedly he said, "Oh, so this is how you're gonna play."

"You know the saying, 'Nothing's fair in love and war.'"

"I didn't know there was a war. I thought there was just love," he kissed my cheek and took my hand, leading me

186

towards the long line for the Ferris wheel.

"Maybe we should come back later," I indicated the line.

"Nah," he shook his head, his shaggy hair shaking. "It'll only get longer."

I reached up and fingered a dark curl on his forehead that had escaped the confines of his baseball cap. "I think you need to get a haircut."

He laughed. "I'll get right on that mom."

Caeden and I were finally seated in the Ferris wheel. Caeden held the panda in his lap.

I gulped.

"I don't think I can do this," my voice cracked.

"What?" Caeden said and then, "*Oh*."

"I'm afraid of heights," I said, unnecessarily.

We lurched upwards a notch and I let out a squeal. Caeden grabbed my hand and with his other cupped my cheek. "Sophie, it's going to be okay. It's too late to get off now."

"I can't do this, I can't do this, I can't do this," I muttered under my breath.

Caeden bit his lip and I knew he was trying really hard not to laugh at me. I appreciated the effort.

"Here," Caeden said, wiggling around in the rickety seat.

I screamed. "Stop! Don't do that!"

"Sorry," Caeden said. "I just thought you might feel better if you tucked your face into my shoulder."

"That might be better," I let him put his arm around me. The seat shook again and I screamed.

Someone said, "Shut that girl up!"

Caeden growled and nothing else was said.

"Sophie, why didn't you tell me you're afraid of heights?"

I stiffened in his arms. "Because, it's a silly fear," I mumbled into his shirt.

"No, it's not," he said, rubbing soothing circles on my

back.

"It is," I said. "I'm sorry."

"Don't apologize," he said and kissed the top of my head. "Silly girl, you have nothing to be sorry for."

The seat continued to lurch upward and shake. "This wouldn't be so bad if it would just stop *shaking!*"

Caeden couldn't contain his laughter any longer and his body began to shake which then shook the seat and me.

I screamed again and bit down on my fist to muffle the sound.

"Sophie, I'm so sorry," he said.

"Not your fault," I said into his shirt, which muffled my voice.

"Yeah it is. I should've known."

"And I should've said something. That makes me the dumbass. Not you."

"That may be true," he said and even though I couldn't see his face I knew his lips were quirked at the corners.

Time seemed to go on forever before my feet touched the ground. "Oh thank God!" I cried and held onto Caeden's arm as a wave of dizziness overtook me.

"Why don't we head somewhere safe?" he pointed to a food stand.

"That's probably the best idea," I said and tried to quell the queasiness in my stomach. I *did not* want to throw up all over Caeden.

Caeden sat me down at a table and came back with a ginger ale and caramel popcorn. I opened the can and stuck in a straw. "Sip this," he said, "it'll make you feel better."

I took the can from him and did as he said. Within minutes my stomach had settled. "Thanks," I smiled.

He leaned over, putting his hand on my face, and tracing my cheek with his thumb. "I will *always* take care of you."

"I've never doubted that for a second."

He was leaning in to kiss me when Bryce showed up.

188

"Hey ya'll, you'll never believe what I just heard! Apparently some girl totally flipped out on the Ferris wheel."

I paled.

"Oh God, it was you wasn't it?" he looked at me and busted out laughing. "It figures."

Charlotte sat down beside me and in her quiet voice said, "Are you okay?"

"I'm fine," I said.

Bryce was still bent over in laughter so Caeden kicked his knee, knocking him to ground. Bryce fussed, "What was that for?"

"What do you think?"

"It was *funny*," Bryce cried.

"You know what else will be funny?" Caeden smiled charmingly.

"What?" Bryce asked and his eyes narrowed.

"When you show up to school on Monday with a black eye."

"You wouldn't," Bryce said.

"Oh I would," Caeden grinned and leaned back in his seat, his hands behind his head.

"You suck! I swear, I'm never allowed to have any fun around you! Fun sucker that's what you are!"

"Dramatic much?" Caeden quirked a brow. "You always did look like a girl as a baby. Is there something you'd like to let me know?"

"I did not look like a girl," Bryce said between gritted teeth. "I just had luscious hair, don't be hatin'." Bryce sat down next to Charlotte and took her hand in his. She looked up at him and for the first time I could truly see the love between them. It was sweet.

"Want some?" Caeden offered me the bag of caramel popcorn.

"Sure," I took a handful. Yum.

As I was munching Caeden said, "Are you going to name the panda?"

I looked over at the panda sitting in a chair next to

him. I shrugged. "You should name him, you're the one that won him."

Caeden pondered. "Perry."

"Perry? Perry the Panda?"

"See? It has a nice ring to it."

Bryce snorted and stood. "Charlotte and I are going to go on one of the rides before you make me ill."

I laughed. "You should hear some of the stuff that comes out of your mouth that makes *me* ill."

Bryce shook his head. "Pure awesomness is what comes out of my mouth. I just have a way with words."

Charlotte shook her head, her red hair flaming around her. She gave me a look that said, 'See what I have to deal with?'

I smiled and twirled my straw around the can.

"Hey!" Caeden called to someone over my shoulder. He waved them over. I turned and saw Logan.

Logan sat down and said, "What's up with you guys?"

"Nothing much," I said.

"Did you hear about the girl-"

I held up my hand to stop him. "It was me." Then, I added under my breath, "Man, news travels fast around here."

"Small town," Logan said. "Everybody knows everything."

"I wouldn't say everything," smiled Caeden. "So, how've you been? We haven't seen you around much," he clapped Logan on the back.

Logan shrugged. "I've just been..."

"Dealing?" I sent him a sympathetic glance. After all, only a few months ago I'd been in his position and I was far from being over it. I tried to put on a brave face and act like it didn't affect me but that wasn't the case. I fingered my scar. *Liar.* Caeden was unaware of the nightmares that haunted me. The vision of Travis looming over me and Peter draining my blood until there was nothing left. All I could do was deal with it.

"Yeah," Logan said, looking at me through long pale blond eyelashes. His green eyes were paler than usual with dark circles underneath. His pale skin was lighter than normal too.

I reached out and patted his hand. He snatched it back as soon as my skin touched his. "Sorry," he said. "I didn't mean to. I know you-"

"It's okay," I held up a hand, "believe me, I understand."

"Yeah, I guess you do," he picked at the frayed knee of his jeans. "You've handled everything a lot better than I am." He swallowed and glanced at the darkening sky.

"I had Caeden," I shrugged. "If I hadn't had him I don't know how I'd act. I certainly wouldn't have handled it as well."

Caeden reached across the table and took my hand. We were both reliving memories that haunted us.

"Well, I'm alone," Logan said. "Always alone."

"No you're not," I cried. "You have us. Your pack. Your sister. You can talk to us Logan. Especially me, I understand."

He ran his hand over his face. "It just sucks because they're right."

"About what?" I raised an eyebrow.

"I am an abomination."

"No you're not," I said with conviction.

"They kill gays," Logan's Adam's apple bobbed. "I'm just going to end up dead."

I wanted to smack Logan over the head for his pessimistic attitude.

"Caeden and I will never let that happen. Neither will Bentley, Bryce, Charlotte, and Christian. We love you Logan."

Logan's eyebrows raised. "I don't see how you can love me. I'm not exactly the nicest person."

"That may be true," I shrugged and then gasped when

191

Caeden kicked me under the table. I sent him a glare. "But we do love you."

His lips lifted in a small smile. It was the biggest smile I'd ever seen him give. "I'll try to be nicer," he said.

I laughed. "I don't care if you're nice or not. I just want you to be *you*. No more pretending. I think it's time we all got to know the real Logan Lyke."

"What if I don't know who the real me is?" he asked.

"Then I guess you better find yourself," I smiled.

"Find myself," he murmured. He smacked his hand on the table and stood, smiling. This was a real smile and I found myself smiling back. "I'll see ya'll later," he said and melted into the crowd.

I looked over at Caeden. "This is turning out to be some night," I said.

He laughed. "And it's not over yet." He picked up Perry and said, "I think we should drop this thing off at the car and walk around. No more Ferris wheel, I promise."

"Sounds good," I stood and stretched. "But don't call him a thing. His name is Perry."

Caeden shook his head, laughing at me. He grabbed Perry and tossed the panda over his shoulder.

"Car's this way," he nodded when I headed in the opposite direction.

"Oh right. Sorry," I blushed.

Caeden put Perry in the driver's seat of Stella Jr. and went as far as to buckle him up.

"If Bryce gets mad and rips Perry to pieces I'm going to rip *you* to pieces," I smiled.

"I can always win you another," he took my hand.

"But then it won't be Perry," I said as we went through the gates again.

"I guess I'll just have to make sure we beat Bryce to the car."

I smiled and stood on my tiptoes to kiss his scruffy cheek. I was enjoying this night so much. It was so nice to go out and just be a normal couple for a little while. I felt like we were never given many opportunities to do that.

I decided to just soak in the night. Remember every detail.

Like the sounds of the games as they clanged and bells went off. Squeals of delight. Groans when someone didn't win. Children's happy shrieks. The whirl of the Ferris wheel.

I sniffed the air and the smells of popcorn and funnel cake flooded me. Underneath that scent was those of the petting zoo, not necessarily pleasant, but I enjoyed it nonetheless.

Caeden and I spent the evening strolling around and stopping to play various games. Caeden always won. I was going to have a nice collection of stuffed animals. I'd never had that before. I smiled at the thought of my bed covered in various stuffed creatures. Caeden ended up buying a bag to put them all in.

"I'm hungry," he announced.

I rolled my eyes. Caeden was *always* hungry.

"Lead the way," I said.

We weaved through the crowd and he stopped in front of one of the various food stands scattered around. This one was selling mini burgers. He ordered a dozen, a mountain dew, and a diet coke for me.

The girl working there handed him a paper bag full of burgers while she looked him up and down. I waited for her to flick her tongue out and lick her lips. I might just rip it off.

Caeden handed her a wad of cash and took my hand. "Soph," he said warningly. "Control yourself. Your eyes are flashing."

Oh Jesus! I squished my eyes closed and took a deep breath before I opened them.

"Better?" I looked at Caeden.

"You're good," he led me to another table like the one we had sat at earlier.

He pulled out a burger and handed it to me. "This will be the best thing you've ever eaten."

I gave him a, 'yeah right', look and took a bite.

"Ohmigod," I moaned in ecstasy. "You're right. This is delicious."

"I told ya so," he said and bit into his own burger.

I grabbed a second.

"So good," I said.

Caeden chuckled and wiped his mouth with a napkin.

We finished eating and Caeden rolled up the paper bag and tossed it into the trashcan over my head. "Score!"

Just then his phone beeped. He pulled it out of his back pocket and scanned the text. "It's Bryce, he says to meet by the car. They're ready to go home."

"Can you drive?" I asked, shuddering at the thought of Bryce driving.

"Do you really think Bryce is going to let me drive Stella Jr.?"

"Gag him if you have to!"

Caeden laughed. "Oh Sophie. Don't you think if he was easy to gag I would've done that a long time ago?"

I laughed as we strolled along. "That's true."

As we were about to leave I saw a cart with balloons. "Ooh! Caeden! Balloons!"

He smirked. "You want one?"

"Yes!"

He chuckled. "Most girls want jewelry. Instead you want a balloon. How did I get to lucky? Which color do you want?"

"That one," I pointed to a pale blue one.

The gray haired man running the balloon cart seemed to find Caeden and me very amusing.

"Mommy! Mommy!" A little kid behind me shrieked. "I want one! Boon! Boon!"

"No," she said, from the tone of her voice I could tell she was exhausted.

"Boon! Boon!" the little girl cried as the mom picked her up and balanced her on her hip.

I looked over at Caeden and saw him holding two

balloons. He grinned. "What? I heard someone else wanted a balloon and I just can't resist a damsel in distress."

I took my balloon from him and kissed him. "I love you."

"Love you too, babe," he grinned.

"I think your damsel's getting away," I nodded towards the thinning parking lot.

"Crap," Caeden said.

I trailed behind him as he jogged to catch up with the mom.

"Ma'am!" he called. "Excuse me," he said when she turned, "I just overheard your daughter asking for a balloon so… here," he thrust the balloon into the little girls tiny hand. "I hope pink's okay?"

The mom smiled and was so overcome by the gesture that I feared she'd cry. She pushed her blond bangs out of her eyes. "Pink's great," she said. "Thank you, that was really sweet and you certainly didn't need to do that. Say thank you Lexie," she prompted the child.

"Tank you," she said.

Caeden smiled at the little girl. Her hair was super curly and pale blond. She was dressed in a pink and green flowered dress and was probably the cutest thing I had ever seen. "Can I have a high-five?" he stuck his hand out.

The little girl smiled, her teeth white a spaced apart. She smacked her tiny hand against Caeden's large one. My stomach lurched with some unknown emotion.

"Thank you, again," the mom said.

"No problem," Caeden waved and returned to my side.

He wrapped his arm around me and kissed the top of my head.

"That was really sweet," I said.

"What can I say? I'm a sweet guy."

"The sweetest."

Bryce and Charlotte were already in the car. Perry was tossed haphazardly in the back seat. I dropped the bag of stuffed animals that Caeden had won for me, on the floor, and held Perry in my lap. As Bryce drove, too fast down the road, the balloon threatened to fly from my hand. If it did, I was going to make Bryce turn around and buy me twelve more.

Bryce skidded the Jeep to a stop in front of Gram's house. Luckily for his wallet my balloon hadn't flown away.

Caeden grabbed Perry the Panda from my lap and the bag at my feet.

"How come you didn't win me anything?" Charlotte asked Bryce.

Bryce looked at the smorgasbord of stuffed critters that Caeden had won for me. "Because babe," he turned to her, "I don't do clichés."

Caeden looked at me and rolled his eyes. He held his hand out to help me down from the Jeep.

"Bye Bryce, Charlotte," I waved.

Charlotte smiled. "I'm so glad you came with us Sophie."

"Me too," I smiled widely. "It was fun to get to do 'town' stuff."

"Just wait for the parade!" she called over the roar of the Jeep as Bryce took off. That boy was going to get them killed if he kept driving like that.

The door to the house opened and Gram ushered us inside. "Don't just stand outside like that," she scolded. "The neighbors are gonna think ya'll are up to no good. Especially with that delinquent brother of yours," she pointed at Caeden. I think Gram thrived on poking fun at Bryce, whether he knew it or not.

I tied the balloon around the doorknob to my room and said, "We're going to bed Gram."

"Night," she said, puttering into the kitchen. Her slippers made little scuffling sounds.

Caeden closed my bedroom door and said, "So how was your first carnival?"

I took my shoes off and tossed them in the closet.

"Besides the whole Ferris wheel thing it was pretty great."

Caeden winced. "Sorry about that," he said as he pulled his shirt over his head.

"It's not your fault," I wiggled into some pajama pants and hid in my closet to change my shirt. I hated how embarrassed I was to be naked in front of Caeden. I mean, he knew what I looked like and I knew what he looked like without clothes, but it was still so *embarrassing*.

I pulled off my shirt and bra and yanked on a baggy shirt that I realized was Caeden's and not mine. Oh, well.

I found Caeden lying on my bed with both the dogs. He was talking to them and petting Archie behind his ears.

It was like our own little family.

I sat down on the bed and unwound my braid. I grabbed my brush off the bedside table and ran it through the tangles.

"Let me do that," Caeden said and put his hand over mine.

"You're going to brush my hair?" I looked over at him.

He blushed. "Yeah."

"Okay," I handed him the brush. He scooted over to sit behind me so that I was resting between his legs.

Caeden was careful not to pull my hair and made sure to get out every tangle.

My eyes quickly became heavy and I had to stifle a yawn.

He finished and put the brush back on the table. He lifted my hair of my neck and kissed the sensitive skin there. I shivered.

Caeden reached over and flicked the light off and wrapped me in his arms. I tucked my head under his neck. He kissed the top of my head and mumbled lowly under his breath, "I love you Sophie, so much, and I'll never let anything happen to you ever again."

NINETEEN.

"I spy with my little eye, Sophie the she-wolf!" yelled a voice behind me, signaling the howls to commence.

"Why on earth did you have to suggest that nickname to them?" I hissed under my breath to Caeden.

We were walking around downtown waiting for the parade to start. It was boiling hot outside and my shoulders were turning red. Now I knew why I had never attended a parade before. Plus, all the people served to make me feel claustrophobic. Apparently this town spent all year waiting for this one day. I guess that's a small town for you.

One of the guys came up behind me and squeezed my shoulders and then smacked a kiss on my cheek before darting away.

"Hands off my girl," Caeden grinned.

"Ah, she-wolf's got a body guard. We better run boys," Shane said.

"Don't worry, I'll give you a head start," joked Caeden.

"We don't need a head start," Evan said.

The rest of the guys fell in step with us.

"Are you excited for the parade, Sophie?" asked Cam.

I shrugged and struggled not to trip over something in the grass. "I've never been to one before so I guess so. It just seems like a lot of hype for nothing."

Cam gasped. "You're kidding? Apple Blossom is like the greatest thing ever."

I laughed. "Sorry guys, it's just not my thing."

"You're crazy," Brody said. His gaze drifted away and focused on a pretty blonde. "I'll see you guys later," he waved half-heartedly.

The other guys snickered. "Poor Brody. When will he learn that Em is never going to go out with him?" Tyler asked.

"Never," Kyle snorted.

"Do you and Caeden have seats for the parade?" asked Riley, tucking his long sandy hair behind his ear.

"Yeah," I said. "In the bleachers. What about you guys?"

"Us too," he said. "Guess you can't be rid of us just yet she-wolf," he winked.

I shook my head and decided to just ignore my teammates and enjoy my time with Caeden.

"Ooh," I stopped in my tracks. "Is that cotton candy? I've never had cotton candy."

"You've never had cotton candy?" a chorus of voices rang out.

"Um… no," I blushed.

"Then you have not *lived*!" Evan cried.

Caeden steered us towards the booth. "Two cotton candies," he told the girl and pulled out his wallet.

She swirled the magical fluffy confection around and around. She handed me a pink one and Caeden a blue one. "Thank you," I told her with a smile.

Caeden nodded to a shady patch of grass underneath a huge oak tree.

"We'll meet up with you guys later," Riley said and they disappeared into the crowd.

I waved and plopped down in the grass beside Caeden. The shade made it feel ten degrees cooler so I was thankful. I crossed my legs underneath me, Indian style, and leaned against the thick wood trunk of the tree. The sun was bright and would've normally blinded me but my shifter eyes adjusted to the different shades of light. There was enough room for Caeden to lean against the tree too, so he sat behind me.

Our spot in front of the tree allowed us to look over at the huge high school that sat next to the parade route. It was a huge stately school with so many steps leading up to the doors it made me dizzy just to look at them. Its football field was located in the front and several dads were currently using it to toss a football with their sons.

Caeden bumped my shoulder with his. "Earth to Sophie," he waved his hand in front of my face.

"Sorry, I got lost in my thoughts."

"Happens to all of us," he smiled and his eyes crinkled in the corners, just the tiniest bit.

I pulled a chunk of fluffy cotton candy off of the stick and stuck it in my mouth. It felt like I had stuck a fluffy, sugary, ball into my mouth. As it dissolved the sugar coated my tongue like sand. It was very sweet. I took another bite.

"This is really good," I said to Caeden.

He finished the last bit of his. Blue sugary fibers stuck to his fingers and he flicked them into his mouth, one by one, to lick it off.

I think I drooled a bit.

Caeden noticed and grinned, his dimple flashing.

Darn him, and his sexy grin. It was only making things worse.

I forced my attention back to my cotton candy and was tempted to give it to Caeden just to see him lick his fingers again.

Nah.

I grabbed another piece of fluff and shoved it into my mouth.

Caeden playfully flicked the ends of my hair.

"Why do you like to play with my hair?" I giggled when one of the strands touched my cheek.

"It's soft," he said and then broke out in a grin. "Why do you like my scruff?"

"I just do," I rubbed his cheek. "Although this," I flicked a piece of dark brown hair from his eye, "is getting way too long."

Caeden pulled a baseball cap out of his pocket, shoved his hair out of his eyes, and stuck the cap on backwards. "Better?" he grinned.

"Not as good as a haircut," I finished my last bite of cotton candy and smiled.

He grumbled, "I hate getting my hair cut." He fingered one of the curls escaping the confines of his hat.

"Do you *want* your hair down to your shoulders?"

"No," he said. Finally, "I'll get it cut." Caeden picked up a piece of grass and tore it to pieces. It sprinkled to the ground like flakes of confetti. He glanced around at the thickening crowd. "The parade's starting soon. We better get our seats," he stood and offered me a hand. I took it and he hauled me up and into my arms. He kissed me quickly and let go, a grin plastered on his face. "This Apple Blossom is already *way* better than last year."

"Why?"

"You're here," he grinned.

I felt my knees turn to jelly. I never thought I'd be one of those girls who swooned over their boyfriend but Caeden was completely, and undeniably, swoon-worthy.

Bleachers are this way," he nodded in their direction, as if I hadn't noticed them.

We weaved our way through the thick crowd. I think the whole town had turned out for this. There were even people that were very obviously tourists, as they snapped pictures of the old buildings. I didn't know who would want to visit this place. To me, it seemed like the smallest, most boring town ever. But I had lived pretty much everywhere, so I guess I just didn't appreciate it.

People began to line the streets and I wanted to scream at them, 'it's *just* a parade', but I didn't think they'd appreciate that.

Caeden and climbed onto the top seats of the bleachers, as luck would have it, next to my teammates. The pack was supposed to be sitting with us but they were still M.I.A.

"She-wolf!" cried Cam.

I rolled my eyes. "Are you guys going to yell that every single time you see me?"

They looked at one another and nodded. "Yeah, pretty much," Shane said.

I saw that Brody was back with them and obviously deflated. Poor guy. I don't think whatever-her-name-was is worth his time. He's a nice guy and could do way better.

Evan leaned towards Caeden. "Do you know who the Grand Marshall is this year?"

Caeden shrugged. "I've got no clue."

"I hope it's some hot chick," Kyle said, "last year they had freakin' Mario Lopez. All the girls were like, 'Aw, look at his dimples!'"

I laughed. "Caeden's dimples are the only ones I want to look at," I poked his cheek.

"Ick," Tyler gagged, "ya'll make me sick."

I stuck my tongue out at him and turned to Caeden. "Mister, you better not be checking out some hot chick on a parade float," I poked his chest.

"It's usually a car not a float," he grinned.

"Same difference!" I threw my hands in the air.

"What are you two arguing over?" Chris asked as she a Bentley decided to grace us with their presence. They were both rumpled so I figured they'd caught a quick make out session somewhere.

Chris slid onto the bleachers beside me and I said to her, "I told Caeden that if this Grand Marshall person was a hot girl, he couldn't look."

Chris laughed. "You know Caeden only has eyes for you." She turned to Bentley, "But same goes to you, anyway, no looking."

Bentley laughed and shook his head, rubbing the side of his face.

"Anyone know where Bryce and Charlotte are?" Caeden asked.

"Uh-" Logan said as he sat down, "I saw them over there." He pointed to several stands setup with various odds and ends things to buy.

"Oh that can't be good," Caeden shook his head.

"Why?" I asked.

Caeden smiled. "Bryce is probably the only sixteen year old boy who still needs a parental chaperone at these things. Lord only knows what he might blow his money on." He shuddered.

The parade was seconds from starting when Bryce and Charlotte showed up. Charlotte had a purple Asian umbrella fanned around her shoulders and Bryce's face was painted up to resemble—a wolf.

Caeden let out a sigh of relief beside me.

I gave him a questioning look.

"This year is mild," he explained. "Last year he was covered in henna tattoos and fake piercings. He nearly gave mom a heart attack."

"He'd give me one too," I laughed.

"I don't know how any of us have survived Bryce," Caeden chuckled. "He's definitely one of a kind."

Kyle tapped Caeden's shoulder. "Isn't your little brother the one who sang the Fergie song at the top of his lungs during that assembly last year."

Caeden buried his face in his hands. "That's the one."

Shane snickered. "I watched that on youtube."

"He did a dance too," Tyler said, and began to, I guess, mimic it. The other guys joined in and they began to sing the lyrics to *Glamorous*.

"Oh God," Caeden croaked. "Youtube?"

They finished mimicking and Shane said, "Yeah, it's on youtube. It's got like a million hits or something."

"A million?" Caeden squeaked.

"I'm tellin' ya, your brother should be a fucking comedian," Tyler said.

"Or euthanized," Caeden muttered under his breath.

I smacked his leg. "Be nice. You know you love him and wouldn't change a thing about him."

Caeden grinned. "I know."

Just then the sound of the band reached us as they rounded the corner.

It amazed me how they managed to march in such perfectly straight lines, while carrying such heavy instruments. Even with my shifter abilities I would've tripped over my own feet and brought the whole thing down.

The band passed and soon a line of cars was going by.

The people in the cars waved to the people in the crowd. They all seemed pretty ordinary to me, no celebrities yet.

More cars and more school bands came by. I yawned.

Caeden bumped my knee. "Having fun?"

"Loads," I smiled brightly.

Caeden laughed. "You are such a little liar." Straightening his baseball cap, he said, "I'm sorry, I know this isn't really your thing."

I shrugged. "It's nice though, you know, to do something like this. A small town thing. But-"

"Not that exciting," he added, just as some horses drawing a carriage walked by.

I smiled in response. Sometimes, I think, Caeden knew me better than I knew myself. It was nice to have a boyfriend that was so in tune to me.

Eventually the parade came to a close. I didn't recognize the celebrity, someone older, but I was thankful that it wasn't some 'hot chick'. My teammates, however, all groaned.

"Dude, that was a waste of fucking time," Evan said to Kyle.

Kyle shook his head. "I think it was still fun. Best thing that happens here all year."

Evan shook his head and looked over at me. "Sophie, you down to play some soccer?"

"Sure," I said, "we don't have any plans."

"Awesome," Evan grinned. "I have soccer balls in my car."

TWENTY.

Four weeks until graduation.

Thirty days.

Wow.

I wiggled in my auditorium seat. The principal was holding an assembly to speak with us about graduation and announce the valedictorian.

I knew what he was saying was important but I couldn't focus.

Caeden put his hand over mine so I'd stop tapping the wooden armrest.

After going over expected behavior and dress for graduation the principal finally got down to business.

He smiled and spoke into the microphone, "I know you're all wondering who your valedictorian is going to be. Let me tell you now, it was a close race. This is a very smart and talented graduating class and in my eyes, you're all winners. But the person with the highest GPA, and therefore giving the speech, is…" he paused for dramatic affect. I held my breath and silently prayed. *Sophie Beaumont, Sophie Beaumont, Sophie Beaumont.* "Caeden Williams."

"What!?" I screamed and every student and teacher in the auditorium turned to look at me. My cheeks flooded with color. I hadn't meant to say that out loud.

Bentley snickered and Chris laughed. Logan's lips quirked at the corner.

Caeden grinned at me and winked. "I told you that you didn't need to worry about my grades."

I bit my lip.

"You?" I squeaked. By now the principal was trying to clear the auditorium but I was rooted to my seat.

"Me," Caeden's grin grew bigger. "I'm that awesome. Boom."

I shook my head. "But you *never* do any homework."

Caeden threw his head back and laughed. "We've been over this before. I do my homework while you're sleep. Besides, I just like to watch you sleep. You talk."

205

"Do not."

"Oh yeah," he smirked and leaned towards me, whispering in my ear, "you say my name over and over again. Some times you even say that you love me. You smile too."

My blush from earlier flamed once again.

"It's cute," he kissed my cheek.

I shook my head and switched back to the earlier topic. "I just can't believe that you're valedictorian."

"You best believe it, babe," he stood and picked up his backpack, slinging it over his shoulder. "And I'm going to write the most epic graduation speech ever. It will be remembered for generations to come."

* * *

The day before graduation we were given a whole block to sign yearbooks in the cafeteria.

Caeden and I were coming up from the math hall and as we were crossing in front of a section of tables a girl let out a squeal. I turned to look, thinking something bad had happened, but instead she was halfway on the table, feet dangling, and staring at Caeden.

"Who's that sexy beast?" she cried.

Caeden laughed. His blue eyes shining with humor.

Shane came up behind us and clapped Caeden on the back. "Looks to me like you have a secret admirer." He shrugged. "Or I guess in this case, not so secret."

"Nah," Caeden shook his head. "That's just Shelby. She's crazy."

Shane nodded to a table. "She-wolf, come over here so you can sign the teams yearbooks. You too Caeden."

We followed him and a stack of yearbooks immediately bombarded me.

"Whoa, guys, slow it down," I took a pen that Riley offered me.

I handed him my yearbook. "Just pass it to the next person when you're done," I motioned to the eagerly waiting guys. The other guys had finally accepted me once they realized they needed me and I was just all around full of awesomeness. I still hung out more with Tyler, Riley, Cam, Kyle, Evan, Shane, and Brody. I had a feeling I'd be friends with those seven guys for years to come.

For the seven, as I liked to call them, I signed:

Lots of Love, Sophie

And for the others I signed with a heart and then my name.

Every time I finished a yearbook I handed it to Caeden for him to sign it. He wrote:

Hugs, Caeden

After signing the stack of my teammates yearbooks, Caeden and I headed to our usual table to eat lunch and exchanged yearbooks with our pack members.

I had packed my lunch, so I pulled out a peanut butter and jelly sandwich, while Caeden bought pizza.

"Give me your yearbook," Bryce said, and snatched it from the table in front of me.

I looked over at Charlotte. "I'm afraid," I said as Bryce scribbled furiously.

"You should be," she handed me her yearbook, "sign mine and see what he wrote."

I opened the front cover and quickly found, scribbled in orange highlighter, *Charlotte, I wish I were your underwear. Why? So, I'd never have to leave your cute bum. Love, Bryce.*

I snorted. "Wow, Bryce."

"It's better than H.A.G.S." He shrugged.

I quickly signed Charlotte's yearbook and then Chris', Bentley's, and Logan's. Bryce passed my yearbook to Charlotte and she passed it to the others. I was a little scared to know what Bryce had written, especially when he kept smirking at me.

Caeden was happily chomping on his pizza and signing the pack's yearbooks. A couple of girls, one of which was the crazy eyed, hyper spastic, Shelby, approached Caeden to sign their yearbooks. "Sure," he shrugged, shoving a chunk of pizza crust in his mouth. They squealed and fangirled like their favorite singer or actor was signing an autograph for them.

I shook my head and took my yearbook back from Logan. I hesitantly opened it. Chris, Charlotte, Bentley, and Logan all signed their names with a quick message but Bryce? Oh, Bryce.

> Sweet Sophie,
>
> I like you. A lot. But you and me? It's just never going to work. You deserve someone better than me. I hope you understand and we can still be friends.
>
> P.S. I have a thing for strawberries now. Not cookies.
>
> —Bryce

I looked up at Bryce and he laughed. He flicked a piece of Charlotte's hair and said, "I just luuuuurve strawberries."

* * *

Caeden scribbled furiously on a piece of paper. I was afraid if he stabbed it any harder it would break in half. He'd gotten his haircut so he didn't have to flick any strands out of his eye every few seconds.

Graduation was tomorrow morning and his speech just *had* to be perfect.

I laid on the bed, stroking Archie's soft head, and trying to keep my mouth shut so I didn't end up getting yelled at.

After a few more minutes of silence I couldn't take it any longer. "I thought you had to turn your speech into Mr. Hines yesterday for approval?" I propped my head up on my hand.

"I did," he bit his tongue.

208

"So shouldn't you, I don't know, leave it alone?"

He tossed the pencil at the wall and shoved the chair back from my desk. "It has to be perfect, Sophie."

I looked at the clock. "It's almost midnight Caeden and graduation is at nine in the morning. You need to sleep."

"I just don't want to sound like an idiot up there."

I climbed off the bed and went over to him, rubbing his shoulders. "You're obviously not an idiot or you wouldn't be valedictorian." My hair fell forward, tickling his face.

"Will you listen to it? Please? One more time?" he asked, giving me those puppy dog eyes that I just couldn't say no to.

"Sure," I fell back on the bed and threw my arm over my eyes. "Go for it."

I think he made it through the first paragraph before I fell asleep.

"Sophie! Sophie!" Caeden ran around Gram's house, his black gown fanning around him. "Have you seen my speech?"

"Check your pocket," I pointed to his khaki pants.

He shoved his hand in and pulled out a clump of papers.

"Told ya," I looked in the hall mirror to straighten my cap.

"What about my tie?"

I grabbed it off the side table and held it aloft. "Right here, remember, you asked if I could put it on you."

"Oh… right," he blushed.

"Come here," I quirked a finger at him. He obliged. I slung the tie over his neck and made quick work of tying the knot.

"How'd you do that," he picked up the silky piece of fabric and stared at it in wonder.

I shrugged. "My dad taught me."

I turned back to the mirror and inspected my hair and makeup. I wasn't normally concerned with such trivial things but graduation called for it. I made sure each chocolate curl was in its place, and that my makeup hadn't melted off. I even inspected my red graduation gown for wrinkles.

"You look perfect Soph," Caeden kissed the top of my head.

I sighed.

"Soph," he said again, noting my sigh, "I'm really sorry your parents couldn't come."

I turned and let him put his arms around me. "I guess I just always pictured them cheering me on when this day finally came. It's weird that they're not here. Plus, I miss them."

Caeden kissed my forehead. "I know Sophie. If I could teleport them here, I would."

"It's fine," I smiled. "Gram is here."

"Darn right!" she called, coming out of her bedroom.

For the first time in all my life, Gram was wearing a skirt.

Oh God, and a pink cardigan.

"Don't you two dare say a thing," she pointed a finger at us, straightening her skirt with the other hand. "Just bite your tongues."

"You look great, Lucinda."

"And you're a liar and should have your mouth washed out with soap," she tugged on the sleeves of her cardigan.

"Nice pearls," I pointed to her neck.

"Didn't I tell ya'll to bite yer tongues," Gram's southern drawl became more pronounced when she was irritated.

Caeden and I worked hard to suppress our snickers.

Gram grabbed her purse off the side table and said, "Don't we need to get going? I thought golden boy here had to be at the school early."

"I do," he said, crinkling the papers in his hand.

"Let's get gone then," Gram motioned us out the door.

I grabbed my cap off the side table. The silver tassel

swayed, flashing the number 2012.

"Let's rock this," I said, sliding into the Jeeps passenger seat.

Caeden laughed and shook his head.

Gram opened the backseat door and said, "I don't know if I can climb in this thing. I need a step ladder."

"You've gotten in here before," Caeden pointed out.

Gram huffed and climbed in with more agility than most twenty year olds had. Crazy lady.

People were just starting to trickle into the school when we got there. Caeden rushed off to find Mr. Hines to get his last minute changes approved.

"I'll see you in a little bit," he kissed my cheek before darting off.

That left me with Gram, who kept messing with her skirt.

"I feel like someone's going to see my hot pocket if the wind blows this thing up a bit."

I snorted. "Gram!"

"What?"

"You know what," I gave her a look.

She smiled and started to laugh. "Well, it's true. Do ya think I can tape this thing to my legs?"

"Um… no," I said.

"Why didn't I just wear jeans?" she said to no one in particular.

"Because that's not allowed," I supplied.

"I might need to talk to dear old Mr. Hines about that. Surly there should be an exception for a women my age."

"You're not that old."

"I'm sixty-two years old Sophie. That's old."

"No it's not," I rolled my eyes.

The school began to fill up with more students.

"I guess I better go get a seat, Sophie dear," she kissed me on my cheek and patted my hand. "I'll be the obnoxious grandma cheering for you."

I laughed. Gram was a hoot.

At eight-thirty Mr. Hines appeared, with a very nervous Caeden at his shoulder, and ushered us into the auditorium. We were seated alphabetically so that when we walked out here and to the football field we wouldn't be mixed up.

"Well seniors, that moment has finally come," he sat down on the stage. "Wow. Can you believe it? Graduation. You'll be off to college in the fall. You have your whole lives ahead of you but this moment," he paused, "is the last moment you'll still be a kid. Once you're handed that diploma you'll out in the real world. No cushion. Just free fall. I'm afraid for some of you, I'm not going to lie," he smiled at a group of trouble makers, "but others, I know you're going to go out there and do great things. I'm proud of all of you. Each and every one. Some of you I know better than others. In some cases, that's a good thing, in others, not so much. But just know, that I know, you warriors will make me the proudest principal to ever grace this school." He turned to some students on his left. "The yearbook department has put together something special. I hope you enjoy it."

The lights dimmed and a projector descended. Images of my classmates as babies, kids, and now flashed onto the screen. Occasionally someone would exclaim but mostly there were a lot of, 'awwws' and tears. A group shot of Caeden, Logan, and Bentley flashed onto the screen. They were laughing, covered in water, and Bentley was holding the smallest fish known to man. They were all missing teeth and looked about eight years old. I joined in the awws, on that one.

The video ended and the lights came back on.

Mr. Hines looked at his watch. "It's almost time but first we're going to walk the halls. This will be the last time you'll ever walk these halls as students. First row," he pointed. We all stood and waited for the row in front of us to leave the room.

Mr. Hines led us through the halls, decorated in red

and black streamers, posters, confetti, and pictures of our time at the school. Music, something I didn't recognize, pumped through the speakers.

From up ahead Mr. Hines called, "You have your teachers and the underclassman to thank for this," he indicated the halls.

We roamed through the whole school before stopping in front of the doors that would lead us out the back of the school, to the football field, where graduation was held.

"Ready?" Mr. Hines asked.

We nodded as a group, everyone too nervous to speak. I shook my hands in an effort to relieve some of the adrenaline coursing through my veins. Who would've ever thought that graduation would be so nerve racking.

"Let's go people," Mr. Hines smiled and led us out the doors.

We turned left and then right to descend the steps to the field. I was amazed by the size of the crowd gathered. The bleachers were packed and people stood all over the surrounding hills. Cameras flashed. I took a deep breath and concentrated on not tripping. As a shifter, the chances of me falling were slim, but I still had a fear of knocking everyone over and the whole class going down like a line of dominos.

We reached the last step and walked straight onto the field and our assigned seats.

I didn't know any of the people around me but Bentley was in the row behind me so I didn't feel completely alone.

Before the speeches started the warrior, our school mascot, rode out onto the field on a horse. He held the spear high before throwing it into the ground where it stuck. With a turn the horse took off back the way it had come, disappearing into the trees. It was the same way the school started home football games but this time it brought tears to my eyes.

I turned my attention from the field to the stage, where Caeden sat while Mr. Hines addressed the crowd.

Caeden's leg kept bouncing up and down and he clenched his speech in his hands.

You're going to rock this. I said to him.

I could see a little bit of the stress leak out of him. *Thanks babe.* He grinned.

"-and now for our valedictorian," Mr. Hines clapped his hands and then waved Caeden up to the podium.

Caeden gulped, took a deep breath, and stood. He strode towards the podium and grinned, flashing his famous dimples.

"Hello class of two-thousand and twelve," he nodded towards us, "families," he nodded at the crowd. Clearing his throat he continued, "It seems like just yesterday we were all kids. Little terrors running around, driving our parents and teachers crazy, eating glue, you get the idea," he winked. "But look where we are today. Graduation. I've known most of you since kindergarten. We've grown up together, matured... Well, some of us have matured," he chuckled. "But we've all been on this life's journey together. Reaching for this one goal. This piece of paper, called a diploma, that suddenly says that we are smart enough to go out into the real world. That's scary. The real world isn't a nice place. In fact, it's a lot like high school. People still lie, cheat, and steal. There's still that awful social pyramid. I think it's time we kick it down, and say 'no more!' I think it's time we realize that we're all just the same. Here we are, embarking on this same journey together. The beginning of the rest of our lives. We have some big decisions coming our way, like, where do we go from here? I don't know," Caeden shrugged. "I'm just as clueless as most of you. I don't know what I want to do with my life. I mean, whatever we decide on now, decides the rest of our life. It's a big decision, where we go from here. There are so many choices presented to us. Which college? Which classes? Bachelor's or Master's degree?" Caeden chuckled. "Most days I can't decide what I want to eat for lunch let alone what I want to do for the rest of my life. Choices, we have so many choices. But enough on that," he shuffled his papers. "It's time to say goodbye. Goodbye to high school, goodbye to the teachers, goodbye to you," he pointed to the Shelby girl, she shrieked in response "goodbye to you guys," he eyed my soccer teammates, "goodbye to all of you," Caeden waved his arms to encompass the whole crowd, "and hello to our futures!"

Everyone cheered and clapped. I stood and waved. "I love you!" I cupped my hands over my mouth. Caeden waved and winked at me.

"Thank you all for your time and I wish you the best of luck with realizing your dreams!"

Since Caeden was valedictorian he was given his diploma first and then the rest of the class was called up in alphabetical order.

"Amanda Grace Banner." The girl in front of me strode forward, her blond hair swishing. She shook hands with the principal and the school board officials before being handed her diploma.

"Sophie Noelle Beaumont." I took a breath a stepped forward.

"Whoo! Go she-wolf!" My team yelled before howling into the clear blue sky.

"Go Sophie!" Bentley hollered from his seat.

"Sophie! Sophie!" yelled a crowd in the bleachers. I easily picked out Gram in her pink cardigan. I also spotted Christian, Bryce, Charlotte, and Amy. Bryce was hooting and fist bumping the air. Ah, Bryce. Then my eyes landed on my parents. My parents! They were here! It took all my will power not to run off the stage and straight into their arms.

With a smile on my face I shook Mr. Hines hand, went down the three steps of the stage, and shook hands with the school board member.

"Congratulations," the lady smiled, handing me my diploma. She moved my tassel to the other side. "I wish you the best of luck."

"Thanks," I said, taking the black diploma case.

I stood in front of my seat and waited for the rest of

my row to return before sitting down, as per instruction.

The names were called surprisingly fast. I cheered when Bentley's name was called, Logan's, and all my teammates.

Mr. Hines called the last name and then said, "I present to you, the graduating class of two-thousand and twelve!"

That was our cue to toss our caps in the air. Red and black caps rained down. It was over. Thirteen years of school, over. Done. Finished.

I smiled, picking up my cap and replacing it on my head before going in search of Caeden.

I easily found him weaving through the crowd and ran into his arms. He swung me around and kissed me before letting me go.

"You did it!" I squealed. "Your speech was amazing!"

"Thanks," he said, taking my face in his hands and kissing me again. "I was so nervous that I think I sweated through my gown."

"I hope not," I poked his side. "After all, it's a rental."

He laughed, and I let the warm, rich, sound of it soak into my bones.

"Your speech was awesome," Bentley came up and gave Caeden that weird guy half-handshake, half-hug thing. Why didn't girls have a cool handshake like that? So not fair.

"Ooh!" I exclaimed and grabbed Caeden's arm. "My parents are here! Even though they said they couldn't make it they're here!"

Caeden grinned, dimple winking. "Did you really think they would miss their only daughter's graduation? They wanted to surprise you, that's why they told you they couldn't make it."

"And you knew?"

"Of course," he smiled.

I hit his arm.

"Ow!" he grabbed it. "What was that for?"

"For making me think that my parents were going to miss my graduation. You all suck!"

Bentley snickered. "You got your hands full with this one don't you Caeden?"

I put my hands on my hips, ready to retort, but was interrupted by Riley. "I told ya'll we should call her Sassy Sophie."

"Or Spunky Sophie," Brody added, winking at me.

I couldn't help cracking a smile.

"I still like she-wolf Sophie," Evan slung his arm over my shoulder. "That's my mom and dad," he pointed to a couple approaching us as families trickled onto the field. "Mom! Get a picture of me and she-wolf?"

"Sure, sure," the strawberry blonde lady said, digging in her purse. "Aha! Here it is. I'm Elaine, Evan's mom," she announced to us. "Now smile!"

I smiled but just before the flash went off Evan kissed my cheek. I gasped in surprise, probably making the funniest face known to man.

Evan snatched the camera from his mom and laughed. "That is totally going to be my facebook profile pic. Take a look she-wolf."

He turned the camera so I could see the image on the screen.

Oh, God.

I narrowed my eyes and pointed a finger at Evan. "You better promise me that, that picture never sees the light of day."

"Well, technically it's already seen the light of day, seeing as it's the morning and all."

"Evan, you know what I mean."

"Fine," he lowered his head, "I won't post it on facebook."

"Or twitter, instagram, or any other picture sharing site. Got it? Maybe you should just delete it now?"

"Nah," Evan grinned. "I'm keeping this forever and

ever as proof that I kissed the she-wolf."

I laughed at him and the heard my mom. "Sophie!"

"Mommy!" I cried and ran into her arms. I didn't give a crap if I was acting like a five year old at my graduation. I had missed my mommy.

She wrapped her arms around me in a tight hug.

"I thought you guys weren't coming," I said into her shoulder.

"We thought we'd surprise you."

"That's what Caeden just told me," I pulled away from her arms.

"Oh yes," she leaned around me to speak to Caeden. "I quite enjoyed your speech."

"Thanks Mrs. Beaumont," he blushed.

"Call me Christine," she said.

I saw my dad coming and ran into his arms just like I had with my mom.

"Careful Soph," he enveloped me in his arms, "you might knock an old man down."

"You're not old," I said, "and you're far from push-downable." I poked his beefy arm to drive home my point.

"Where's Gram?" I looked around.

"Probably fussing about her shoes. Do you know that I've never seen her wear a skirt?" Dad smiled.

I laughed. "I must be pretty special."

"Darn right you're pretty special," Gram hobbled up, her short little heels sticking in the dirt, "but if I wasn't required to dress up I'd be in jeans, no matter how special you are." She patted my cheek.

"Thanks Gram," I laughed.

"Alright guys," my mom waved her arms around, "I need pictures! Lots and lots of pictures!"

"Oh no," I looked at Caeden, "we'll be here for two hours."

"We better not be," Caeden eyed my mom.

She laughed. "An hour, tops, I promise," she held up one finger.

"Let's get one with my teammates," I told her. "Hey guys!" I called and waved them over. "Do you mind taking a picture?"

"Nah, of course not. Anything for our she-wolf," Brody grinned. His dark wavy hair was escaping from the confines of his cap.

I looked over at Evan. "And no stealing anymore kisses."

He tilted his head back a bit. "You ruined my plan."

"Squish together," mom said, bringing her hands together as if she could move us herself. "Now smile." The flash went off. "Let's do one more, and this time no funny faces." Flash. "Great, thanks. Now I want one of Sophie by herself," she dismissed the guys.

"Bye," I said to them. "I'll see you guys this summer right?"

"Oh yeah," Riley grinned. "You'll see us. Hey dad!" he disappeared into the crowd and the others with him.

"Smile Soph," she said. "Yeah, just like that. Oh that's a keeper. I'm going to put that one somewhere I can see it. Caeden, get over here."

Caeden came over, putting his arm around my waist.

"Smile!"

Flash.

Flash.

Flash.

"My eyes hurt now," Caeden whispered in my ear.

"My face hurts," I said. "Mom, I think you have enough pictures."

"Sophie, don't spoil my fun. I wasn't here for prom."

Amy showed up then, the pack on her heels, and pulled her camera out. "Pictures!" she squeled.

"Oh God," Caeden and I said simultaneously.

* * *

"I think my face is frozen," I poked my cheek as Caeden drove out of the school parking lot. We had posed and smiled for a good hour. Separately, together, and with the pack. I was utterly and completely exhausted just from taking pictures.

"I thought they'd never give it up," he clicked his blinker on.

"Are we not going back to Gram's?"

"No," he shook his head. "Everyone's going to my mom's house. She's put together a joint party for all of us."

"That's really nice of her."

Caeden grinned crookedly. "It may be nice, but expect lots of crying."

"I hope you have tissues."

"I told Bryce to stop at Walgreen's and get some," he grinned.

"I hope he remembers."

"It's Bryce, so probably not. I guess she can always use my shirt," he plucked at the blue button down, tucked into gray slacks. It was a drool-worthy look on him.

"Who all's coming?"

"Lucinda, your parents, the pack, the pack's parents, and I also invited your teammates and their parents. I hope that's okay? I should've asked you first," he gave me a sheepish glance.

"Of course that's fine," I laced my fingers with his. "It just might get a little rowdy."

Caeden chuckled. "Soph, it's already going to be rowdy with Bryce in attendance."

"True."

There was already a crowd of cars at Amy's house. Caeden took my hand and instead of leading me into the house, led me to the edge of the woods. He held a branch up above my head. I gave him a questioning glance.

"I need to talk to you," he fidgeted. "In private."

"And we can't do it in the car?"

"No."

"Alrightie then," I ducked under the branch. "Lead the way."

TWENTY ONE.

The earth crunched beneath my feet as I followed Caeden deeper and deeper into the woods.

"Where are we going?" I asked, taking Caeden's hand so he could help me over a log.

"Patience," he flashed me a crooked grin and I relaxed a bit. "We're almost there."

After a few more minutes of walking he stopped. "Hang on a sec," he rummaged through his pockets. "Crap," he muttered and began untying his tie.

He started wrapping the fabric around my eyes and I laughed, "Caeden, what are you doing?"

"I think that's pretty obvious. I'm blindfolding you, silly girl."

He secured the knot on the back of my head. "You better not mess up my hair," I warned.

"Never," he took my hand.

I tripped over some unseen obstacle but Caeden caught me before I could hit the ground.

"I'm just going to carry you," he swept my legs out from under me, and the air whooshed out of my lungs, "I don't want you tripping and ruining that pretty dress."

I held onto Caeden's neck with one hand and used the other to keep my dress from flashing my fanny at any unsuspecting woodland creatures. The sight might shock them to death.

Caeden walked a short distance before setting me down with a steadying hand on my lower back.

"Can I take this off yet?" I tugged at the blindfold.

"Not yet!" His hands grabbed mine. "I'll tell you when," he tightened the knot so that it wouldn't slip.

"This isn't some weird training exercise where ya'll are going to jump out at me and see who I tear into first, is it?" I could hear the sounds of a stream trickling nearby. The peaceful sound of it calmed my nerves.

Caeden laughed. "No silly girl. You're not even close." He shuffled around, the twigs crunching underneath

---

221

his feet. "Ow!" He cried.

"Caeden?" I almost tore the tie off my eyes.

"No, no, no! I'm fine. Leave it on."

"What happened?"

"I cut myself on a stick. Don't worry, it's already healing." He took a deep breath, "Open your eyes."

I opened my eyes and was greeted with the most beautiful sight. Red poppies were growing everywhere, even coiling themselves around the trees. There reddish orange color was so bright against the greens and browns of the forest. The small little stream I had heard, trickled through and around the flowers. The white and gray pebbles gleamed from the sun shining through the clearing. "Caeden, this place is beautiful," I turned to look for him but he was gone. He cleared his throat and my gaze fell. "Oh my God," tears stung my eyes.

Caeden was down on one knee surrounded by the bright red poppies, and a ring was held tightly in his hand.

"Caeden?" a tear fell from my eye.

He cleared his throat and then swallowed. His jaw clenched and unclenched in nervousness. He took my hand in his free one.

"Sophie," he let out a breath, "I've wanted to marry you ever since I first laid eyes on you in the cupcake shop. I knew then, that you were far too good for me, but I also knew that you were mine. Not because we're mates but because we will always, in any universe, belong together. You were a shining light when I was bathed in darkness. You were my miracle, sent to save me. I'm so lucky to call you my shooting star, my she-wolf, my mate, and I hope… my wife. Will you marry me, Sophie?"

Tears coursed down my face and I knew I was a very unattractive snotty mess. But none of that mattered. What mattered was this moment and what it meant to me, to Caeden, and to the rest of our lives. I lowered myself to both knees and put my hands on each of his scruffy cheeks. He was waiting, as if I would have any other answer, so I said,

"Yes."

Caeden whooped and wrapped his arms around me.

"Yes, yes, a thousand times yes," I said and kissed him.

Our mouths melted together. Softly. Lovingly. His fingertips caressed my skin. I breathed him in. Pine, cinnamon, citrus, and wood, engulfing my lungs. I was still crying, I couldn't help it, and my tears coated our lips.

Caeden pulled away and I was surprised to see tears falling from his eyes.

"I hope it fits," he held up the ring. "It was my grandmother's."

"It's beautiful," I held my hand out for him to slip the ring on.

"Perfect fit," he said when it slid easily over my knuckle, settling on my ring finger, where it would stay forever.

"It's perfect," I breathed, tracing the marquise shaped diamond, and then the unique vine and leaf like band.

"I thought so. It's-" he searched for a word. "Naturey."

I smiled and kissed his cheek. "When you blindfolded me, I never in a million years, imagined you'd propose to me." I cupped his cheek and leaned in so that our lips brushed when I spoke, he let out a shaky breath. "And by the way, *you* are my miracle." My fingers tangled in his wavy brown hair.

He swung me around, the poppies brushing my feet. "I should let you know though. There's a bit of a... catch, to marrying me."

"A catch? What do you mean?" My eyebrows narrowed.

He leaned in close. "You have to marry me before we start our first semester of classes."

My mouth fell open a bit. "Caeden, that's less than three months from now."

"I know," he said. "But I don't want to start college

223

as a bachelor. I gotta let the ladies know I'm taken," he grinned, his eyes squinting.

"You're full of it," I said as he took my hand and held it in the air, his other hand rested on the small of my back and we began to dance to our own music.

"I'm serious Sophie," his blue eyes darkened. "I'm ready to be married to you. I want to call you my wife." He leaned towards my ear and whispered, "And I want to make love to you until your toes curl."

I gasped.

"Three months, Sophie. That's all you've got to plan a wedding. Can you do it?" He bent, plucking a poppy from the ground, and sticking it in my hair.

"Of course," I stuttered, still recovering from his previous statement. A delicious sense of excitement had settled in my stomach.

He grinned and then dipped me down. My hair brushed the poppies and a ladybug whizzed by.

Caeden lifted me up and held me so our whole bodies were touching. Smiling he said, "We've got a party to attend."

* * *

I kept looking at my ring as we walked back to the house. It truly was beautiful and I loved the fact that it had belonged to Caeden's grandma. I traced the leaf and vine design on the band with my thumb. It fit the fact that as shifters, we spent most of our time outdoors.

"Does anyone know?"

"Know what?" he asked.

"That you were planning to propose to me."

"No," he shook his head. "I didn't tell anybody but… I did ask your father for permission."

"What?" my jaw dropped.

Caeden blushed. "It didn't feel right *not* to ask him," he shrugged his shoulders.

"When did you ask him?"

"While we were in Germany."

224

"Oh," I said, several things clicking into place. The mysterious conversation that I had not been privy to.

Caeden lifted me over the fallen log; my red ballet flats skimmed the top.

"I didn't get a chance to tell you that I love this dress," Caeden fingered the sleeve of it. "Red is definitely your color."

I blushed and looked down at the red dress with little white birds on it. "Thanks."

The house came into view and Caeden took my hand. "My mom is gonna freak," he said.

"Your mom? What about my mom and Gram?"

Caeden laughed. "I'm sure Gram will burst into her 'no baby' talk."

"Oh God, I hope not," I put my head in my hands. "Especially in front of everyone."

"Lucinda has no filter," he grinned, leading me to the front door.

It opened just as Caeden put his hand on the knob. "There you are," Amy huffed. "Everyone was wondering where you were. This is your party."

"It's everyone's party, mom," he said, leading me past her and into the family room. "Besides, I needed to talk to Sophie."

"You talk to Sophie every day," she followed us.

"Thank you oh wise one."

Everyone was gathered in the family room, holding drinks, and munching on food.

"Oh my God," Amy gasped from behind us.

Caeden squeezed my hand and whispered, "I thought it would take her a little longer to notice."

"You're engaged!" she screamed and the whole room went quiet. I turned as red as my dress as every pair of eyes in the room turned to me.

My mom dropped her cup on the floor. Thankfully it was empty. "You're getting married!"

"Caeden decided to put a ring on it!" Evan joined in.

225

He and my teammates started to do the *Single Ladies* dance.

The pack came over to congratulate us. Bentley's smile was the biggest of all as he hugged Caeden and then me. "I'm so happy for you guys. You deserve to be happy."

Charlotte and Christian squealed before they both squeezed me tightly. They then did the same with Caeden, who seemed at a loss as to what to do.

Logan said, "Congratulations."

And Bryce. Oh, Bryce.

"Does this mean ya'll are going to be even more grossly in love?"

"Probably," Caeden laughed.

"Yuck," Bryce said. "I think I'm going to throw up."

"There's a trash can over there," Caeden pointed to the corner of the room. "Help yourself."

Bryce rolled his eyes and walked off after Charlotte. I watched him take her hand and kiss her cheek. I was so happy to see those two together.

My dad came up to us, and Caeden's arm stiffened around my waist. I wondered if he would ever get over his fear of my father.

"Congratulations," he hugged me, kissed my cheek, and then hugged Caeden. "I can't wait for you to be a part of the family," he clapped Caeden on the shoulder. "My daughter couldn't have found a more perfect mate and I know there's no one on the planet that could ever love her more than you do."

Caeden blushed and toed the ground to avoid eye contact. "I really do love her," he pinched my side, "more than anything."

"I know," Dad smiled and squeezed his shoulder. "Your mom has prepared a feast. The food's in the kitchen… if there's any left," he smiled and walked back towards my mother. She had her back to him and he wrapped his arms around her. She leaned back into him and kissed his chin. I hoped that was Caeden and I were that happy eighteen years from now.

"Food?" Caeden tilted his head towards the kitchen.
"I'm starving."

Caeden led me into the black and white kitchen. Food was everywhere; Amy had really outdone herself. I picked up a mini hotdog and squirted some ketchup and mustard on it before popping it into my mouth.

Caeden hopped up on the counter, shoveling macaroni and cheese into his mouth. I climbed up beside him, careful to keep my legs together.

"I'm sorry about that," he swallowed.

"About what?" I picked up a mini burger.

"I'm just sorry you were bombarded. I thought it would take everyone a while to notice, if they noticed at all, and we'd be able to announce it later."

I bumped his shoulder with mine. "I'm happy that everyone knows, and that we were all together."

"Good point," he grinned and I leaned over to kiss his dimple.

Gram came into the kitchen, twisting her skirt around. "What was all that screaming about? I had to pee."

"Thanks for that information Gram," I laughed, grabbing a napkin to wipe my mouth.

Gram rolled her eyes. "Now what was all that squealing about? You're mom didn't get you some sports car did she?" Gram looked at Caeden. "Those things are dangerous."

"No Lucinda," Caeden chuckled. "Your granddaughter has agreed to marry me."

"Oh!" Gram snatched my left hand. "Engaged?" tears formed in her eyes. "You're both growing up," she patted my hand before releasing it. She looked between us. "Now just don't go making me a great-grandma before I'm ready," she scolded, before turning on her heal and disappearing.

Caeden laughed into my shoulder. "I called it."

"You did," I grabbed a cake pop and stuck it in my mouth.

"That looks good," Caeden said and grabbed the cake

pop from my mouth and stuck it in his. He waggled his eyebrows.

"Hey!"

"Come and get it."

"I don't think so, mister," I grabbed another.

Evan and Brody came into the kitchen to get another plate of food.

"You two are getting married, huh?" Evan lifted an eyebrow. "I guess Caeden here couldn't handle a little competition." We all laughed.

"So," Brody said, "are ya'll going to Beach Week?"

"Nah, I don't think so," Caeden shook his head. "It's a bit too rowdy for us. We have a house at Virginia Beach so I was thinking we might all go there," he addressed me.

"That would be great. I'd love to go to the beach," I smiled.

Evan snorted. "It figures Mr. Moneybags would have a beach house. I mean, look at this place."

"Beach?" Bryce stuck his head in the doorway. "Did someone say beach?"

"Yeah," Caeden said. "I was thinking we'd all go to the beach house."

"This isn't a joke right?" he asked. "Because if it is, you're really cruel."

"It's not a joke."

"Yes!" Bryce fist-bumped the air. "Charlotte! Babe, wait up! We're going to the beach!" he called after her.

"Is it just me or is he really excited to go to the beach?" Brody asked.

"That's Bryce," Caeden and I said simultaneously and then laughed.

Caeden ran his fingers through his hair and said, "Bryce can build the most epic sandcastles you've ever seen."

Bryce sauntered back into the kitchen. "He's right, and this year I plan to build a life size castle."

"Bryce, I think that's impossible," Caeden said.

"Watch me, big brother, and when I do you must bow down to my superior marvelousness."

"I don't think so," Caeden said.

Bryce shrugged. "Fine, now bowing. But you'll still have to admit to my marvelousness."

"Sure, sure," Caeden waved his hand.

"Hey guys," Amy came into the kitchen. "Did ya'll bring your swimming trunks? I've got the outside set up now."

"We remembered," Evan said.

"Great," she clapped her hands together.

"Caeden and Sophie," she teared up when she looked at us. "I'm so proud of you both. You've graduated high school and now you're getting married. I'm going to cry. Does anyone know where the tissues went?"

"Right here mom," Bryce pulled out one of those portable packs from his pocket.

"Oh, thank you sweetie," she took it from him and dabbed the corner of her eyes. "I just have so many emotions." She ran from the kitchen sniffling.

"Should we go after her?" I asked Caeden.

"Are you kidding? That'll only make it worse."

"Hey man," Brody said, "where can we change into our trunks?"

"Bathroom's down the hall. Bryce will show you."

"I will?"

"Yes," Caeden eyed his younger brother, "you will."

"This way," Bryce said.

"I don't have a bathing suit," I told Caeden.

"Don't worry," Caeden winked. "I've got you covered."

He hopped off the counter and helped me down. He took my hand and led me to his room. He picked a bag off of his bed and tossed it at me. I opened the bag and found several swimsuits in it.

"I got a couple so you'd be able to choose."

"Thanks," I dumped the contents out on his bed.

I picked out a multi-colored chevron patterned tankini with black bikini bottoms.

"Darn," Caeden grinned. "I was hoping you'd pick one of these," he held a bikini top on the end of his finger.

"I don't think so, mister. Not with all these guys here."

"Good point," he dropped it back on the bed.

I headed into the bathroom to change and Caeden rummaged through the drawers for his trunks.

I lifted my dress over my head and folded it, along with my other clothes, so I could change back into it later. Unless, Caeden decided he wanted to sleep here tonight.

I opened the door a crack and stepped into his room.

Caeden was collapsed onto one of the beanbags. His swim trunks were green with white piping, making him look even more tan. I wondered how much tanner he'd get when we went to the beach.

"Ready?" he jumped up, giving me an amazing glimpse of his perfect chest and abs, coated in a light dusting of hair. The hair grew thicker at his belly button and disappeared into his swim trunks.

Do not hyperventilate.

"Do you have a shirt I can where over this?"

"Yeah, sure," he opened a drawer and tossed a gray batman shirt at me.

I slipped it over my head and took his hand.

Everyone had disappeared from the downstairs and ventured outside. Caeden opened the French doors leading out back and my jaw dropped.

The pool was crystal clear, surrounded decorative rock to give it a natural vibe, and it even had a waterfall. My eyes ventured upward and took in a swirling slide and even a rope swing. A hot tub was adjacent to the pool. There was a pergola with wispy white netting, an outdoor kitchen, and a TV.

For the party, Amy had music pumping through the speakers, and red, black, and white balloons everywhere, even in the pool. There was more food and a cake in the shape of a Warrior.

"First, your backyard is amazing," I told Caeden, "and second, if this is how your mom plans a graduation party, I'm giving her free reign for the wedding."

"Better not do that. We might end up getting married in a spaceship."

"She-wolf!" Riley called. "Get in this pool before I come get you."

"I'm coming!"

Caeden let go of my hand and ran at the pool before jumping in the air, doing a flip, and diving gracefully into the water.

"Show off!" Tyler yelled when he came up for air.

Caeden shook his head, sending water everywhere, and sticking his hair up in every direction.

"Come on babe, just jump."

I tore his shirt off and tossed it on a nearby chair and decided to take his advice and just jump.

TWENTY TWO.

Two weeks later.

"Babe, are you packed?" Caeden came into my room. Before I could answer he twisted me around to face him and dipped me before planting a kiss on my lips. "Or should I say, *fiancé*, are you packed?"

I giggled. "Almost."

He kissed my cheek and let me go. "We leave in five minutes," he playfully smacked my butt.

I added a few more tank tops and shorts to the bag. Plus a sweatshirt that Caeden had gotten me, just in case the nights and mornings were chilly. I looked around my room, making sure I hadn't forgotten anything, and couldn't help but smile when I saw Perry the Panda sitting on my bed.

I looked in my closet and grabbed two dresses just in case we went out anywhere fancy. I grabbed a pair of black sequined flats too and added it all to my bag.

I couldn't get the bag to zip so I called for Caeden. "Caeden! I need your manly strength!"

He appeared in the doorway. "How can I help you? My name is Caeden and I am at your service," he kissed my hand.

I laughed. "I can't get my suitcase closed."

"Easy peasy," he zipped it in one swipe. "Are you ready to go now?"

"Yep," I said, tightening my ponytail and yawning. "I'm glad you're so awake. I'm ready to go back to bed," I looked at my bed longingly.

"I have to drive, therefore, I have to be awake." He grabbed my suitcase off the bed. "Oh and your mom and dad are here."

I walked out into the living room and found them sitting on the couch. "Hey guys," I sat down in between them. "Your flight leaves tomorrow right?"

"About that…" dad said.

"What?"

Mom patted my knee. "Your dad and I found a house

232

here and we've decided to move back here. With the Grimm's mostly eliminated we should be fairly safe."

Caeden came back in and stopped in his tracks, face stricken.

"Are you okay?" I asked him.

He shook his head. "Uh... yeah... fine." He went into my room and came out with Archie in his arms.

"That's great news," I hugged them both. "I've missed you guys so much, you have no idea. It'll be so awesome having you live here."

"We're still flying back to Germany to settle everything there before we settle here but we've already made a deal on the house so we should be moved in by the end of the month," dad said.

"This is just so great," I hugged and kissed them.

"You better get on the road," mom said. "You want to miss the traffic."

"I love you guys," I said and went to say bye to Gram who was furiously cooking scrambled eggs.

"Bye Gram," I kissed her cheek.

"I love you Sophie, ya'll be careful."

"We will."

"No babies."

"Gram!"

She smiled and patted my cheek. "Get your cute toosh outta here."

"Will do," I said and shook my butt.

She laughed. "Call and let me know you get in safe. Call your parents too."

"I know," I said and hugged her. "Love ya Gram."

I hugged my parents again and grabbed my purse up. "I guess I'll see you soon."

Caeden was waiting in the car, Archie sitting on his lap, and poor Murphy in the back.

"Bryce, Charlotte, and Logan are going to drive down later today so we're going to pick up Bentley and Christian."

"Are we going to have enough room for all the

dogs?"

Caeden frowned. "We'll have to stick our bags on top of the cages."

"Sounds like a plan," I buckled up.

Chris was at Bentley's house so we only had to make one stop. We had to maneuver things around a bit but we managed to fit the three large dog cages in the trunk with our bags.

"You guys hungry?" asked Caeden.

"Starving," said Bentley.

"McDonalds?"

"That's fine," Chris said.

"Yeah," said Bentley.

"You okay with that?" Caeden glanced at me.

"I'm cool with whatever."

He turned into the drive thru and ordered enough food to feed fifteen people. I only hoped it was enough.

Caeden paid and grabbed the food, plopping it in my lap. I took our food and handed the rest to Bentley and Chris.

I handed Caeden a biscuit and hash brown.

"Can you put a napkin on my lap? I don't want to get crumbs all over me."

"Sure," I grabbed a napkin, fluffed it open, and spread it across his lap.

"Thanks."

We ate and talked, and then turned on the radio and sang along.

It was an almost five hour drive but went by surprisingly fast. Caeden pulled into the driveway of a beachfront property. It had a two-car garage, full front deck on the second floor, and it was three levels. The front was a mix of stone and medium blue siding. It was fairly large, more than enough room for all of us.

"Home sweet home," Caeden sighed, turning off the car.

I climbed out and let Archie down.

Caeden opened the trunk and put all our suitcases on

the ground before helping the dogs out. The three large dogs stretched their stiff muscles. We'd stopped and let them walk a couple of times but it just hadn't been enough to satisfy the large familiars.

We let the dogs run around for a bit before we headed inside.

The house was decorated in calming whites, beiges, and gold's, with hints of teal. The floor was white washed and covered in different rugs to add softness. The walls were painted an off white and the couch, a large sectional, was also white but dotted with teal pillows and throws. The open kitchen was done in black cabinets with white countertops that had flecks of sea glass in it.

"This house is beautiful," I told Caeden.

"I'm glad you like it. Just hang here for a second. I'm going to show Bentley and Chris their room."

He took them down the hallway and I could hear him pointing out where different things were located.

Caeden came back down and grabbed both of our suitcases. "And our room is upstairs," he grinned.

"Oooh, does that mean more privacy?" I followed him up the steps.

"It does," he looked back at me and grinned. The dogs happily followed us. Caeden opened a set of doors. "Tada!"

"Wow," I breathed.

The room was huge, obviously the master, and decorated much like the rest of the house. The bedspread was a sand color and so fluffy I just wanted to fall face first on it. The carpet was so plush under my feet that I was tempted to kick my flip-flops off and scrunch my toes in it.

The walls were papered in a damask pattern that reflect gold depending on how the light hit it. The furniture, a large armoire, end tables, and a dresser, were all off white. Teal vases were scattered about.

A settee was placed in front of the bed and that's where I plopped myself.

235

"I can't believe you guys own this," I gasped, in awe.

Caeden sat down beside me and the dogs hopped up on the bed. Murphy flicked his long tongue out and licked Caeden's ear.

Caeden's right leg began to bounce, a sure sign of nervousness.

"Caeden?"

He turned to me; his blue eyes were pale and scared. "There's something I need to tell you."

"What?" I asked, my brow furrowing in wonder.

"I didn't kill Travis. He's alive."

EPILOGUE. TRAVIS.

I marched into the house, pushing the door open with enough force that the hinges cracked.

Thanks to Caeden's pack mine was dead. And silly, silly, Caeden had thought he'd taken care of me. He should've known I wouldn't go down that easy. I just gave him a vacant eyed stare, made a last gurgling breath, and feigned death. The dumb ass hadn't even bothered to stay behind to see if I reverted to my human form, as all shifters do when they die. But Caeden's stupidity didn't transfer to his pack. They killed Hannah and Robert, eliminating my pack, but I still had the older wolves.

I smirked.

Older wolves meant more experience.

I stepped into the living room where they were gathered. I slid my sunglasses into my pockets, crossed my arms over my chest, and smirked. I was dressed in jeans, t-shirt, and a leather jacket despite the summer weather.

"Travis," growled Jack. "What are you doing here?"

"I'm your Alpha. I have a plan to eliminate Caeden and his pack once and for all."

My plan was perfect. Nothing could foil it. Caeden and his pack wouldn't know what hit them when I released my creations on them.

Mary stood up, her mousy brown hair fanned around her head. "We've been talking," she started, her voice shaking and her eyes averted to the ground.

"Without me?" I frowned. "I'm hurt," I added sarcastically.

"We won't follow you," she said, now looking into my eyes. Her voice was stronger, louder.

"Excuse me?" I snapped. "You are my pack! I am Alpha! You do as I say!" I yelled and pointed at my chest.

"Not anymore," Jack said in that irritating gravelly voice of his. I wanted to rip out his throat and then his wild gray hair.

"We renounce you as Alpha and as a part of our pack.

237

You're on your own now Travis," Lewis said.

"No, no," I said in disbelief. But I could feel it, their presence leaving me, and soon I was completely empty.

"You have ten seconds to get out of my house before I kill you," Jack said. "Ten, nine, eight, seven, six, five, four, three, two-"

I ran.

My clothes burst from my skin as I transformed form man to beast.

The forest floor thumped beneath my feet.

I ran and ran and ran.

This was bad.

So bad.

This wasn't supposed to go this way.

But then a thought struck me like lightning.

This was good.

So, so, good.

A lone wolf is a more powerful wolf.

They're stronger, more aggressive, and far more dangerous.

Yes, this was a very good thing.

And most importantly, I didn't have anything to lose.

BOOK THREE IN THE OUTSIDER SERIES
NOW AVAILABLE

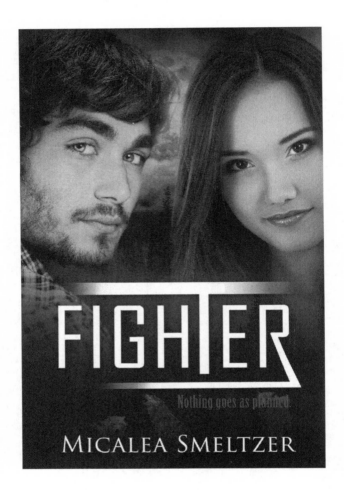

FIGHTER

Nothing goes as planned.

MICALEA SMELTZER

CONTINUE FOR AN EXCLUSIVE LOOK AT
THE FIRST CHAPTER OF DESTINY OF
SILIS BY SYDNEY PROCTOR AND SOME
INSIDER EXTRAS!

ACKNOWLEDGEMENTS

First, I want to thank my amazing Mawmaw for putting up with me and my constant writer babble and shrieks of, "Leave me alone! I'm writing! Remember, angry bear in a cave!" I'm surprised she didn't kick my grumpy butt out. Haha. I love you so much MawMaw!

Thank you to my mom and dad for not thinking I was a crazy person for wanting to write. And thank you for not lecturing me to, **insert snippy voice**, "Go to college and get a *real* job." Your support means the world to me; you have no idea. I love you both! (And mom! You better have read these books by now or I'm coming over there!) Haha.

Thank you to my cousin Britni who has been so supportive of my writing endeavors! Thank you for believing in me when a lot of people didn't. I hope I get to see you sometime soon since I haven't seen you since I was in like... 1st grade. I'm sure I had missing teeth. I promise, they're all here now!

Thank you to my brothers Noah and Hunter. Wait... why am I thanking you? Do you two even know I write books? Never mind. I unthank you.

Thank you to my aunt Janiece and uncle David for being so supportive of my writing. It means so much to me!

Thank you to my best friend Shelby who hates to read but read Outsider in just a few days. I was shocked. Haha. I'm so happy you loved it (and Caeden) and that I have your support. Now let's go to Five Guys. ;)

Thank you to my amazing fans! All of you are wonderful and I love hearing from you! Reading your emails and comments makes my day! You're the greatest! In particular I want to thank my DJs Emily and Brianna. You both suggested some awesome music. (Brianna suggested what became the Insider 'theme song', *Never far Away* by Rush of Fools. I love it!) I also want to thank Kathryn for being so sweet and asking how Inside was going and if I was well. Thank you to Megan for your enthusiasm about the

Outsider Series and for your love of dogs. (Thank the lord I'm not the only crazy dog lady, haha) All your support really means a lot to me, not just the people I named, but all my fans. Thank you!

Thank you, thank you, thank you!

(Especially to everyone who had to put up with my grumpy bear attitude, you're a saint)

And lastly, all I want to say is:

Once a warrior, always a warrior.

The Destiny of Silis

Sydney Proctor

What if your friends told you they weren't human. That you weren't human. Dmitri has only liked one girl, Maia Vicks. Maia has only liked one guy, Dmitri Marcal. So when Maia and Dmitri find out they're not human, that they have to lead a race of people, they wonder what else has been a lie. Danger is on the way and they have to decide whether to face it- or run and they have a destiny to fulfill.

The Destiny of Silis

Sydney Proctor

This is for all the authors out there who have inspired me such as J.C Isabella. To all my friends, but more specifically Katie. You listened to me chatter away about this book and more importantly you read it and told me what you thought.

Chapter One

Dmitri

Maia Vicks. Her long brown hair and big blue eyes stopped me dead in my tracks. It was the first day of my senior year and Maia happened to be in my gym class. I had known Maia since freshman year though I hadn't really talked to her because I couldn't build up the nerve. The one time I had talked to her was junior year when she dropped her books and I helped her pick them up muttering 'you're welcome' when she said thanks. I seem to only get nervous when I'm around her or thinking about her which tended to be a lot recently.

"Dmitri! It's rude to stare dude. I know she's the only reason you don't date," My best friend Marcus had said. He was right though. In all honesty I didn't date anyone because I cared for Maia too much even though we didn't associate.

"Sorry. Wait!" I said as realization dawned on me. "How do you know I like her?"

He smirked. "Everyone knows it except her. It's pretty obvious when you stare at her all the time."

"Well I'm glad you decided to tell me," I said with a smartass tone.

We headed off to the locker rooms, which didn't smell like sweat which was nice but I knew would change. Five minutes later Marcus and I walked out the rooms and headed to the upper gym. Since it was the first day of gym everyone who had gym this period would head to the upper gym to be paired with one of the two coaches. When Marcus and I sat on the bleachers I immediately searched for Maia. When I spotted her I noticed she was wearing a sky blue shirt and a pair of shorts that sure too small to have me feel at ease. Her long tan legs were stretched out on the bleachers in front of her when I was hit in the back of the head by Marcus. "You're staring again. Please tell me this is the year you build up the nerve to ask her out ." "I can't even talk to her! Plus, I bet you she doesn't even know I exist." This, I was pretty sure was true. Though we had talked that one time I bet she didn't remember me now.

"If you don't ask her out now someone else will and you'll be pissed you didn't ask her first." I opened my mouth to continue our conversation when I heard my name being called.

"Dmitri Marcal you will be with Coach Wilder."

Maia

I was on the bleachers nervously awaiting my gym teacher fate. I felt a pair of eyes burning a hole in the back of my head but didn't turn around. "Maia Vicks please join Dmitri Marcal with Coach Wilder." Wait, did she just say Dmitri? Of course she did. I got up on my legs that seemed to be made of rubber at the time and walked over to my new coach. After everyone was divided to be in our assigned groups for the year we headed out to the track. Luckily, I was a good runner and I didn't sweat. I set off at a smooth and easy paced jog, thinking about Dmitri. You see I had, well have had a crush on him since freshman year. His jet black hair and bright green eyes made me like him even more. I'm shy so I haven't really worked up the nerve but I believe that if we had talked I'm sure we would get along. If he talked to me I don't think I'd be shy at all- it's just getting up the nerve to start talking. All of a sudden I'm on the grass and something, no someone is on top of me.

"Oh my God I'm so sorry!" When I opened my eyes I noticed it was Dmitri. He rolled off of me.

"It's ok. Just what happened?" I asked curiously.

"Well since the school is too cheap to repave the track properly I tripped over the uneven parts." I laughed and so did he. I couldn't help it because what he said was absolutely true.

"Yeah, you're definitely right about that!" I was trying to grasp the fact that Dmitri was previously on top of me and we're now talking like old friends. He stood up and stretched his hand out to me. I stared at his hand awhile before grabbing it. When I stood next to him I realized he was taller than me, he was about 6'1". I'm pretty sure I looked stupid staring at him and probably looked really small compared to him since I was only 5'7". I looked away and started to jog. I heard Dmitri behind me. "Hey, wait up!"

"Um...hi?" I definitely sounded stupid now. I wasn't asking a question. "Hey. I'm Dmitri. I'm really sorry about falling on you." "I know who you are and by the way I accept your multiple apologies." He looked surprised a minute before recovering.

Dmitri

The fact that Maia knew my name was very surprising. Then again I knew her name but she was beautiful. "You're Maia right?" It was her turn to look surprised. Every guy knew who she was because of her athletic ability and her looks. "Yeah...I guess I am Maia."

"Are you saying you don't know your own name?"

"Oh believe me I know my name I'm just shocked you knew it." "Well Maia it seems to me I owe you. After all you did cushion my fall." I truly hoped this worked. I knew that if I wanted any kind of relationship with her she should at least get to know me.

"I'm glad you survived though you don't owe me anything."

"Oh but I do. How about I take you out to lunch today?" I was wishing she'd say yes but I didn't want to freak her out. The closer I got to her the more I noticed how good she smelt. She smelt like coconut and vanilla.

"Um, ok I guess."

"Great I'll meet you at your locker." She agreed and jogged ahead of me. Marcus jogged up to me shortly after. He smiled at me knowingly. "You were all over her. Literally."

"I tripped over the crappy pavement but if it makes you happy I asked her out to lunch."

"You, Dmitri Marcal asked out Maia Vicks?" I smiled. "Yeah I did." He smiled at me and we jogged the rest of the way silently. Where was I going to take her? McDonalds was too cheap and the 99 was too fancy so I settled on chinese food at a new restaurant that opened up. I was going to have a relationship with Maia whether it was as friends or as something more- starting with today.

INSIDER EXTRAS

DETENTION
SOPHIE'S POV

I looked over at Caeden, snoozing peacefully. He was on his stomach with his face turned towards me. His eyes flitted beneath closed lids and his freckle-covered shoulders rose and fell with each breath. A curl fell over his forehead. I wanted to brush it away but I feared I might wake him.

With a sigh I stood up from the bed and grabbed my backpack up off the floor. I was already dressed and ready for the day. I had to arrive at school early today in order to serve detention.

Detention. I'd never had detention before. This was really going to suck.

I closed the bedroom door as quietly as possible and grabbed a cereal bar from the kitchen before snatching my keys off the side table.

I marched out to the car with a determined gait. I would not let Mrs. Harding ruin my morning or my day by giving me detention.

After all, who gives someone detention because they say math makes them happy? The woman is freakin' crazy and needs a chill pill… or three.

I ripped the paper off the breakfast bar and took a big bite before starting the car. It was still dark out, I yawned, wishing I could go back to bed and snuggle up to Caeden.

I forced myself to put the car into reverse and back out of the driveway. I drove the two or so minutes to school and parked. The student parking lot was empty except for my car.

I shook my head and grabbed my backpack, heading into the school, all the while I fussed under my breath about demon teachers.

The door was, of course, locked and I had to knock on it until one of the gym teachers took mercy on me and let me inside. I thanked him profusely and looked at the large clock on the wall. I had forty-five seconds to make it to Mrs. Harding's classroom without being late.

I glanced around, checking for any teachers, when the coast was clear I sprinted down the hallway at a pace a normal human could never meet.

When I rounded the corner to the math hallway I slowed to a walk. My hair was a bit ruffled and I quickly fixed it. I knocked on Mrs. Harding's door with twenty seconds to spare.

She opened the door, grinning, her teeth were yellow and I could smell the distinct odor of cigarettes on her breath. Ew.

She ushered me inside and I picked a desk in the front. I dropped my backpack down beside me.

A sense of dread pooled in the bottom of my stomach.

Mrs. Harding waddled over to her desk. She shuffled a large stack of papers until they were perfectly straight. She picked them up and dropped them on my desk. The papers made a loud thwacking sound.

"Using a red pen I expect you to grade every single one of these tests before the morning bell rings," she thrust her index finger against the papers. "I suggest you get started," she smirked.

I stared in disbelief at the stack of tests in front of me. There had to be at least sixty of them, four pages each. I shook my head and dug a red pen out of my bag. I'd probably get shot if I used a pink or purple one.

I removed the cap and tapped the pen against the desk.

"Ms. Beaumont, none of that tapping!" she yelled.

I ceased the tapping.

I grabbed the first test off the pile and scanned the first problem.

What the hell was this?

"Uh, Mrs. Harding?" I raised my hand.

"Yes?" she rolled her eyes.

"This is college level."

"I'm aware of that."

I gaped. "But... but... I don't *know* this kind of math."

Mrs. Harding smiled like the cat that ate the canary. I could easily picture her plucking small yellow feathers from between her teeth.

"I suggest you learn real fast then."

Oh crapsicles.

I looked at the clock and hoped that Caeden was awake.

Caeden!

Soph? Is everything okay?

Ugh, no... this old hag expects me to grade her college level tests. There's like sixty of them here. I fanned the tests and Mrs. Harding glared at me. *Can you call Bryce? I can tell you the problem and what the answer is and you can ask him if it's right.*

Sure, I'm in the car. Let me call him. A few seconds went by before Caeden said, *I've got him. What's the first one?*

I told him and he relayed the information to Bryce.

By the way, I'm pretty sure if I don't get this done she's going to make me serve detention again.

We better hurry then. I don't like being without my snuggle buddy.

I snorted.

"Ms. Beaumont? Is something funny?" Mrs. Harding

narrowed her eyes at me.

"No. Nothing."

"That's what I thought." She went back to playing angry birds. Angry birds! Geez.

Snuggle buddy? I said to Caeden.

Yep, you're my snuggle buddy. What's the next one?

With Caeden and Bryce's help I finished with two minutes to spare. I straightened the pile of papers, like she'd done, and handed them to her.

"Did you grade *all* of them?" she huffed and glanced at the clock.

"Yes," I danced on the balls of my feet, ready to flee.

Her eyes narrowed and she flipped through the tests, scanning for red marks.

"I guess you're free to go then."

I turned on the charm. "I just hope I helped you Mrs. Harding. It must be so difficult having to grade all of those tests. I don't see how you ever have time for yourself."

"Well," she straightened in her chair; plucking on her button down shirt that was stretched so tight I was afraid if a button flew off it might blind me. "It is certainly difficult but I do try to find the time to enjoy the occasional bingo game."

"I sure hope so," I patted the end of her desk. "Everyone needs a night off." I grabbed my backpack off the floor. "I'll see you tomorrow Mrs. Harding," I smiled for affect and opened the door.

"Close the door behind you, Ms. Beaumont."

I closed the door with a soft click and ran down the hall to where Caeden was waiting.

He was leaning against the wall and looked oh so delish in his jeans and pale blue polo shirt. "You're alive!" he grinned.

"With you by my side I'll always make it out alive," I kissed his cheek and took his hand.

"Then I guess you better never leave me," he squeezed me to him.

"That's a promise I can easily make."

PERMISSION
CAEDEN'S POV

I was trying to listen to what Mr. and Mrs. Beaumont were saying but it was so hard when I only had one thing on my mind and a small box burning a hole in my back pocket. Sweat beaded on my brow and I hoped no one would notice.

I swallowed and cleared my throat. "I...we," I clarified, "need your advice on how to handle the Grimm's."

My hand moved up Sophie's arm and traced the word engraved in her skin. *Liar.*

Just looking at it made me sick to my stomach. It was my fault she was scarred by Travis. I'd let him hurt my mate. It was my job to protect her and I had failed in the worst way possible. I wouldn't make the same mistake twice. I would protect her with my life. She was my everything.

Mr. and Mrs. Beaumont looked at each other before Mr. Beaumont shrugged. "I don't know what to tell you. They've always been a little strange-" Mrs. Beaumont smacked his arm. "Except for your mother of course," he corrected, smiling at Sophie. "She's perfectly sane."

Mrs. Beaumont turned her gaze to Sophie. Her eyes were filled with tears and I braced myself for an all out cry-fest. Someone grab a bucket.

"I'm so sorry for what my brother did to you," she began to choke up. Tears coursed down her cheeks. I felt bad for her. This had to be hard on her. "I'm sorry," she ran from the room.

Sophie looked between me and her dad; no doubt weighing whether or not I'd be alive when she came back. Deciding I'd be safe she squeezed me knee, "I should go talk to her."

I nodded and rubbed my hands together. This moment

had come much sooner than I expected. I didn't know whether to be relieved or scared to death. "That's okay. I'd... uh... actually like to talk to your father in private."

Sophie narrowed her eyes. That was never a good thing. "Why?"

"Nothing important," I looked down at my shoes.

"Uh-huh sure," she turned on her heel and headed after her mom. I knew she was going to chew me out later; she just had that look in her eye.

I looked over at Mr. Beaumont. Sweat coated my hands and I wiped them on my jeans. I thought I might throw up.

"Why don't we head to my office?" he nodded down the hallway. "More privacy that way."

I nodded my head in agreement before I thought it might be safer to do this out in the open. I really hoped he didn't have a gun in there. It might not kill me but it'd be a pain in the butt to heal.

I followed Mr. Beaumont into his office with my head hung like a man about to be sent to the guillotine.

"Have a seat," Mr. Beaumont motioned to a plush leather chair.

I sat down. My knee bounced up and down restlessly.

Mr. Beaumont ventured behind his desk and opened a cabinet. He bent down and came back up with a glass of scotch. "You want anything?" he asked.

"No," I waved my hand. "I'm not old enough to drink."

"Oh, right," he nodded. He swirled the liquid around. "It doesn't do much good anyway. Our metabolisms just burn it right up." He took a large gulp and sat down in the chair beside me.

Thank God, I thought he might be going to sit behind the desk and if he did there's no way I could ask him my question. I'd feel like I was making a business proposition or something.

I scooted around in the chair, the leather squeaking,

and cleared my throat.

"What was it you wanted to talk about?"

"Um…" I gaped like a fish.

Dang gone it, I'm an Alpha! I can do this!

I straightened in the chair and looked into his eyes. "Mr. Beaumont-" I started.

He downed his drink and waved his glass. "Please call me Garrett. Mr. Beaumont makes me feel old." He smiled, easing a tiny bit of my discomfort.

I took a deep breath.

Do it already!

"I wanted to ask you for permission to marry your daughter," I let out a gust of air I hadn't realized I was holding in.

Garrett sighed. "I knew this day would come I just didn't think it would be so soon-"

I clenched my jaw. Was he mad?

"But how can I say no? You're my daughter's mate and I know you love her more than anyone else ever could. You're a good man Caeden and I know you'll take good care of my baby girl." His eyes filled with tears. It was very moving seeing someone like Garrett near tears. It made me realize that it's okay to be emotional.

"I'll never let anything hurt her ever again."

Garrett chuckled and rubbed his face. "You best not say that. Sophie may seem like the kind of person to stay in the background but let me tell you, she's got fire, that one. Don't think for a second that you'll be able to control her and keep her away from danger."

"I would never try to control her," I shook my head. "But I'll try my hardest to keep her away from anything dangerous."

"Good luck with that," Garrett chuckled and stared at his empty glass. "Sophie's not going to let you go out and have all the fun. She's not going to be one to wait behind while you go out and do the dangerous stuff. She'll want to be in the thick of things. Right now, it may not seem like

---

255

that, but she's just learned about this life. She's only just begun to shift. It won't be long until she's front and center. Trust me, my daughter's a Beaumont, she'll be a force to be reckoned with," his lips quirked. "I wish you luck."

We sat in silence for a few moments before Garrett broke the silence.

"Do you have a ring?"

"Yeah," I pulled it out of my back pocket. I popped the case open and showed him the ring. "It was my grandma's."

Garrett smiled. "It's beautiful Caeden. Sophie's not a jewelry person but she'll love this."

"I hope so," I took the ring back and stuck it in my pocket.

"When are you going to propose?" he went behind his desk to pour some more scotch.

"I don't know. Whenever the moment feels right I guess. Until then I'll just take it everywhere with me," I patted my pocket.

Garrett lifted his glass in salute. "Cheers to you."

ABOUT THE AUTHOR

Micalea Smeltzer is an author from Virginia. She is permanently glued to her computer writing one of the many books swirling around in her head. She has to listen to music when she writes and has a playlist for every book she's ever started. When she's not writing, she can be found reading a book or playing with her three dogs.

You can email Micalea at:
msmeltzer9793@gmail.com

Like her facebook page to stay updated on all the latest book news:
http://www.facebook.com/MicaleaSmeltzerfanpage?ref=hl

Follow her on twitter:
https://twitter.com/msmeltzer9793
NOTE: She rarely uses her twitter, so you're better off to contact her another way.

Website:
http://micaleasmeltzer.com/

Made in the USA
San Bernardino, CA
29 April 2016